A PRIVATE EDUCATION

A
Private Education

Carol Anderson

HEADLINE
Liaison

First published in 1997
by HEADLINE BOOK PUBLISHING

A HEADLINE LIAISON paperback

10 9 8 7 6 5 4 3 2 1

ISBN 0 7472 5518 0

Typeset at The Spartan Press Ltd,
Lymington, Hants

Printed and bound in Great Britain by
Cox & Wyman Ltd, Reading, Berks

HEADLINE BOOK PUBLISHING
A division of Hodder Headline PLC
338 Euston Road
London NW1 3BH

A
Private Education

Chapter One

Professor Gerrard Gottlieb picked up the album from his desk. The pages fell open to his favourite print; a sepia-tinted photograph he had been assured was from a genuine Victorian plate. It showed a pale, dark-haired girl manacled between ornately carved bedposts. Facing away from the camera, her body was caught in silhouette, revealing the sumptuous curves of her hips, the slimness of her waist, the dimples on her alabaster shoulders – an erotic hour-glass that always gave him a little shiver of pleasure.

The girl was peeping back over her shoulder, glittering eyes revealing a heady mixture of fear and expectation. He had studied the print so often he knew every detail – the discarded tumble of clothes at her feet, the small tasselled lamp throwing a delicate glow onto her rounded buttocks, the dark inviting places between her milk-white thighs, almost, but not completely, obscured by shadow.

Gottlieb smiled, replaying the image in his mind. He closed the book and turned to watch the retreating figure of Phoebe Williams as she hurried across the college green outside his window.

Under the trees she hesitated for an instant and glanced

1

back towards Gottlieb's office. Even from this distance he could make out the expression on her face; the same heady mix of fear and expectation. What a shame she couldn't have stayed a little longer.

Gottlieb glanced down at his tutorials list. His next student was someone called David Liscombe. A sallow-faced youth no doubt.

Reluctantly he slipped the leather-bound photo-album back into his desk. In the drawer alongside it were a set of custom-made manacles, lovingly crafted copies of those worn by the girl in the photograph. For an instant he imagined closing them with a satisfying click around the slim, delicate wrists of Phoebe Williams. With a sigh, he slid the drawer shut and went to the door of his new office.

David Liscombe was waiting in the hall, clutching an untidy bundle of notes tied around with bright orange string. Gottlieb grimaced and waved the boy – as sallow and spotty as he had feared – into the warm confines of his office.

'Good afternoon, Mr Liscombe,' he said flatly, indicating a chair by the desk. 'As you've no doubt heard your usual tutor, Dr Manley, has had to leave us temporarily due to ill health. My name is Gottlieb, Gerrard Gottlieb. Now, what have you got for me amongst that sad pile of papers, young man?'

On the far side of the university campus, Phoebe Williams slipped quietly into a seat just inside the door of the lecture theatre and pulled out her notebook. Below her at the podium the speaker was already in full flow. Phoebe stared ahead, struggling to regain her composure – pretending to be engrossed in Dr Dart's sonorous monologue on the effects of the railway in nineteenth-century industrial Britain.

In the seat next to her, a long-haired boy was shredding a tissue into confetti. She disliked arriving late and hated sitting with the students at the back who had crept in out of the rain. Even her friend, Nina King, had managed to arrive on time and was sitting near the front, with her knees resting on the seat in front of her.

Phoebe gazed down unseeing at Dr Dart, who was busily unfurling a huge chart on the display board, and wondered what on earth she was going to do without her tutor, Audrey Manley.

Strong-willed yet sympathetic, Audrey Manley had taken up the halls of academe in the same way some women took the veil. Now she had been unexpectedly replaced by Gerrard Gottlieb. Even his name sounded contrived. Phoebe shivered and tried to concentrate on Dr Dart's voice but found it impossible.

Her tutorial with Gottlieb had been a disaster:

'Come in,' Gottlieb had said, waving his hand in her direction. 'You must be Miss Williams, do take a seat.'

Phoebe had been so surprised she could barely speak and stood uneasily in the open doorway staring into Audrey's office. It was unrecognisable; gone were the baskets of dried flowers, the Laura Ashley curtains, the family photographs and the whisper of perfume in the air, to be replaced by a hideous twisted metal sculpture perched in the bay window on polished bare boards. For a few seconds she had wondered whether she was in the right place.

3

Gerrard Gottlieb peered at her across the desk from behind his wire-rimmed spectacles. He had huge brown eyes framed by thick bushy eyebrows and heavy, sinister, Mediterranean features. He smiled wolfishly and ran his fingers through a great leonine mane of black-and-silver hair.

'Two thirty?' he said reflectively, his eyes not leaving hers.

Phoebe coughed. 'I'm sorry?'

Gottlieb glanced at the clock on the antique pine desk. 'You're a little early.' He looked her up and down. His intense stare was disconcerting. 'You're normally on time for everything, aren't you, Miss Williams? A bourgeois little habit, picked up from your parents, no doubt.' He opened a folder of notes on his desk, puckered his lips into a little moue of displeasure before leaning back, resting his fingertips together and blowing thoughtfully between them.

Phoebe flushed scarlet. 'I ... I ...' she began, trying hard to work out some sort of parry to counter Gottlieb's attack. Nothing came.

The man got to his feet and extended a large hand.

'Gottlieb,' he said, striding towards her. 'Gerrard Gottlieb, taking over temporarily from Audrey Manley, pleased to meet you. Why don't you come in and take a seat? Or does Dr Manley normally hold her tutorials with her students hovering in the doorway?'

He was tall, in his late thirties, broad-shouldered and he smelt of woodsmoke. Phoebe suppressed a tremor as he engulfed her small hand in his. There was something raw and untamed about him. He smiled, revealing a row of perfect white teeth, then stalked back to his desk and picked up a file.

'Now, let's get on with this bloody dissertation nonsense. Tell me, wasn't part of the reason you came to university to broaden your horizons? Open up those blue eyes to a set of wider possibilities?'

Phoebe would have spoken but Gottlieb cut her short.

'. . . Or was it just to get a nice safe degree that would lead to a nice safe job – a nice safe way of life?'

She took another breath but Gottlieb was too fast for her.

'Safe, safe, safe,' he snapped furiously. 'Dr Manley preferred the safe options. I've seen half a dozen of her acolytes and they're all the same: tight-lipped and buttoned down. Final-year students and not one of them shows an ounce of flair. No passion.' He spun round and glared at her. 'I had really hoped for better. Now, let me see.' He flicked through the pages of notes on his desk. 'It says here you are a mature student.' He looked up at her again, this time his eyes resting more thoughtfully on her face. Under his appraisal Phoebe found herself blushing furiously.

Gottlieb sniffed. 'How old are you? Twenty-three? Twenty-four?'

Phoebe nodded.

Gottlieb hadn't noticed. 'Mature ought to imply something more interesting than the passage of years. Let's see if we can do something adventurous with this final work of yours, Miss Williams, something which will make the burden you bring into my life here a little less onerous.'

Phoebe coughed to clear her mind as much as her throat. Gottlieb's gaze made her feel uncomfortable; it was as if he could see inside her mind. What was even more disturbing, and despite her discomfort, there was something unnaturally compelling about him.

'What do you suggest, Mr Gottlieb?' she said in an unsteady voice.

He smiled, revealing sharp predator's teeth, and leant forward on his elbows. 'Oh, I have lots of ideas,' he said in an undertone. 'Lots and lots of ideas.'

Phoebe looked away, feeling Gottlieb's dark eyes moving slowly across her body.

'Such as?' she managed to stammer.

He grinned. 'Don't worry, Miss Williams, I shall be coming to that in a minute,' he purred.

In the lecture hall, Phoebe reddened. Gottlieb had thrown her totally. He'd unsettled her so much that she'd thought that she might have to miss Dr Dart's lecture. She could still feel the way his eyes had lingered on her body, as invasive and compelling as a caress.

She shuddered and forced her attention back to Dr Dart, who was pointing to his chart. Dr Dart was sixty if he was a day and as comforting and unchanging as a family dog.

Later that evening, in the university library, Phoebe Williams barely registered the tip-tap of high heels across the wooden library floor behind her. She glanced up again at the computer and mouthed the words on the screen, back-spacing to correct a spelling error.

'You're not *still* here, are you?'

The sound of Nina King's voice made her jump.

'Jesus, calm down,' said Nina, palming a stick of chewing gum into her mouth. 'I thought I'd catch you after dear old Dart's lecture but you were off like a rabbit. Have you got any idea what time it is? You said you'd meet me at the flat at eight, remember?'

Phoebe stared blankly at Nina, who lifted her hands above her head and jiggled her hips provocatively. Her heavy breasts echoed the rhythm.

'Oh, come on, Phoebe – Thursday night? Party time? Robert Fellowes' house? All coming back to you now, is it?'

Phoebe groaned and rubbed her eyes. 'Oh God, I'd forgotten everything about the party.'

Nina pulled a face. 'So, what's new? I knew you'd be in here. What are you working on?' She peered myopically at the computer screen.

Phoebe began collecting things from the table and saving her work onto a floppy disk.

'The notes for my final paper. I've got to submit a new title by the end of term – or do examinations always pass you by?'

Nina pouted, pulling her scarlet lips into a tight little bow. 'No need to be so bitchy.' She paused for a second as Phoebe pushed things into a bag.

'It's not like you to be doing it at the eleventh hour – cramming isn't really your style, is it?' Nina grinned, her voice dropping to a conspiratorial whisper. 'Or is the new man in your life – the quiet but *very* sexy Shaun Rees – taking your mind off your work?' She mimicked a cat meowing. 'Nice catch.'

Phoebe glared at her. Nina laughed and held up her hands in mock surrender.

'Okay, okay. How did your tutorial go, then? If you don't want to talk about Shaun, tell me all about the lovely Gerrard Gottlieb instead.'

Phoebe stared at her. 'You knew who they'd got to replace Audrey, didn't you?'

Nina grinned. 'Everybody's talking about him. He's a research fellow or something. Go on then, spill the beans, what's he like?'

Phoebe stopped and stared past her thoughtfully. 'He's a complete and utter bastard. He threw my dissertation ideas out and then . . .' she stopped and took a deep breath. 'He just gave me the creeps. I'm going to have to say something about him.'

Nina stared at her in disbelief. 'That's not like you either. What's the matter with him? I thought some wild-eyed dedicated academic would be right up your street.' She lifted an eyebrow. 'Good-looking too, or so one of the social work students told me. Good-looking in a danger-ous sort of way.'

Phoebe bit her lip, imagining Gottlieb's dark uncanny eyes. 'I really didn't notice,' she lied.

Nina snorted. 'Don't tell me, you prefer Shaun Rees.' She pulled a face and aped a huge yawn. 'Nice but very, very straight. Whereas Gottlieb by all accounts . . .'

Phoebe blushed, dragging her coat off the back of the chair. 'I really can't believe Audrey's left,' she said in-dignantly, cutting Nina short. 'We're half way through a term.'

Nina had already turned on her heel and replied over

her shoulder. 'One of the other girls said she thought it was a nervous breakdown. They've got no idea when she'll be back, so you'd better get used to Gottlieb.'

Phoebe stared at her in astonishment.

'Come on, you've got to get changed, unless of course a woolly skirt and that manky old sweater are your party outfit,' said Nina, tap-tap-tapping on her spiky heels towards the door. 'We'll miss all the food if we're much later.'

Phoebe hurried after her, struggling with the rest of her bags.

Outside the university library, in the biting winter wind, Phoebe's head spun. She wasn't certain whether it was the change of temperature or Gottlieb's influence on her. Nina broke into an ungainly trot, heading towards the accommodation block.

As they got close to the flats, Phoebe waved Nina on. 'Look, thanks for coming and getting me. Why don't you go ahead? I'll meet you there.'

Nina peered at her. 'Are you sure? You will come, won't you? I thought you'd arranged to meet Shaun there, I want you to introduce me to his flatmate.' Nina shimmied suggestively. 'I'm banking on it.'

Phoebe laughed in spite of herself. 'Give me an hour.'

Nina pointed into the gloom. 'Talk of the devil.' She rolled her eyes as Shaun Rees, Phoebe's new boyfriend, hurried across the green towards them, grinning a warm hello.

'Hi,' he said, 'I . . .'

Before Phoebe could say anything or Shaun could finish his sentence Nina veered off across the path.

'Don't mind me, young lovers,' she said flatly and turned towards Phoebe. 'I'll see you at the party. Don't be long. Remember, I'm counting on you.'

Shaun grinned and slipped his arm through Phoebe's. There was something deeply reassuring about his touch. She smiled as he snuggled close to her.

'Hi, how's it going?'

Phoebe grimaced. 'Don't ask. I've had a lousy day.'

'I wondered if you'd got lost or something,' he said walking towards her flat. 'I've already been over to Robert's place. I thought you'd be there already.'

Phoebe bundled her books under her arm and unlocked the door. 'Sorry, I was working late. Have you heard Audrey Manley's left?'

Shaun nodded. 'The whole place is buzzing with it.' He squeezed under the cover of the porch and leant forward to kiss her tentatively. His arms snaked around her, pulling her into the warm confines of his coat. She brushed his lips with hers and was rewarded by yet another grin.

'I thought maybe you'd changed your mind. Stood me up,' he said softly. As he spoke he moved closer, eyes glittering, and kissed her a little more fiercely.

Phoebe shook her head, easing herself away from him. 'No, I'm just running late. Do you want to come in for a little while?'

'I wouldn't say no, it's too cold to stand around out here.'

Phoebe opened the door to her tiny flat with Shaun no more than a breath behind her. Their relationship was very new, not yet easy or familiar. Shaun shuffled uncomfortably in the doorway, unsure whether to sit or stand – or leave.

She flicked on the lamps and stacked her books and bag on the desk. 'Would you like some coffee? I've just got to get changed. It won't take me long.'

Shaun nodded, eyes moving across the tidy bookshelves that reached from floor to celing along the wall of the cramped sitting room.

'That would be great. I thought maybe you were held up.' His voice followed her into the kitchen.

'No, I'm fine, really, I just lost track of time. Nina came to get me.' She switched on the kettle and pulled two mugs out of the rack.

'I'm surprised you know Nina, she doesn't seem like your type . . .' Shaun began. 'I mean . . .'

Phoebe couldn't see his face but sensed his hesitancy. She knew exactly what he meant. Phoebe's mother would have said Nina King was the kind of girl men practised on – Phoebe was the kind they married. She glanced back into the sitting room while waiting for the kettle to boil. Shaun was thoughtfully studying the rows of books. The lamplight picked out his distinctive profile and muscular torso encased in a white collarless shirt. A tendril of dark hair curled enticingly into the curve of his long neck. Phoebe's mother would approve of Shaun Rees despite his nod towards fashionable student grunge.

'Nina and I work together, at Don Giovanni's, you know? The restaurant in Helm Street? she said, carrying the coffee back into the sitting room. Shaun was now sitting outstretched in the one comfortable armchair. As she came in he scrambled to his feet and then reached out for the mug. For a fraction of a second their fingertips touched and Phoebe felt a tiny scintillating pulse of desire.

She felt her colour rising and wished that in some ways she could be more like Nina King. Shaun Rees was beautiful.

'Thanks,' said Shaun. Around his eyes the skin crinkled into soft humorous lines. He sipped the coffee and smiled. 'Umm, that's good. So when you're not a student you're a waitress, then?'

Phoebe smiled. 'That's right. Got to do something to make the money go around. Look, I'm just going to take a quick shower. Would you like to put some music on or something? I won't be very long.'

Shaun nodded and Phoebe hurried into the bedroom feeling uncomfortable making him wait for her. She could hardly ask him to leave, after all he'd come to pick her up. But she didn't like the uneasy, prickly feeling she had in her stomach, that lay somewhere between discomfort and desire. She wished the relationship was six months down the line, when they would know exactly what to say and how to act with each other.

Slipping off her clothes, she switched on the shower and stepped into the torrent. The first blast of water was bitterly cold and made her gasp with surprise. A second or two later it warmed, etching silvery rivulets on her small slim body. She glanced down at the ripe curves of her uptilted breasts and imagined Shaun stepping in behind her, soaping her nipples, hands circling her narrow waist as he pulled her closer. She closed her eyes as the fantasy took on a life of its own. She could almost feel his kisses, wet and hot on her neck and the press of his insistent hungry cock. The thought rooted her to the spot.

Despite being alone, the fantasy made her blush. She ran a hand down over the taut muscles of her belly, brushing the dark triangle of her sex. She and Shaun weren't lovers yet but she knew eventually they would be.

It would take Shaun time: supper, nights at the pictures, parties with friends, coming home together for endless cups of coffee, tentative steps forward, a kiss, a touch – until one night . . . she shivered. How much simpler it would be if she were as self-assured as Nina King, who would have no such inhibitions. Nina would just call out and invite Shaun Rees to join her in the shower. Gottlieb would undoubtedly approve of Nina's lack of inhibitions – her passion.

Phoebe thrust her head under the torrent of the shower, trying to wash away the erotic images; they refused to leave. Gerrard Gottlieb had unsettled her. She turned her face up into the stream of water and realised with a start that part of her ached to be touched. She swallowed hard, imagining Shaun pressing her up against the cold tiles, lifting her legs around his waist so that he could slip deep inside her.

She snapped the temperature control back onto cold and let out a tiny gasp as the icy burst of water hit her like needle points, driving away the inner heat that was gathering low in her belly.

Shaun Rees was like every other man she had ever dated; gentle, kind, and most definitely not the kind of man who would step uninvited into a respectable girl's shower cubicle. Everything between them was so new that Shaun would be shocked – stunned – even if she could bring herself to invite him in, which of course she knew, she never would.

Turning off the shower and wrapping herself in a towelling robe she could hear the soft tones of Vivaldi coming through the closed door; he *would* choose that. She dressed quickly in a long soft cotton dress, tying the belt loosely before towelling her sensible shoulder-length bob dry. A few more minutes and with the lightest touch of lipstick she would be ready.

She stared thoughtfully at her reflection; calm blue eyes stared back, taking in the details of her slim body in its understated and sensible dress. She lifted her hands above her head and swung her hips as she had seen Nina do in the library.

'Party time,' she murmured under her breath picking up a handbag. The jiggle made her feel ridiculous.

Shaun got to his feet as she came into the sitting room. 'All set?' he said cheerfully. 'I wondered whether you'd like to go for a drink first? We could go to The Ploughman's, it's on the way.'

Phoebe nodded, picking up her cardigan. 'That would be great.'

Shaun smiled. 'I was going to ask you if you'd like to come to supper with me tomorrow night? Do you know Tony and Beth Goodman?'

Phoebe shook her head; she didn't know them, but she knew the form. They would be Shaun's friends and they wanted to check her out.

She smiled. 'I'd love to come. What time?'

'Eight.'

'That'll be fine.' She picked up her bag. 'I think I'm more or less ready, if you are.'

Shaun pulled on his jacket. 'Great.' He glanced at his

14

wristwatch. 'We really ought to be going.' He tipped her face towards his for the briefest of kisses and for a split second Phoebe felt a compelling need to possess him.

Breathlessly she stepped away. 'I'll just go and get my coat,' she said quickly.

In his elegant town house close to the river, Gerrard Gottlieb, massage almost complete, rolled over onto his back, revealing muscular bands of hirsute flesh glittering with fragrant oil. In the lamp light the little Eurasian whore clambered up beside him on the couch and guided his great arcing cock into her tiny blood red mouth. He tucked his hands behind his head, and surrendered to the sensations, hissing softly as her eager lips tightened around him.

He'd brought the girl home from Bangkok as his house-keeper – not that she could keep house – but it mattered little. She welcomed him home each day dressed in no-thing but a thin pink wrap that he had made for her from a roll of sheer translucent silk. As she opened the door it would drift apart to reveal the plump almost hairless mound of her quim; ever ready, ever obedient. The dark peaks of her nipples shadowed through the silk, making his mouth water.

On the couch in front of the log fire he shivered as she cupped his scrotum, running knowing fingers along its sensitive centre seam, gently mouthing his distended testi-cles between her lips. She made soft animal noises of pleasure while her lips and fingers worked on and on. The sounds vibrated through Gottlieb's cock, settling in his belly like a warm caress. He strained now, breath coming

15

in strangled panting gasps as she ran her tongue across the angry red glans, working her tongue into his cock's sensitive eye before dragging him deeper into her mouth, teeth nipping gently to add to his excitement.

He arched up towards her and instantly she slid her hands beneath his muscular buttocks, pulling him into her, drinking from him, kisses electric and wild, sucking him on and on until he thought that he might explode at the point of orgasm. Explode he did. As her lips closed over him, a tidal wave of semen roared through him on its unstoppable journey, filling his mind with a blinding flash of white light and flooding his little mistress's mouth.

She giggled and pulled away. The long pink robe was pulled back to frame her pert dark-tipped breasts, a trail of glittering pearly seed trickling down her chin. She ran her tongue around her lips as if she were hungry, not wanting to miss a drop of the feast he had given her.

She looked up at him coyly from beneath coal-black lashes. 'You like?' she purred. 'Maya make you much happy?'

Gottlieb snorted. 'Of course I liked it. Talk in English, Maya, not street pidgin.' He swung his legs over the edge of the couch and pulled his dressing gown around him.

Maya pouted miserably. 'Don't be angry with me, Gerrard,' she said in a soft cultured voice.

Gottlieb poured them both a glass of wine.

Maya crept up beside him. 'Dinner will be half an hour. I've made a pot roast, your favourite.'

He shook his head; sex and food, the only things his diminutive companion had any real passion for. He watched her turn and teeter away on her little high-heeled mules, oblivious of her near-nakedness.

16

He sighed and sipped his wine. Maya presented no challenge. Her upbringing, the culture in which she had been raised, engendered submission. Maya spent her whole life making him happy, waiting for him to come home so that her life could begin.

The wine warmed his belly. He realised he had no idea how she spent her days. He often thought of her as a wind-up doll, only truly alive when he was there. Maya's unquestioning obedience was both deeply flattering and at the same time frustrating.

They had been together almost five years. At first, barely more than eighteen, she had been afraid of him as he had schooled her to meet his needs. He'd felt like a true master then, taming a little wild beast to obey his every command – but it had been too easy. It saddened him to realise that, in spite of everything, he was bored with her.

Maya had always given everything he wanted, whenever he wanted it, without question. He had anticipated that when she became anglicised, confident in her new lifestyle, she would rebel against his strictures and he would have the pleasure of breaking her again. He had intended to introduce her to the arts, literature – until finally he would have the perfect, educated, intelligent, but ultimately compliant companion.

He sighed; the reverse was true. Now she aped fear and obedience and had no interests beyond the ever-present promise of food and sex. Familiar with his desires she would tremble at his feet, crawl towards him on her knees.

He topped up his glass, slumped in the armchair by the hearth and let his mind wander.

Phoebe Williams. He repeated the name thoughtfully. She might prove a real challenge. Buttoned up tight, with her dark hair caught up in a bun, soft stray wisps framing her delicate features, she exuded an understated sensuality, so subtle that he wasn't sure she was aware of it.

He closed his eyes and immediately visualised her sitting primly in front of his desk, tucking her skirt tidily around her long legs. She had been dressed for warmth; a soft wool skirt draped over her thighs, subtly revealing their contours, and a sensible sweater that had done nothing to disguise the beautiful taut outline of her small rounded breasts.

And her eyes – he smiled to himself – eyes that betrayed a glitter of fear and curiosity. He knew he had unnerved her, it had been his intention. At the end of their tutorial he had held out a hand in invitation and made her look into the full-length mirror that hung from the wall in his study.

'When you look at your reflection in the mirror, Miss Williams, what exactly do you see?' Standing behind her he could see that she was trembling.

'I don't understand,' she had said unsteadily, staring at herself. 'What are you trying to do?'

Gottlieb had smiled. 'Awaken you,' he'd said in an undertone. 'Awaken passion, make you truly understand yourself. Surely that is what real education is about, Miss Williams? Helping us to understand our strengths and weaknesses so that we can harness them.' He lingered over the word harness. Phoebe had turned away from the mirror, clutching at the back of the chair.

He had seen a glittering flash of anxiety in her eyes. She

sensed what he meant and it had nothing to do with her final paper. He had indicated that she should return to her seat. Without a word, she had followed his instruction and sat staring at the floor while he thumbed through the rest of her notes. Her silence excited him.

Quietly he had closed her file. 'I think that will be all for today, Miss Williams. Perhaps we can meet early next week to discuss where we go from here.'

Constrained by good manners, Phoebe had thanked him for his time and hurried out of the office with barely a backward glance.

Phoebe's former tutor, Audrey Manley, had said Phoebe was a particularly gifted student – which had instantly aroused his curiosity. Her grades weren't that remarkable but he sensed Audrey had seen something in Phoebe that appealed to her.

Ruefully Gottlieb took another sip of wine. Audrey Manley had a taste for compliant well-educated female flesh – it was an open secret on campus. Perhaps it was desire which had drawn Audrey to Phoebe Williams.

He let the fantasy take shape behind his closed eyelids. Audrey Manley with her heavy thighs and bloated pendulous breasts astride the lovely Phoebe, who was strapped to a bed. The older woman's bristly quim rubbed roughly against the girl's pale skin as her fingers teased Phoebe's fleshed nipples into erection.

He felt the familiar stirring in his groin as his imagination invited Audrey to place a long lingering kiss between Phoebe's open thighs, the older woman's tongue snaking into the fragrant folds of the girl's tight sex. Phoebe arched up instinctively, opening herself for Audrey's attentions, grinding her pubis into Audrey's face. The girl's mouth was slack, eyes closed as she submitted without question.

Gottlieb didn't hear the door to the sitting room open, nor the approach of Maya, but was grateful beyond measure when he felt her smooth warm flesh brush against his as she climbed astride him. She moaned softly and guided his renewed throbbing erection into her quim. Her sex closed around him like a tight fist, drawing him deep inside her body.

He had no trouble sustaining the image of Phoebe Williams in his mind. Her eyes were open now, revealing a stunning mixture of pleasure and revulsion while Audrey nipped and lapped at her clitoris which peeked between the lips of the girl's sex like a scarlet bead.

Gottlieb shivered and pushed the imaginary Audrey aside as Phoebe writhed and bucked in a maelstrom of pleasure. He imagined guiding his cock into her wet welcoming quim, thrusting himself deeper and deeper until he was buried to the hilt.

Above him, Maya ground her hips against him but in his mind's eye it was the delightful Phoebe Williams who brushed her sopping quim against Gottlieb's groin, moaning softly, impaling herself again and again as she rode him out towards release.

Chapter Two

The following afternoon, Nina King was leaning against the door frame of the flat when Phoebe opened the door.

'I was just about to knock.' Nina grinned salaciously. 'And where did you two get to last night? I knew you wouldn't come to the party once lover boy turned up.' She lifted an eyebrow questioningly. 'That's why I didn't come round first thing this morning. Didn't want to disturb you. So go on, tell me.'

Phoebe stared at her. 'Tell you what?'

Nina groaned. 'Oh, come on! Did you do the wild thing? Jump on his bones. Let's have all the grim details.'

Phoebe, who was pulling on her coat, snorted. 'We went for a drink at The Ploughman's and just talked. Neither of us fancied going to the party so he walked me home.'

Nina rolled her eyes heavenwards. 'Right, I should have known. You're so predictable. I was counting on you to help me with Shaun's flatmate.'

Phoebe laughed. 'You really think you needed my help? How was ...?' She glanced at the clock. 'Oh, come on, we can talk on the way. I'm late. I've got a lecture at two.'

Nina groaned. 'You worry too much. I just came to remind you we've got to go to work early on Saturday night. I'll call round for you if you like.'

Phoebe, juggling a bag and her files shooed Nina out of the flat and locked the door.

'Here hold these, will you?' she said, buttoning up her coat.

Nina peered at the notebooks. 'Gottlieb?'

Phoebe nodded. 'That's right. Two o'clock, lecture theatre four. Are you coming?'

Nina grinned. 'Actually I was going to see Mark.'

Phoebe peered at her. 'Mark?'

Nina grinned. 'That's right. Shaun's flatmate. I managed to trap him without you. But I'll walk you as far as the admin block if you like. Mark said he'd meet me there.'

Phoebe found a seat near the front in the lecture theatre and waited for Gerrard Gottlieb to arrive. The stage was set, a single spotlight picking out a carved oak lectern. When, a few minutes after two o'clock, he strode on, clutching a pile of cards, she couldn't quite suppress a shiver of anticipation. He stared up into the audience like a hawk amongst a flight of doves, weighing his chances of a kill. There was a respectful hush amongst the other students: Gottlieb's reputation preceded him. He cleared his throat.

'Good afternoon, ladies and gentlemen,' he said in a low even voice. 'I'm sure those of you who know me will realise that I am not unused to presenting myself and my ideas in this manner, but for the foreseeable future, I am, so to speak, filling the shoes of your beloved Dr Manley. It would appear that I am to regularly amuse you with some discourse on the vagaries of social structure.' Gottlieb looked pained. 'So, rather after the fashion of a Presbyterian pastor I shall take, as our text for the day, the *bon mot* of Virginia Woolf who said, regarding feminism, "The history of men's opposition to women's emancipation is more interesting perhaps than the story of that emancipation itself."'

Phoebe could barely hear the words above the sound of her heart beating. She sensed Gottlieb searching her out amongst the faces. His eyes scanned left and right, out over the rows of students, until finally she knew he had seen her. For an instant their eyes met, though his expression didn't change. She felt a tiny unnerving tingle in her spine as he stared at her; assessing her, drinking her in. The gaze seemed to last for an eternity until finally she could bear it no longer and looked down at her feet, blushing madly.

When she looked up again Gottlieb licked his lips, took the first notecard from those he held and stalked back towards the lectern, his dark eyes moving slowly across the rest of the assembled audience.

'What is it we are all so afraid of, gentlemen?' he said slowly. 'Why this compulsion to suppress? What do we fear? Our desire, our passion? Men of letters and men of God have, for centuries, been terrified of losing their minds to the magic of a woman's sexuality; to be enslaved by the unstoppable compulsion to possess, to have, to consume ... to be sucked down into that compelling ocean of desire.'

Gottlieb's voice was hypnotic and sensual, as smooth and dark as the sea. Phoebe watched him move around the stage and imagined him in his office. Willingly she stepped into the fantasy, slipping off her coat and standing before him. His eyes glittered while his great hands travelling across her shoulders, unbuttoning her blouse. She stood, frozen, as each button slipped through the thin fabric. His face was impassive as he slid the material back over her shoulders so that he could cup her breasts, his fingers working back and forth across her nipples which hardened under his touch.

In her mind, he commanded her to undress for him; and without hesitation she slipped off her clothes, exposing herself for his pleasure. He was fully dressed. The contrast of his dark heavy clothes and the smooth vulnerability of her nakedness was both startling and at the same time deeply exciting. Slowly he circled her, all the time his eyes moving across her body, as tangible and electrifying as the touch of his fingers.

She shivered as the fantasy took hold. Gottlieb's lecture faded away until it was no more than a distant abstract link with her imagination.

The fantasy Gottlieb ran his hands over her chest, a fingertip idly toying with the stiff sensitive buds of her nipples. Now he trailed the single finger down over her ribs, making every nerve-ending in her body glow white-hot.

His touch was speculative, exploratory, until finally his hand slipped between her legs, dipping into her, opening up a passageway to pleasure for them both. She shivered as she imagined him moan softly as he discovered the heat of her excitement. His fingers brushed her clitoris, parting her thighs wider and wider until it seemed that she would break in his eagerness to explore every part of her.

She was being suffused with warm ripples of need and hunger; an almost animalistic desire that built low down in her belly. Each ripple, each wave added to the others making the sensations so intense that she could barely breathe. She knew she was wet for him, his fingers no longer just dipping into her sex but bathing in an ocean of pleasure that ran down over her thighs onto his fingers.

Slowly he sank to his knees in front of her, lips pressing kisses to her belly and the sensitive plains of her thighs. When he finally parted the lips of her quim with his tongue she let out a thin low sob. His mouth closed around the dark swollen bud of her clitoris, sucking at it, nibbling, lapping like a baby at a breast. Just when she thought that she couldn't take any more he moved back and stood up. She watched him, as helpless and vulnerable as a lamb in the maw of a wolf, as he unzipped his trousers and slipped out his cock. It reared up for an instant in front of her; a scimitar, straining and livid.

He moved closer, his great bulk overshadowing her, his cock nudging at her belly, demanding to be taken in. With one engulfing movement, he slipped his hands around her buttocks and pulled her up onto him, impaling, driving deep inside in a seamless terrifying thrust.

Almost instantly she could feel the first wave of her climax rushing headlong through her body, a great roaring desperate tidal surge that took her to the edge of consciousness. Between her legs, Gottlieb thrust again and again, pulling her down onto him. The coarse material of his trousers ripped and rubbed against her thighs, while deep inside her his cock grew and grew, filling every atom of her, taking over her whole body.

When he came he seemed to tear her apart. He was raw, angry, unstoppable, driving her own pleasure on to heights that took her to the very shores of madness . . .

Phoebe gasped, and her eyes snapped open. To her total horror she realised she was still in the lecture theatre. On the stage below Gottlieb was talking, bringing the lecture to its conclusion. He laid the pile of notes back on the lectern and invited questions from the floor. She looked around nervously; to her relief, the students around her seemed totally enrapt in Gottlieb.

On her lap her notebook was blank; other than the opening few sentences she hadn't heard a word. Between her legs she could still feel the delicious rawness and the compelling afterglow of orgasm, a slick trail of excitement oozing out onto her thighs. She shivered, struggling to regain her composure. She could hardly believe what had happened to her, the images had been so vivid, so compelling.

On stage, Gottlieb finally called enough.

Hurriedly, Phoebe threw her things into her bag and rushed towards the back of the hall. She was almost at the door when she heard Gottlieb call her name and would have ignored it except the students around her parted so that Gottlieb could make his way up towards her.

'Miss Williams?'

Phoebe turned slowly, looking down, feeling that if Gottlieb looked into her eyes he would see every fantastic thought.

'I wonder if you have a few moments?' he said pleasantly. 'Have you got another lecture this afternoon?'

Phoebe shook her head and fell into step beside him.

'I've been thinking about you,' he said, as they walked across the windy green.

Phoebe stiffened. 'Really.'

'This final paper. The titles have to be in by the end of this month. Have you had any thoughts on the things we discussed?'

Phoebe made an effort to regain her control. 'My theme lacks passion,' she said unevenly.

Gottlieb snorted. 'It does, Miss Williams. Have you had chance to come up with any other ideas?'

As they approached the door to his office Phoebe hesitated. He turned towards her, his expression as wolfish and hungry as the Gottlieb in her fantasy.

'Come in,' he said indicating that she should go ahead of him. Phoebe swallowed hard and stepped inside, trying to suppress the growing sense of *déjà vu*. Gottlieb sat down and stared at her. He took a cigarette from a case on his desk and lit it.

'Did you enjoy my lecture?'

Phoebe tried to avoid meeting his eyes. 'Yes,' she said softly.

Gottlieb grunted his approval and then leant closer. 'Passion,' he said slowly. 'Look at the effects of desire on our lives, wild, animal passion that drives us on to the very heights of achievement.' He picked up the notes she had given him the previous day. 'This thing here is as cold and lifeless as a cadaver. You need to choose something that inspires you, excites you, astonishes you. What astonishes you, Miss Williams? What is it that makes your pulse race and your mind reel?'

Phoebe wasn't certain whether he actually wanted an answer; up until then he'd done all the talking. If he'd been trying to provoke a response it didn't work, she was so stunned that she could barely think. There was a difficult pause. Gottlieb stared at her.

'Well?' he'd said more calmly. 'Why don't we start by you justifying exactly why you want to do *this*?' He waved a dismissive hand towards her bundle of notes.

Phoebe swallowed hard, trying to order her thoughts. Intense images of her fantasy kept flashing through her mind. She took a deep breath, struggling to clear her head.

'Audrey, Dr Manley . . .' she began.

Gottlieb snorted but Phoebe continued unsteadily. ' . . . She thought it was important we produced something of social relevance. She wanted us to explore . . .'

Gottlieb's expression dried the words in her throat. He sat on the edge of the desk now, overbearing and dangerous. 'Miss Williams, one thing your friend Dr Manley did not want any of her students to do was explore. Exploration requires some degree of risk, some crossing of unknown frontiers. Let me tell you about exploration . . .'

'So what did Gottlieb say? Did he suggest an alternative to the nursery report?' said Shaun Rees.

Phoebe shook her head as they hurried across the campus towards the car park. It was early evening and they were on their way to supper with Shaun's friends. A bitter easterly wind gave the night air a razor's edge.

Shaun slid his arm through hers as they made their way along the path. He had called for her after she got back from the office. She hadn't meant to mention Gottlieb but the memory just wouldn't go away. She couldn't make sense of why he disturbed her so much and her fantasy in the lecture theatre made her blush with embarrassment.

'Nothing really,' she said, quickly changing the subject. 'What are Beth and Tony like?'

'They're nice. You'll like them. Beth's a technician here and Tony's doing a degree in Computer Science. They live over on Almond Road.' Shaun guided her towards a battered VW and opened the door. She slid gratefully into the dark interior. For a few seconds she wished they could stay there, shut in against the cold together. He turned towards her and leant closer, his lips brushing hers.

'I'm really pleased you said you'd come,' he whispered.

She felt a tiny ripple of expectation as he lifted his hand to cup her face.

Shaun pulled back. 'Are you cold?' he said, turning the key in the ignition. 'It'll soon warm up once the engine's running.'

Phoebe stared out of the windscreen. Gottlieb's face hung in her imagination like a silent observer. Irrationally she felt a prickle of tears in her eyes. She wasn't cold, Shaun's light touch had stirred the unfulfilled desire in her belly. She wanted to tell him, to say... She shivered again. Shaun was safe and unthreatening. She wondered if that was why he couldn't sense the passion she felt. She pulled her coat tight around her and tried not to think about Gerrard Gottlieb.

Tony and Beth's house was on the other side of town, a small terraced cottage, tastefully decorated in hippie chic, everywhere cluttered with low lamps and Indian rugs.

Phoebe slipped off her coat as the introductions were made, feeling Beth assessing her at every turn. Tony scuttled around opening wine, playing the host. Their house had a comfortable lived-in feel but, even as she made polite conversation, Phoebe couldn't quite shake the lingering ghost of Gottlieb's eyes drinking in the details of her body.

'What are you studying?' said Beth, settling them in the untidy sitting room while Tony poured everyone a glass of wine.

'Social Studies.'

Beth nodded her approval. 'Interesting course. It's a shame about Audrey Manley.'

Phoebe stared at her. 'You know about her leaving?'

Beth nodded. 'It's all over the campus. Everyone's talking about it.'

Shaun sipped his wine. 'They've got someone called Gottlieb in to cover.'

Beth rolled her eyes heavenwards. 'Bloody hell. Rather you than me.'

Phoebe took a long warming pull on her wine. 'Why do you say that?

Beth snorted. 'Have you met him yet?'

Phoebe didn't trust herself to speak. She nodded.

'Then you know exactly what I mean,' said Beth archly. 'He's thrown the title for my final paper out.'

'Doesn't surprise me, the man is a complete anarchist. What did he say?'

Phoebe shook her head and tightened her fingers around the wine glass. 'It really doesn't matter. I'm going to see him again on Monday to sort something out,' she said lamely, wondering why the man seemed to be haunting her.

'You'll come up with something. Will you excuse me a minute? I just want to take a look at supper.' Beth clambered to her feet. 'Just have to check on the bolognese.' Tony vanished into the kitchen along with Beth.

'Are you okay?' asked Shaun. 'You seem really quiet.'

Phoebe nodded. 'I'm fine,' she began, trying hard to suppress a shiver as Shaun moved closer.

'I think Beth likes you,' he said, softly sliding his arms around her waist. He turned and glanced towards the open door before kissing her.

'Pasta,' he said, nodding toward the kitchen. 'Beth's speciality. Don't let this Gottlieb thing get to you. Things will work out once you get used to him. Just give yourself a little while to adjust.'

Phoebe wasn't so certain. She struggled to put a name to the emotions Gottlieb had stirred in her. He had implied she was boring, safe, repressed. While her first reaction was to feel indignant she knew he was right – a stinging blow – the fantasy she had had in the lecture theatre had astonished her. She'd never experienced anything so vivid or disturbing in her life. Every time she tried to push it away the memory came flooding back in stunning detail. Even now the thought of his fingers on her body fired a soft heat in her belly. She ached for more.

Shaun tentatively pressed his lips to her neck, feeling his way forward, inviting her to stop him. She eased nearer, enjoying the sensation of his body against hers. He smelt so good, he was gentle, undemanding, safe. She flinched as her mind formed the word.

Shaun's looked confused and then he smiled. 'Too much? I'm sorry. I didn't mean . . .' his voice faded.

Phoebe shook her head and looked up into his kind eyes. Not enough, she thought miserably, that was the problem. Outside the weather was horrible – a wet, miserable night too cold and dark to be alone.

'No, it's all right.' She wished there was some way to stop playing everything by the same unspoken set of rules. She wanted Shaun to take her, desperate with a sexual hunger that was unstoppable. She imagined his lips on her breasts while he forced her thighs apart, frenzied and wild, longing to impale her, driving them both to the limits of passion . . .

Shaun looked down at her and smiled, mistaking her tense expression for nervousness.

'Relax, they're really nice people. Here, let me get you some more wine,' he said pleasantly, teasing the glass out of her fingers.

Blushing crimson as the sexual fantasy took on a life of its own, Phoebe wondered where the frantic images had come from. From the kitchen she could hear muffled voices; obviously a conference of approval. She perched on the edge of the settee and tried to concentrate on the rich smell of food.

'You look a bit flushed,' said Shaun, returning with another glassful.

Phoebe smiled. 'I'm fine, really.'

Shaun looked past her towards the window. Late autumn rain, trying hard to be snow, coursed down the grimy panes. 'It's really foul out there,' he said, unaware of the thoughts coursing through Phoebe's mind. She stood up to join him, staring absently at the street lights. What she really wanted was to exorcise the dark demon of Gerrard Gottlieb's derision.

'What did you think of our lecher in residence, then?' said Beth, blowing a plume of cigarette smoke across the table in her sitting room. The table, decked with candles, was littered with wine bottles and the remains of supper.

Phoebe reddened. 'I'm not sure,' she said uncomfortably.

Beside her, Shaun was picking at the last of the pasta. On her left Tony was topping up his own glass. He had consumed most of the wine and sat with his shoulders slumped forward, struggling to follow what the others were saying.

Phoebe turned her glass thoughtfully in her fingers. She tried to sound relaxed. 'I shouldn't really judge yet.' She paused. 'He's very different from Audrey.'

Beth laughed. 'You can say that again. I went to his lectures last term. Those eyes of his strip you naked. He really gave me the creeps.' She shuddered and stubbed her cigarette out. 'He's quite brilliant apparently. What was it he said about your final paper?'

Shaun laid his fork down and groaned. 'You may be getting into dangerous waters there, Beth.'

The wine had brought a bloom to his face and made him

bolder. Under the table Phoebe could feel his thigh pressing lightly against hers. She could feel the heat of his body, his desire emboldened by the alcohol, and didn't resist as his hand moved softly, tentatively, up onto her leg.

Beth, oblivious, eyes bright from the wine, snorted. 'Sorry, sore subject?'

'Not at all,' Phoebe said quickly, as Shaun's hand slipped nervously into the warm junction between her thighs. She didn't look at him, afraid that he might stop.

'What Gottlieb said was probably right; it's too safe, too dull. He said I ought to be writing something with more fire in the belly. Something with passion.'

Beth laughed uproariously. 'That sounds just like him. Have you given any thought to what you're going to do instead? You haven't got a lot of time.'

Phoebe shrugged. 'I'm not sure.'

Tony, who until then had been engrossed in finishing off another glass of wine, looked across at her. 'I'd watch him, Beth says he's got a pretty dodgy reputation.' He grinned, face flushed with alcohol. He leered drunkenly across the table, peering lecherously down the front of her dress. 'Pretty dodgy.'

Phoebe could sense Tony's undisguised lust, exposed by alcohol, animalistic and indiscriminate; a dog hungrily eyeing an unclaimed bitch. She stared at him in astonishment.

Beth glanced heavenwards. 'For God's sake, Tony,' she snapped and then turned her attentions to Phoebe. 'Just ignore him. He's had too much to drink – again.' She sighed with resignation. 'I don't know why he does it. He says it's because I won't let him get a word in edgeways.'

Phoebe smiled ruefully; it was probably true.

'What were Gottlieb's lectures on?' asked Shaun conversationally, trying to take everyone's attention away from Tony, who had begun to hiccup.

'Sex,' said Beth quietly, staring into her glass. 'Politely veiled, of course. Had all the first years baying in the aisles.'

Phoebe was still staring at Tony.

'Gottlieb's totally obsessed with it, you know.'

Rapidly recovering, Phoebe laughed. 'I'll bear that in mind. I don't understand why I haven't seen him before – everyone else seems to know all about him.'

Beth sucked a stray piece of pasta out of her teeth. 'He's doing research work out at Morrahills and only gives the odd lecture. I'm amazed they've got him doing Audrey Manley's job. I thought he was intriguing – in a weird sort of way – but not...' She paused. 'Well, not the sort of man who would get involved in helping lesser mortals through the rigours of the examination process, if you know what I mean. Unless of course it suited him for another reason.'

Beth pulled a face as if trying to conjure up the memory. 'He was doing this stuff on sexual politics; women's rights, all the usual well-ploughed furrows and then he got onto the class he'd taught in the States.' She paused again as if trying to recollect the details. 'I can't remember exactly where he said he was now – Los Angeles? California? Somewhere hot and amoral-sounding anyway. He told us that half the girls in his group were paying their way through college by stripping, lap-dancing or working as escorts.' She snorted. 'He seemed quite impressed.'

Tony laughed drunkenly. 'I bet his tutorials were fun.' He stumbled to his feet and began to hum 'The Stripper', thrusting out his pelvis in an exaggerated impression of bump and grind. The performance was aimed squarely at Phoebe.

Beth flushed scarlet. 'You've had too much to drink, Tony,' she snapped furiously. 'Sit down!'

Chastened, Tony slipped back into his seat. Phoebe stared at him.

Across the room, Beth was apologising profusely, fussing around, offering to make coffee, mopping up the puddle of wine Tony had spilt as he'd sprung up from the table.

Phoebe barely noticed, her mind racing with memories of Gottlieb's intense hungry face no more than a few inches from hers as they had stared into the mirror in his office. Tony Goodman was wearing the same expression. She realised with a start that Gottlieb had been assessing her; weighing her up in a way that had nothing to do with dissertations or education. He had been assessing his chances of possessing her, like a trophy; a scalp. She shivered; the look in his eyes had been that of a predator stalking potential prey.

She was hardly aware of Shaun's hand, brushing the front of her skirt. Encouraged by her apparent compliance he grew bolder still, stroking the mound of her sex. A single touch snapped her back to reality and a tiny electric flare of pleasure coursed through her as he brushed her clitoris. She could feel herself blushing and wished that she had had less wine or an awful lot more; it was so tempting to let go.

And Gottlieb wanted her too; it was a revelation. She flushed crimson, imagining some unseen lover gathering up her skirt, slipping a finger into her quim; wet now, open. She shivered and tried desperately to pull her concentration back to what Beth was saying as she handed out cups of coffee.

As Tony excused himself, Shaun leant closer and pressed a soft kiss to the sensitive skin behind Phoebe's ear, his finger working more enthusiastically. She shivered and turned to smile at him.

'We could leave early, if you like,' Shaun said in a low whisper as if he could see into her mind. 'Tony's pretty far gone.' He nodded towards Beth, who was giving Tony orders through the door. 'Though I did say we'd stay and play Trivial Pursuits.'

Phoebe fought to suppress a laugh. 'I'd rather we went home,' she said in a thick throaty voice, that sounded as strange to her as it must have to Shaun. As she spoke she lifted her hips a little, opening her legs so that his hand slipped round to cradle her sex.

He gasped, eyes never leaving hers as she began to move slowly against his fingers. It was as if she had ensnared him. He glanced accusingly at the empty wine glass in front of her.

'Have you had much to drink?'

Phoebe threw back her head and giggled. 'No, not very much at all. Why, have you?'

Shaun shook his head a little too enthusiastically. 'No, no,' he said. 'I'm fine.'

Across the room Beth was on her feet and heading towards the hall to rescue Tony.

Shaun, with a bemused expression leant forward and kissed Phoebe.

'That feels good,' she whispered, pressing his fingers tight up against her body. 'Why don't we leave these two to have the row that's brewing and go back to my flat instead?' She was surprised by her own words, but it was too late to claw them back.

Shaun stared at her, eyes bright with a mixture of desire and surprise. 'Are you sure?' he said uneasily. 'I mean . . .'

Phoebe smiled to cover her uncertainty and pulled him closer so that she could kiss him into silence. She didn't want to talk, instead she slid her tongue between his lips. His kisses tasted of wine, and she tried to imagine what it might be like to lose herself in the feelings that bubbled up inside her. The idea sent a little thrill of something wild and compelling up her spine.

'I'm fine,' she said softly, trying hard not to lose the raw sense of urgency. It would be all to easy to let the desire slip through her fingers. 'Let's go. Please,' she whispered.

She was afraid to look at him in case her courage failed her. Shaun pressed a soft kiss to her throat and wrapped his arms around her.

'Are you sure about this?' he murmured as she pressed her body against him.

It was the last question on earth she wanted to hear. She wanted to be free of words and rules and expectations. She kissed him again, fingers stroking his chest. He groaned softly and took her hand in his, kissing each fingertip in turn. The air between them crackled as the seconds passed, charged with unspoken promise. His eyes darkened.

She bit her lip and nodded slowly. 'Yes,' she said unevenly. 'I'm sure.'

Shaun seemed almost afraid to let her go in case she changed her mind. Finally he nodded towards the door. 'I'll just go and make our excuses to Beth and Tony.'

Beth waved them off from the doorstep. Phoebe pulled her coat around her and fell into step beside Shaun. There was a strange pulsating silence between them that she was afraid to break. She looked left and right along the narrow side street, trying to remember where they had parked the car. Shaun slipped his arm through hers.

'It's just round the back here,' he said, as if reading her mind.

As they turned off the main street into a dimly lit alley he turned and kissed her gently. 'Are you sure you want me to come back to your flat?' he said, eyes glittering in the lamp light. 'We could go for a drink instead if you want.'

Phoebe shook her head, still afraid to speak. Gently, in the deep shadows of the alley Shaun slid his hands up under her coat and pulled her into his arms. She shivered as he encircled her waist and his lips sought hers. She could feel the low earthly pulse of desire in his body. His kisses began as delicate invitations, reassuring and generous. He pulled away, smiling down at her.

'I really don't want to push you into anything you're not ready for,' he said softly.

While his voice said one thing, his body said something

totally different. The heat of his chest pressing against her seemed furnace-bright, compelling and delicious. She didn't resist as his hands moved down to her hips, fumbling, eager, working down over the swell of her buttocks.

She gasped as he kissed her again, harder now, his breath burning on her cheek as she felt his excitement rising. A flash of bright hungry need arced between them, glowing like a comet. She returned his kiss, pressing her lips to his, sliding her tongue into his mouth, pulling him close, every fibre of her body suddenly begging him for more.

He moaned and guided her deeper into the shadows, fingers working eagerly between her thighs. The walls behind her sucked the heat from her body. Shaun murmured something and then slid her dress up, fingers tracing a hot pattern over her belly. She whimpered, feeling as if she were drowning in excitement.

'Please,' she murmured thickly, 'please—' not knowing whether she was begging him to stop or go on.

He moaned appreciatively, easing aside the thin lacy fabric of her knickers. It seemed as if his hands and lips were everywhere. Moving closer he pushed her legs apart with his knee and buried his face in her dark hair.

'Oh God, oh God,' he hissed as he traced out a delicate spiralling pattern, stroking the moist divide of her sex with cold fingers.

Phoebe moved against his caresses, shivering as he slid his hand further between her legs. She was wet and sensed his growing pleasure as his finger explored the damp fragrant scrap of fabric that divided him from her. For an instant he pulled away, eyes alight.

'Are you sure about this?' he whispered thickly.

Phoebe almost wanted to cry out in frustration. 'Please, Shaun,' she said softly, 'please, don't ask me again – just touch me.'

Shaun groaned and kissed her, the tip of his tongue parting her lips. Gently he took one of her hands and guided it between his legs. She gasped as she felt the impressive bulge in the front of his trousers. Her hand lingered, cupping his shaft, wondering whether she had the courage to free it.

Shaun's kisses moved down into the curve of her neck, breath quickening against the thin fabric of her dress. Cold fingers struggled with the little pearl buttons that fastened the bodice, fingers working just a fraction ahead of his tongue and lips. His kisses worked over the sheer lace of her bra, until he found her tight hard nipples.

The sensation of his breath and tongue through the thin material made her gasp. She whimpered, pushing her hips toward him. Eagerly he gathered up the soft fabric of her skirt, slipping under the band of her panties, tugging them down over her slim hips. They dropped to the floor unnoticed as he stroked the pulsating, glistening outer lips of her quim.

'God, you're so wet,' he whispered. 'It feels like heaven—'

She opened her legs a little more, leaning back against the wall to concentrate on the sensations he had ignited in her. His touch was compelling, astounding – breathtaking. His thumb grazed the throbbing bud of her clitoris making her quiver. Moving her hands, she heard rather than saw him undo his flies and then gasped as he guided his cock between her legs.

'We must be mad,' she gasped nervously. 'What if someone sees us?'

Shaun's reply was a throaty growl. 'I don't care. You feel wonderful.'

She trembled as the head of his shaft nuzzled between the delicate folds of her quim. Her whole body ached for him. She could feel the moisture gathering around him, tendrils of anticipation shimmering low in her belly. He eased closer, sliding himself home a fraction at a time, teasing, tempting. She whimpered again and grabbing hold of his buttocks, pulled herself onto him.

He let out a thick grunt as he slid home, gasping in delight before plunging deeper and deeper, pressing her roughly against the brick wall. Grinding into her sex, he dragged her skirt higher so when she glanced down she could see the erotic image of his engorged wet shaft sliding in and out of the hot confines of her body. He undid the rest of the little buttons on the front of her dress, pushing the fabric aside to reveal the small pert curves of her breasts. The dim street lights leeched the colours away so that their bodies seemed to be rendered in the most delicate translucent ivory.

While Shaun lapped at her erect nipples, his fingers caressed the sensitive bud nestling amongst the glistening corona of her pubic hair. Phoebe moaned and writhed at the power of her pleasure as it grew. He circled the sensitive hood, varying the pressure and intensity of the strokes until she was breathless with excitement.

He leant back to look at her, eyes reduced to glittering pinpricks in the half-light with the sharpness of the bitter night air nipping at her naked skin and Shaun's insistent cock buried to the hilt inside her. The taste of his kisses was overwhelming and she let out a long throaty sob.

He grinned and plunged into her again, jerking her towards him, driving her mind out beyond the heavens, while great crashing waves shuddered through them as they were swept away on the riptide of orgasm.

Phoebe, gasping for breath, felt as if she was regaining consciousness when the last of the aftershocks trembled through them. Shaun stepped away, sliding out from her still-pulsating body.

He looked at her almost shyly, drinking in the details of her exposure. Her dress was undone to the waist, revealing her small breasts and tight hard nipples. Her skirt was gathered up around her hips, framing her sex.

'My God,' he whispered, 'you are astounding.'

Phoebe blushed furiously and started to button her dress, looking around frantically for her panties. Shaun caught hold of her wrists. Her delight was momentarily replaced by a great wave of embarrassment and self-consciousness. She looked away, her skin prickling with apprehension; what had she done? What would he think of her? She imagined the thoughts in his head and her colour deepened from red to crimson as she fought the ridiculous compulsion to apologise.

'That was amazing,' he said breathlessly. 'Here, let me help you.'

She laughed with relief as he tugged her coat back together, his fingers unable to keep away from the wet, glistening lips of her sex. He moved closer and kissed her again, this time so gently that she thought she would cry. Stroking her neck he held her tight as if he would never let her go.

Chapter Three

When Phoebe opened her eyes the next morning Shaun
Rees was still asleep, his arms curled protectively around
her waist. His body was deliciously warm, his breath a
delicate kiss on her shoulder-blades. The evidence of
seduction was all around them; her dress discarded on the
rug, her underwear, shed like rose petals in a colourful
trail leading from the door to the bed.

She felt the insistent press of his cock against her back
and blushed furiously, astounded that she could have been
so wanton. It was too late now to undo what had been
done. She turned over slowly so they lay belly to belly.

Shaun, hardly conscious, encircled her with his arm and
pulled her closer.

'Morning,' he murmured. 'What time is it?'

Reluctantly Phoebe peered at the bedside table,
vaguely annoyed by the intrusion of real time and real life.
For a few hours she had driven Gottlieb out of her mind,
driven everything except the compelling pursuit of passion.

'Nearly eight.'

Shaun groaned, rubbing his eyes. 'I really ought to be
going,' he said half-heartedly.

Phoebe felt a little flutter of panic, now she had given him what he wanted was he going to hurry away? She ran a hand over his chest, down over his muscular belly to the hot aching contours of his cock, closing her fingers around the shaft. He smelt divine, warm and inviting, a subtle mixture of male musk and the heady perfume of their night's lovemaking.

Shaun's eyes snapped into focus. 'You are amazing,' he murmured, staring at her. 'You're so different to how I imagined.'

Phoebe felt her colour rising. 'Are you complaining?' she said defensively.

Shaun shook his head. 'Hardly. I've dreamt about this so many times.' He made a soft sound in his throat and ran his hands over her sleep-warm nakedness. 'You're wonderful,' he purred.

Phoebe laughed nervously. 'I think I surprised myself as well. How long have you been thinking about getting me into bed?'

Shaun grinned and ran his fingers through his hair. 'Since the first time I saw you.'

Phoebe screwed up her nose. 'You said you saw me the day we started here. That's nearly two and a half years ago.'

Shaun reddened slightly. 'That's right. I'm a very patient man.' Playfully he rolled over on top of her, straddling her waist. He took her by surprise.

'But I didn't ever imagine it would be as good as this. I—' He stopped as she stretched up to kiss him, sliding her arms around him, her fears receding in the face of his undisguised approval. The tip of his cock nestled between the damp curve of her thighs. Shaun gasped as she lifted her hips and slowly guided him into her, a fraction at a time, relishing the way his cock slid seamlessly into her quim.

'Please, don't talk, just kiss me,' she said, her voice no more than a whisper, followed by a throaty mew of pleasure as her sex closed around him hungrily.

Wordlessly he arched his back, driving deeper, lighting every nerve-ending in her body. At first his progress was tentative; soft kisses nuzzling at the pulse in her throat before his lips moved lower, seeking out the sensitive peaks of her breasts.

She shivered, feeling a familiar glow of pleasure ignite low in her belly. There was a momentary flash when she visualised Gottlieb's burning dark eyes, but they were soon forgotten as Shaun drove them both on the stunning journey towards release.

His hips ground against her, friction and heat electrifying the engorged ridge of her clitoris. The sensations hit her like a summer storm; one minute distant, with just a promise of what might follow, the next explosive and all-engulfing. She reared up to meet his thrust, astonished that the pleasure could be so intense. He buried his face in her hair, murmuring words of delight and encouragement.

An instant later Phoebe felt the first, breathtaking, lightning flash of orgasm, followed an instant later by another and another, until she thought she might drown in the sheer intensity of the sensations.

'My God,' she hissed between gritted teeth, pulling Shaun closer. 'This is amazing.'

Shaun grinned down at her, his expression triumphant as he held back until the very last instant before joining her in the crashing floodtide.

'Bloody hell,' he murmured and drowned out her soft throaty gasps of pleasure with his kisses.

Finally, as they snuggled side by side in the grey morning light, he brushed a stray tendril of dark hair back from her face. 'Are you all right. I mean, really all right?' he said earnestly, on a soft outward breath. 'You seem quiet . . .' He paused. 'You don't regret doing this, do you?'

Phoebe shook her head. 'I've been thinking about what Gottlieb said, maybe I was too safe, too unadventurous.'

His face split into a warm grin. 'I like you just as you are, you don't have to prove anything to me.' He planted a tender kiss on her forehead before rolling out from amongst the tangled sheets. 'I really have to go though, I promised I'd go jogging with Tony this morning.'

'You think he's going to be up to it after last night?'

Shaun smiled as he retrieved his trousers from the bedside chair. 'He'll be fine.'

Phoebe nodded, noticing the way his eyes lingered hungrily on the contours of her body. She was tempted to pose, to stretch artfully. For a split second she was reminded of Gottlieb's mirror. What had he hoped to see reflected there? Quickly she dragged the duvet up around her shoulders.

'Is it all right if I come back this afternoon?' Shaun said, his eyes never leaving hers as if he couldn't quite believe his luck.

She nodded. 'I'd like that but I've got to do some work.'

Shaun pulled a face. 'Spoil-sport.'

He was almost dressed, pulling an Arran sweater on over a soft chambray shirt. Combined with faded jeans and his mop of dark hair, he looked almost edible. Phoebe felt a tiny ripple of desire in her belly. Shaun Rees was beautiful. She couldn't quite believe she felt so excited by him or that he had shared her bed so soon.

'If you're still in this mood—' he began mischievously. Cat-like he sprung onto the bed beside her and pulled her into his arms. 'Maybe I could persuade you to leave the work until tomorrow,' he whispered.

Phoebe felt herself melting until the abstract voice of reason bubbled up amongst the unfamiliar erotic images in her mind.

'I've got to get my notes up to date,' she whispered unsteadily, 'then try and come up with something for my final paper and I'm working at the restaurant tonight.'

She pulled the bedclothes tighter and returned his smile. 'So you'd better go and drag Tony out of bed.'

Shaun lifted a hand in farewell. 'See you later then.'

When he'd gone, Phoebe wrapped herself in the duvet and stood in front of the mirrored wardrobe. Slowly she let the cover fall to reveal her breasts, the soft swell of her belly, the dark almost sculptural triangle of hair between her thighs. Her skin seemed to have a bloom to it, as soft and enticing as ripe fruit. Her body still glower from Shaun's touch. She stared at her reflection as if seeing it for the first time. Turning slowly, she let the morning light caress her, highlighting her pert nipples and the sensual curve of her hips.

49

Mesmerised, she turned back and forth, watching herself, observing the shadows fall and lift across her until finally the cold made her pull the duvet back up over her nakedness.

'What do you see when you look at your reflection, Miss Williams?' she said softly.

What she saw was passion, a sensuous raw hunger that needed satisfying. She closed her eyes and forced the images to recede. Reaching across the bed she pulled on her robe, eyes still firmly closed. Passion would have to wait. She wanted to get as much study done before Shaun came back as she could.

By mid-morning Phoebe was busy on her computer, gnawing her lip as she re-read the notes that had taken all morning to compose. Open on the desk was a book of quotations. Glancing away from the screen, she slipped through the dog-eared pages again. She often used it to look for some new idea, something to inspire her from amongst the thoughts of the late, the great and the outrageous.

The Marquis de Sade. She sighed thoughtfully and ran her fingers back through her dark hair. There had to be something in his obsessive sexual journeying that would convince Gottlieb that she was neither safe nor repressed but a creature of real passion.

Between her legs she was damp – even after a shower. The remains of Shaun's lovemaking lingered, a subtle indication that she could surprise herself. Halfway down the page a quotation caught her eye and, staring down at the keyboard, she began to type it in:

'Woman's destiny is to be wanton, like the bitch, the she-wolf; she must belong to all who claim her.'

Marquis de Sade (1795)

When she had added the page reference she pushed away from the desk. She wasn't altogether sure why she had chosen it – perhaps Gottlieb would be able to tell her.

Shaun arrived back at Phoebe's flat at almost the same time as Nina King. Nina was dressed in her interpretation of a waitress's uniform: a tight black mini-skirt and sheer white blouse that did nothing to disguise her heavy breasts. As Phoebe opened the door to them she looked first at one and then the other. Shaun was holding a small posy of flowers and smiling, while Nina was clutching two freshly laundered frilly white aprons and lazily chewing gum.

Phoebe grinned and waved them inside.

'I began to think you weren't coming back,' she said mischievously to Shaun, as he kissed her hello.

Shaun coloured. 'Sorry, Tony and Beth had a row last night after we left. I thought I ought to stay and listen. Here, I brought you these.' His eyes were alight.

Phoebe smiled and took the little posy, trying to avoid looking into his expectant gaze.

'They're lovely.'

Shaun grinned. 'You too,' he whispered, kissing her again.

Phoebe glanced at Nina, who winked theatrically before slipping past them into the kitchen and filling the kettle.

'And I wasn't expecting you so soon,' Phoebe called to Nina's retreating figure.

Nina groaned. 'I told you we've got to go into work early, or have you forgotten that as well? There's a conference party in the function room tonight.'

Phoebe nodded. 'I know, but I didn't think that started until seven.'

'I've volunteered us to set up the tables.' Nina rubbed her thumb and forefinger together enthusiastically. 'A couple of hours extra – cash in hand.'

Shaun kissed Phoebe again. 'Bad timing. Look, I can come back later if you like. Would you like me to pick you up from work?'

Phoebe shook her head. 'I'm not sure when we'll be finished.'

Shaun looked nonplussed. 'Tomorrow then?'

Phoebe could almost see the same doubts and fears in his mind as she had had. She pressed herself against him, gently rubbing the rise of her sex against his thigh. Even as she did it she felt herself reddening. Shaun cupped her face in his hands and kissed her long and hard.

'I've already told you,' he whispered in an undertone. 'You've got nothing to prove to me. I'll be back tomorrow.'

Phoebe lifted a finger to outline his lips. 'Thank you for the flowers,' she whispered.

When he'd gone Nina came in with two mugs of tea and the biscuit tin which she prised open as soon as she'd put the tray on the table.

'Yum yum,' she said, peering into the tin with undisguised avarice. 'Chocolate digestives, living rather high on the hog, aren't we?'

Phoebe snorted. 'Help yourself.'

Nina threw herself into the armchair, exposing a mile of black stocking-clad leg. 'Well then, what have you got to tell me?'

Phoebe laughed as she tidied away her books. 'Absolutely nothing. I'm just going to go and get my uniform on. Don't eat all those, will you?'

Nina grimaced. 'Oh, *come on*. Shaun Rees looks like the cat who's got the cream, he followed me up the path whistling for God's sake – and flowers, too.' She rolled her eyes theatrically. 'I'd like all the sordid details.'

Phoebe laughed and threw a cushion at her. 'I'll be five minutes. Make sure you leave me some of those biscuits.'

Don Giovanni's upstairs function room was smoky and hot. It had been a long evening. After serving coffee and liqueurs Phoebe stood in the little service area near the kitchens and eased off her shoes with a sigh of relief. Nina swooped past her with a tray of empty glasses which she slid into the dumb waiter before lighting up a cigarette.

'Don't tell me you're shattered, kid,' Nina said, taking a long pull on the cigarette. 'I thought we'd go on to a club after this. That place in the arcade is open until three—'

Phoebe groaned miserably. 'Please. The only place I want to go is home to bed.'

Nina grinned. 'Really, I didn't think Shaun was coming round until tomorrow. Was he that good?'

Phoebe flushed crimson and, rather than meet Nina's eyes, she peered out through the porthole on the service doors into the dining room.

'It surprises me,' she said. 'All those fat little executives have got such beautiful wives and girlfriends.' She paused for a second. 'Is it a power thing? Are they attracted by their status?'

From behind her, Nina snorted. 'You can be such a twit,' she laughed, sidling up to stand alongside Phoebe. 'Those aren't their wives, you idiot. Their wives are all safely tucked up in suburbia. Here.' She pulled a folded brochure out of her apron pocket and handed it to a mystified Phoebe and then continued, 'Those girls out there are professionals brought in by the bus load for the evening.'

Phoebe stared blankly at the brochure and then at Nina, who pulled a face before pointing to the print. 'It says on the back there, "Escorts provided by Bad Company."'

Phoebe looked blankly out of the window again and then she saw with blinding clarity. The girls she had taken as wives and girlfriends were all stunning, immaculately dressed, not a hair out of place. Seated around the tables they were giving the men their undivided attention in a way no-one in a real couple ever did. She felt herself reddening furiously. Each girl was issuing a subtle message, their expensive clothes and elegantly coiffured hair didn't quite disguise the sensual undertones of the way they moved and looked.

'They're being paid?' she hissed in disbelief. 'But some of the delegates are women.'

Nina wrinkled up her nose in amusement. 'Where have you been all your life, Phoebe? Yes, some of the delegates are women, and some of the escorts are men. Look at that guy over by the door. He wouldn't be seen dead with an old crone like that if he wasn't being paid.'

Phoebe looked again, seeing the things she had missed before: the looks, the erotic body language, the way the escorts moved. How many other things had she missed? She shivered.

'Do they sleep with them?' she whispered in an undertone.

Nina snorted and stubbed out her cigarette.

'Buggered if I know or care, let's just get the rest of the tables clear, I can hear clubland calling me.' With that she snatched another tray off the counter and backed out of the double doors. For a few seconds Phoebe stared into the dining room then folded the brochure carefully into her pocket before following Nina.

'Bad Company personal services.' The next morning Phoebe stood in the hallway of the accommodation block and mouthed the name as she wrote down the telephone number from the local directory. She ran a finger down the column to see if there were any others.

'Hi, how's it going?'

Shaun's familiar voice made her jump. He was smiling.

Hastily Phoebe closed her notebook. 'Fine. How are you this morning?'

Shaun crossed the hall in a couple of strides. Phoebe couldn't suppress a little flutter of excitement as he lifted a hand to stroke her face. He was so close she could see the delicate tracery of lines around his eyes, feel his body heat, smell him. She blinked – where was all this coming from? It was as if she had tapped some great reserve of desire she never knew she had.

Shaun was staring at her. 'Are you okay today?'

She nodded dumbly, tucking the directories back onto the shelf, almost afraid to meet his eyes in case he could somehow read her thoughts.

Shaun screwed up his nose, studying her and then leant forward to whisper in her ear. 'You know, you look incredibly, amazingly sexy. Just seeing you makes me want to make love to you. Right here—' His tone was full of both surprise and delight.

Phoebe laughed. 'It's all in the mind,' she said quietly. Whose mind was the question.

Shaun kissed her lightly on the cheek. 'I'm really not complaining.'

There was a tiny electric pause when Phoebe felt another shiver of pleasure. She could feel Shaun's desire simmering just below the surface and knew she had only to give him one single word of encouragement, one look and he would follow her anywhere. She stared down at the cover of her notebook.

'I've still got some work to do,' she said briskly, trying not to be swept away by the newly discovered sensations. Shaun was still frozen to the spot, as if he had been captivated by some scent, some intense unseen signal that she was unwittingly giving off.

'I've been thinking about you all morning,' he said thickly and caught hold of her hand. She didn't resist as he guided it under his coat and wasn't in the least surprised to find his cock was pressing hard and angry against his soft faded denim jeans.

'Look what you're doing to me, I can't think about anything else,' he said with mock distress.

She felt him tremble as she stroked the outline with her

fingertips. When she looked up his face was scarlet; a heady mixture of pleasure and embarrassment. She smiled and ran the flat of her palm along his constrained shaft.

'Good thoughts?' she whispered.

Shaun's colour deepened. 'Not exactly,' he said wryly between tight lips. 'I keep thinking about Friday night. It's never been like that before.'

Phoebe didn't move her hand, instead she closed her fingers around him. He swallowed sharply. She edged a little closer. 'And what did you think of it?'

Shaun was trembling, she could feel an exciting electric hum beneath her fingertips. He shook his head, at a loss for words. She tightened her grip making him groan softly. Between her legs she could feel a soft liquid heat. She stared into Shaun's eyes.

'Well?'

He shivered. 'I don't know what to say,' he stammered lamely. 'Is this all to do with Gottlieb?'

Phoebe laughed. 'I'm not sure.'

Her fingers moved again making Shaun writhe miserably. He looked up and down the hallway in desperation. 'Are you going to invite me into the flat or am I going to have to screw you here?' he whispered thickly.

Phoebe laughed and removed her hand. 'I'm supposed to be working.'

Shaun groaned without meeting her eyes. 'I'm not sure I can wait.'

Phoebe nodded and pressed herself against him. 'Who says you have to?' she murmured, handing him the key to her flat. 'I've just got to make a phone call. Why don't you let yourself in? I won't be a minute.'

Without a word Shaun took the key from her fingers and turned on his heel. When she heard the flat door close, Phoebe dialled Bad Company before her courage failed her.

'Phoebe?'

Phoebe stretched and looked up from the computer screen at Shaun. He was hastily buttoning his shirt, tucking it into his jeans. She turned off the Walkman beside her and pulled off her headphones. 'Hello, I didn't hear you get up. What time is it? Would you like some coffee?'

Shaun didn't look as if he had coffee on his mind. 'Didn't you hear the door? There's someone outside to see you.'

Phoebe peered past him. 'Who is it? I really want to get this printed out,' she whispered.

Shaun blushed. 'She says you contacted her?' He lifted his hands helplessly. 'But . . .'

Phoebe pulled a face. 'I contacted her? Did she say what she wanted? What's her name?'

Shaun shifted uneasily from one foot to the other. 'Storm,' he said quietly.

Phoebe pulled a face, brushing her sweater as she got to her feet. 'Storm what?'

'I'm not sure.' He hesitated again. 'She's a bit . . . odd. I told her to wait outside.'

Phoebe's unexpected guest was curled provocatively on the sofa in the foyer of the accommodation block, twisting a tendril of shiny black hair around a scarlet fingertip. Intelligent brown eyes weighed Phoebe up in a single glance.

'Phoebe Williams?' she said in a deep, cultured voice.

Phoebe stared at her; no wonder Shaun had looked uncomfortable.

Phoebe coughed. 'How can I help you?' she said nervously, glancing out of the main doors. Parked against the fence was a low-slung cherry-red sports car.

'You rang Bad Company this morning?' said Storm. 'Something about doing some research?'

Phoebe held out a hand. 'You'd better come in,' she said. The woman followed her. Phoebe showed her into her sitting room, glancing nervously at Shaun, who was heading off towards the kitchen. He seemed to sense Phoebe looking in his direction and smiled.

'Coffee?' he said pleasantly.

Storm lifted a hand in agreement.

'Yes, please, that would be great,' she purred in a voice that came from somewhere below her navel. She was dressed in an elegant tailored cream suit that owed its pedigree more to *haute couture* than the high street. Elegant or not, the outfit couldn't disguise the sensuality of its wearer; it clung to every curve. She looked uncannily like the girls Phoebe had seen the previous night at Don Giovanni's.

Storm teased a cigarette packet from the pocket of a camel coat she had draped across the arm of the chair.

Phoebe held up her hand. 'I don't,' she said quickly, trying to get a grip on the situation.

Storm lifted an eyebrow. 'Not a problem,' she said and pushed the packet back out of sight.

Shaun hadn't moved, his attention focused on Storm's legs, which were clad in sheer black silk stockings and scintillating five-inch spiky high heels.

Phoebe took a deep breath. 'I hadn't expected anyone to contact me so quickly.'

Storm smiled and glanced down at the pile of folders neatly arranged on Phoebe's coffee table. 'You wanted to talk to someone – a professional escort? That's right, isn't it?' As she spoke she cast an appraising eye over Phoebe, who was suddenly very conscious of her comfortable floral leggings and warm sweater. 'Your final paper?'

'That's right,' Phoebe said in a quiet controlled voice. Shaun, still playing musical statues, made an odd breathy noise.

'I left my name and address so that someone could contact me. I hadn't expected anyone to turn up here.'

Storm smiled. 'Sorry, would you like me to leave? I was over this way. I had a booking at lunch time and thought I'd drop in on my way back.' She looked at Shaun who still hadn't moved. 'Is this a bad time?'

Phoebe shook her head. 'No, no it's fine, really. I'm just a bit surprised that's all.' Her voice faded as Storm slid a business card out of her clutch bag.

'I suppose I should have rung first,' Storm said. She leant across the coffee table and handed Phoebe the card, revealing a stunning expanse of cleavage that peeked from between the lapels of her jacket. Phoebe stared down at the card rather than the intimidating curve of Storm's breasts.

'Storm Brooks, PhD?'

Storm nodded. 'That's right, I took my doctorate in behavioural science. I thought perhaps you'd like me to help you. Technical details, the right contacts.' Storm smiled pleasantly.

Phoebe was knotted up like a corkscrew. 'I haven't actually got anything organised yet,' she managed to splutter defensively. 'It's just an idea at the moment.'

Storm got to her feet. 'That's okay. I thought maybe you'd like to get it right. First hand.' Before Phoebe could complain she whipped a cigarette from her pocket and lit up.

Phoebe sighed and collapsed into the armchair. 'Could I have one of those?'

Storm nodded and lit one of her own. 'When did you give up?' she asked sympathetically.

Phoebe took a long head-spinning drag. 'I've only tried it once before,' she said on the edge of a choking cough.

In the doorway Shaun coughed in sympathy.

'I'll make this coffee and then I'll be off,' he said and before Phoebe could protest he vanished into the kitchen.

When the tray was on the coffee table, Phoebe showed him to the door.

Shaun kissed her tenderly. 'This morning was amazing,' he said.

She smiled. 'You sound as if you're addicted.'

He blushed. 'Maybe that's what it is.' He nodded back towards the sitting room. 'Has she got anything to do with this Gottlieb thing?'

Phoebe shook her head. 'I'm not sure, it's only an idea I've got.'

Shaun pulled her close and kissed her again. 'I've got to go, can I see you tonight?'

Phoebe laughed in spite of herself. 'You really are hooked, aren't you? I'm not sure what this Storm character has in mind.'

Shaun nodded. 'Okay. I'll drop by later.'

When Phoebe went back into the sitting room Storm glanced up at her. 'Actually I've got a party booked for this evening,' she said, draining her mug.

'Oh, I'm sorry,' said Phoebe quickly, regretting that Shaun had left so quickly. 'I didn't realise I was holding you up.'

Storm shook her head. 'That wasn't what I meant. I wondered if perhaps you'd like to come along for the ride?'

Phoebe stared at her in astonishment. 'Sorry?'

'See what the job's like first-hand.'

Phoebe began to protest.

Storm held up a hand to silence her. 'It's really no big deal.'

'I'm not sure. I mean your clothes, the way you look, I . . . ' Phoebe's voice faded. She was so surprised by Storm's invitation that she didn't really know what to say, or think.

'That's nothing that couldn't be taken care of.' Storm studied her thoughtfully. 'At the moment you look like an off-duty social worker, none of the girls I work with will take you seriously dressed like that. If you want to interview them, this is the perfect opportunity to make a few contacts. The host is one of our regulars, he really won't mind if you tag along.'

Storm uncrossed her long legs and stood up before plucking a set of keys from her handbag. 'Clothes really wouldn't be a problem. I could take you to my place. I'm sure I can find something to fit – it's up to you . . .'

Phoebe hesitated for a second and then nodded. 'All right,' she said decisively. 'Why not?'

Storm Brooks turned her radiant, enticing smile on Phoebe. 'Why not indeed? Do you want to leave a note for your boyfriend? I didn't catch his name.'

Chapter Four

'Oh my God, what have you done to me?' Phoebe gasped, when she finally got a chance to look in the mirror of Storm Brooks' dressing-room. Storm stubbed out her cigarette in a dish on the dressing-table and stood back to admire her handiwork.

'Think of it as a disguise. You look great. After all, if you were going on safari you'd wear camouflage, wouldn't you? You've got to blend in if you want to do this properly.'

Phoebe stared at her reflection in disbelief. Gone was the comfortable woollen sweater and leggings, gone the sensible shoes. Actually, she did look . . . her mind scrambled around for a suitable adjective.

'You look really foxy,' said Storm, reading her mind. 'We'd have to beat the men off with a stick if you went cruising like that.'

Phoebe flushed crimson. Her transformation had taken less than an hour. She turned around admiring her reflection in the full-length mirror.

Storm had driven them across town to an elegant detached house just behind the park. The house itself had taken Phoebe completely by surprise.

'Is this yours?' she'd said as Storm turned the key in the lock and tapped a security code into the burglar alarm.

Storm nodded. 'Certainly is. I bought it last spring. Do you like it?'

Phoebe nodded dumbly.

Inside, every surface seemed to be painted in a soft warm cream, tables were arranged with tiny boxes and elegant lamps. The whole place looked like something out of a Sunday colour supplement. Storm waved her towards a door in the hall.

'Put your coat in there and then we'll go upstairs.'

As she spoke, a small dark woman appeared from the shadows.

Storm smiled. 'Hello, Mim. This is Miss Williams, Phoebe – my housekeeper, Mim Forbes.'

The woman smiled and nodded a greeting. Storm slipped off her coat and hung it over the banisters.

'Mim, could you bring us some tea, please?'

The woman nodded again and wordlessly vanished back into the depths of the house.

Upstairs, Phoebe had been overwhelmed by the air of refined luxury. After a shower, Phoebe sat wrapped in a thick towelling robe while Storm teased her sensible shoulder-length bob up into a tumult of curls. When Storm was satisfied, she'd presented Phoebe with a small box – inside was a black lace teddy that fitted Phoebe like a second skin, while at the same time displaying her breasts like a restoration banquet. Black silk hold-up stockings with a thick band of frothy lace around her thighs, black patent spikes, and a stunning make-up job

66

had transformed her small even features into cover girl material. Storm Brooks, PhD really knew her stuff.

'Well?' said Storm, leaning back provocatively against the dressing-table. 'What do you think?'

Phoebe shook her head at the image in the mirror. 'I don't believe it.'

Storm laughed. 'I told you it wouldn't take a lot, didn't I? So are you ready?'

Phoebe blew out her lips thoughtfully. 'I'm not sure, can you guarantee this won't wear off at midnight?'

Storm grinned. 'I've never thought of myself as a fairy godmother before. Let's find you a dress.' From one of the wardrobes she produced a floor-length metallic blue sheath that glittered like oil as she laid it across her arm.

Phoebe pulled a face as she slipped it on. 'Are you sure about this? I don't know what to do . . .'

Storm smiled 'Relax, you'll be fine. Just smile, make polite conversation. Let the men take the lead. You'll be okay, honest injun. Maybe next time around your boy-friend would like to come with us as well.' She grinned. 'I could give him a make-over too, not that he'd need much. He looked pretty hot as he was. Lots of our clients are ladies, he'd knock 'em dead.'

Astounded, Phoebe blushed crimson. 'Shaun?'

Storm grinned and lit another cigarette. 'Why not? Are you all set?'

'I think so.' She glanced nervously back at the mirror and the pile of familiar clothes folded up on the dressing-table.

Storm grinned. 'Relax, you look just fine, don't panic. I'll find you a coat downstairs. We'll put the rest of your things in a bag.'

Phoebe gazed at her reflection and whispered, 'Whore about town.'

Storm was tidying away the tray of make-up. 'Relax. If you wait downstairs I'll just go and get changed. It won't take me long, we've got a party to go to.'

'I'm really still not sure about this,' said Phoebe apprehensively as she climbed the steps of the elegant mansion on the outskirts of a small town. Below her, a coloured guy with a body that looked as if it had been carved out of granite, was valet-parking the cherry-red Stag that had brought Phoebe and Storm – extremely fast – on a motorway journey into a leafy green belt not far away from London.

Storm grinned, opened her bag and took out a breath freshener. 'Here.'

'My breath smells?' said Phoebe incredulously.

Storm shook her head. 'Vodka, have a good belt and then I'll give you a mint. Relax, you look perfect. Let me do the talking until you get the feel of what's going on. I rang the guy who's throwing the party while you were in the shower, he really doesn't mind.' She beamed cheerfully and mounted the final few steps. 'Come on!'

At the door an elderly woman was working the coat check. She smiled when she saw Storm. 'How nice to see you again, my dear. Are you well?'

Storm hit her with a smile the size of a small battleship. 'I'm fine, how are you?'

The woman looked away, hanging coats. 'Not so bad. Who's your friend?'

Phoebe shrank down into her five-inch spikes, trying to

cling onto her composure and look inconspicuous.

Storm slipped her coat down over her milky white shoulders to reveal a tiny black evening dress that barely – just barely – covered her breathtaking curves. Phoebe blushed scarlet; she had wondered what Storm had been doing upstairs before they left.

'Take your coat off, Phoebe. It'll be taken good care of. This is Phoebe Williams, she's doing research,' said Storm calmly, dropping Phoebe a long slow conspiratorial wink.

The old lady looked up at Phoebe in amazement. 'Really? Ooh, how interesting.' Her face contorted in delight.

Phoebe parted reluctantly with her borrowed leather trench coat.

'Not working tonight though, sadly,' added Storm. 'Bad back.'

The woman sighed theatrically. 'Ooh, I know what you mean. Mine gives me so much jip, you wouldn't believe it. If you're not working you'd better have one of these.' From under the marble table she took a little black arm band.

Phoebe hesitated until the woman pressed it into her hands. 'There we are, my dear. Have a lovely time.'

'We will,' said Storm, lifting a hand in salute. As they walked into the sumptuous main hall Phoebe started to pull the arm band on. She desperately wished it was a long sensible black dress. Coming to the party with Storm had been total madness. She looked around wondering if there was any way she could make a discreet exit.

Storm sighed. 'For God's sake, don't put that on. It's like a red rag to a bull. You'll have every man in the place after you.'

Phoebe paused mid-stride. 'I'm not with you, I thought it meant I wasn't available?'

Storm looked heavenwards. 'It's supposed to, but haven't you ever heard of forbidden fruit? They'll be all over you trying to find out why you're out of bounds. A friend of mine always brings her own black band to kick-start trade on a slow night. Here, give it to me, I'll stick it in my bag.'

Phoebe meanwhile was trying to take in the scene that was rapidly filling every sense. The hallway was a vast oval with a fountain in the centre, the walls were cream and maroon marble and, in front of them, a huge sweeping staircase rose up towards a galleried landing. Understated luxury it was not; it crowed opulence and over-indulgence loud and clear.

'My God,' Phoebe whispered on an outward breath. In one wall a set of doors were being discreetly minded by two good-looking gorillas in dinner suits that fitted them in a way that suggested they were far more at home in muscle vests and shorts.

The tallest one, six foot plus, with a spiral perm that brushed his shoulders and tan too deep to be natural, grinned at Storm. 'How's it going, babe?'

Storm smiled warmly. 'Joe! I didn't know you were on duty tonight.'

The man shrugged and pulled a face. 'They wanted the best, what can I say?' As he spoke he eyed Phoebe speculatively, quietly taking in every square inch of her flesh, exposed and otherwise.

Storm gave her an encouraging smile. 'Phoebe Williams, I'd like you to meet Joe Blenheim. Joe's in security.'

Nervously Phoebe extended a hand which Joe pressed to his lips with an unnerving flourish. 'Delighted,' he purred, eyes alight with something Phoebe had just learnt to recognise; lust, handsomely packaged and very, very close to the surface.

Storm sighed and disentangled Phoebe's fingers from Joe's. 'Oh, please,' she sighed. 'Give the girl a bit of leg room. She's new to this. Here for research purposes only.'

Joe lifted an eyebrow. 'Really? Maybe I could give you a guided tour of what's on offer,' he said, his eyes not leaving Phoebe's. She wondered if anyone had really ever died of pure embarrassment, if her face got much redder she thought, she might just explode.

'Who's here?' said Storm, finally dragging Joe's attention away from Phoebe.

'Huh? Oh, Phillipa, Helen, Daisy, most of the usual faces.'

'And men?'

Joe groaned theatrically. 'Why do you always have to spoil it, babe? Gordon, the party animal, has invited everyone from Sonny Grayson upwards.' He smiled at Phoebe again, his white teeth seemed wolfish. 'Are you sure your friend is off limits? There are men in there who would sell their soul for a slice of something oven fresh.' He paused. 'Not to mention one or two out here who're gentle, kind, and can show a lady a wonderful, wonderful time.' His eyes moved over Phoebe's breasts like warm hands. It was all she could do to suppress a shudder.

Storm cheerfully slipped her arm through Phoebe's. 'Time to party.'

As Joe opened the doors for them, Phoebe hissed, 'What do I say to keep them away?'

Storm grinned. 'Use your imagination. You're the student. But don't be too keen to turn it down. I mean, there's nothing says you can't change your mind.'

The double doors opened to reveal an enormous split-level room, the whole of the far wall made up of glass doors which opened onto a floodlit terrace.

Phoebe glanced left and right trying to absorb everything. The room was furnished with comfortable settees and low tables, groups of people moved around talking in subdued voices, while uniformed staff circulated, carrying glasses of champagne.

Phoebe sighed with relief; since they had arrived her imagination had been working overtime. She'd wondered if they were going to walk in on a full-blown orgy but this was like a cocktail party. Feeling more confident she followed Storm, who was making for a small group of men standing near the buffet table.

They looked up as Storm approached and one man – a great bear with a shock of white shoulder-length hair – grinned a broad welcome. 'My dear Storm,' he said, 'how very nice of you to come.' He embraced her, kissing each cheek with enthusiasm. He glanced at Phoebe. 'And this must be your student friend.' With equal warmth he embraced her.

Phoebe smiled. 'It was nice of you to let me come.'

'My pleasure, my dear. I hope you have a wonderful time. Let me introduce you to my friends. This is David—' He nodded towards a tall balding man who grasped her hand, eyes alight. The introductions moved on around the group, each man smiling and shaking Phoebe's hand. None of the men were under thirty, their manner and dress suggesting they were well-established, wealthy executives.

'And what did you do before you were Storm's student, my dear?' asked David, as the waiter offered Phoebe a glass of champagne.

She smiled, he looked a pleasant-enough man, distinguished – a doctor or a teacher maybe.

'Actually I worked as a classroom assistant,' she began, sipping her drink. 'The staff encouraged me to take a degree, I . . .' From the corner of her eye she saw Storm drawing a slender finger across her throat. The words caught in Phoebe's throat.

Storm stepped forward and touched Phoebe on the shoulder. 'Take no notice of her, David, she's just teasing you,' Storm purred. She winked discreetly at Phoebe. 'No need to be so coy, Miss Phoebe, you're amongst friends here.' She turned back to David who was staring at Phoebe with barely concealed interest.

'Miss Phoebe is a very strict disciplinarian – an extremely accomplished mistress of correction.' She aped a whip cracking and made a sharp hissing sound like leather cutting through the air.

David brightened visibly. 'Oh really,' he whispered, the colour rising in his weather-beaten features. 'How very interesting.' He smiled coyly at Phoebe. 'Perhaps you and I might get together some time, Miss Phoebe. I've been a terribly naughty boy.'

Phoebe could feel her face reddening as Storm continued conspiratorially. 'Great shame, David, but she's out of commission tonight. Exhausted after a very hectic afternoon.' She tapped the side of her nose and David positively twinkled.

'Well, of course, I do understand,' he blustered. 'My apologies. Perhaps another time, Miss Phoebe. Might I give you my card?'

He pulled a business card from the inside pocket of his dinner jacket. Storm took it from him and wheeled Phoebe away.

'If you'll excuse us, gentlemen, I think we really ought to circulate.'

Their host beamed at Storm. 'Of course, my dear, see you a little later.'

Storm skilfully guided Phoebe towards the far end of the buffet. 'Rule one,' Storm whispered, lifting two more glasses of champagne from a passing waiter. 'Never tell the clients anything about yourself.'

Phoebe stared at her. 'What? What do I say to them then?'

Storm grinned and handed her a glass. 'Lie. They want magic and mystery, wild fantasy – they most definitely do not want the truth. You're not likely to see any of them again, so you can be exactly who you want for a few hours.'

Storm plucked a plate from the buffet table and continued, 'Re-invent yourself. I spent a very enjoyable evening as a white Russian princess being hand-fed caviar and vodka by an extremely attentive and very rich client.'

Phoebe stared at her. 'Are you serious?'

Storm grinned. 'Of course, you can be anything or anyone you want while you're here.'

Phoebe took a thoughtful pull on her champagne.

'Heady stuff,' said Storm, teasing a tiger prawn from

amongst a mouth-watering display of shellfish.

'The champagne?' said Phoebe, staring into her glass.

Storm shook her head. 'No, my little innocent – the fantasy. Now fill up your plate and I'll introduce you to some of the other people here.'

By the time Phoebe had been guided under Storm's eager hand around the party her senses were reeling. The girls were stunning and exuded an easy but still intimidating sexuality. They were all dressed in evening gowns that must have cost the earth, all beautifully made up and coiffured – a selection of tasty morsels as enticing and inviting as the sumptuous buffet.

The men seemed deferential and polite, though this didn't quite disguise the way they appraised Phoebe's body with the eyes of potential purchasers.

Storm grinned as they finally completed a circuit around the huge room. She lifted her glass towards the little group of men Phoebe had met first, smiling warmly as she spoke.

'David has obviously been spreading the word.'

'What word?' said Phoebe, taking another long pull on her glass.

Storm stared at her. 'Where have you been all your life? They think you're a dominatrix.'

The expression on Phoebe's face gave away her non-comprehension.

Storm shook her head in disbelief. 'Whips and chains? Leather gear? Rubber? They think you discipline clients. Sado-masochism? Is this ringing any bells?'

Phoebe nearly choked on her champagne and flushed scarlet. 'You've got to be joking,' she hissed, struggling to swallow her drink.

Storm shrugged. 'Not at all. It's not to everyone's taste so most of the straight guys will stay clear of you. By telling David you've been working this afternoon none of the submissives – who would be interested – would dare ask you for a good thrashing in case they upset you. Now, come on, there's someone I'd like you to meet. After all, I *am* supposed to be working.'

As they crossed the floor Phoebe realised that the mood in the room was subtly changing; earlier it had seemed like a subdued cocktail party, now – though nothing had visibly changed – there was a different feel to the party, as if the air was suffused with a volatile erotic charge.

'Do you sleep with any of the clients?' Phoebe hissed in an undertone.

Storm smiled wolfishly. 'What do you think?'

Phoebe already knew the answer, officially or unofficially, she certainly did.

Outside, the night was darkening, the lights dimming, and the intimacy between the couples was bubbling to the surface. At the tables the women were moving imperceptibly closer to the men. Here and there a man was touching his companion – not overtly but with the promise of things to come.

In a secluded corner by a pillar, a tall man in a dinner jacket was slowly turning a glass between his long fingers. As they approached, he looked up and smiled. Storm seemed to change up a gear, her walk subtly altering as the man watched their progress across the crowded room. Phoebe hesitated as the man got to his feet but Storm shooed her along.

'Come on, he won't bite – at least not in public.'

'Good evening, Storm,' said the man, his voice betraying the merest hint of a foreign accent. 'How are you this evening?'

Storm slid into the seat beside him and kissed him gently on the cheek. 'Geno, how lovely to see you again. This is my friend, Phoebe Wiliams. Phoebe, this is Geno.'

Introductions over, Phoebe stood by the table feeling extremely uncomfortable. It was obvious that Geno and Storm were more than just friends, and she was unsure whether to sit down or leave them alone together.

Storm indicated a chair but Phoebe shook her head.

'No, I think I'll go and get something else to eat,' she said awkwardly.

Storm lifted an eyebrow. 'Are you sure?'

Phoebe nodded. 'I'll be fine. I won't be long,' she added with a confidence she didn't feel and headed back across the room towards the buffet table. As she did so, the lights in the room dimmed and for the first time Phoebe noticed that in the centre, near the French windows, was a stage. A split-second later a spotlight flicked on and music which until then had been no more than a background noise, rose in volume.

The conversation in the room faded to a low hum and Phoebe stared in disbelief at the stage. The spotlight picked out a tall, slim woman clad in a leather body-harness. The heavily studded straps circled her shapely breasts, exaggerating their heavy contours, crossing over her navel. Below, the dark leather framed her sex before ending in thick bands, strapped around her slim but muscular thighs. Her long legs were clad in thigh-length shiny black boots, her face obscured by a leather mask, set with silver studs.

The music rose again and the woman thrust her pelvis forward dramatically, while one long gloved finger stroked the open lips of her trimmed pussy. With the other hand she lifted an intimidating whip and, as her finger found the tight bud of her clitoris, she cracked it like a thunder bolt, threw back her head and howled like a wolf.

Phoebe was completely stunned and stood open-mouthed as the woman prowled around the small stage, cracking the whip. In the centre of the stage stood a bentwood café chair, over which were draped a pair of handcuffs.

Phoebe couldn't believe her eyes and blinked, trying to clear her head.

The leather-clad woman suddenly leapt off the stage and grabbed one of the escorts, a slim blonde girl in a scarlet mini-dress, who was sitting at a table amongst a group of other guests. The girl screamed and writhed, fighting the tall woman, who relentlessly dragged her towards the stage. As they struggled their way into the spotlight, the masked woman seized the top of the girl's dress and, with a single violent movement, ripped it down, revealing the milky white curves of the girl's bosom.

There was a hiss of approval from the audience as her tormentor cupped one heavy breast in her gloved hand and squeezed it speculatively, tweaking the ripe pink nipple. The girl sobbed and writhed miserably but the woman did not stop. She guided the girl towards the chair, all the time her fingers working at the girl's body, ripping away the remainder of her evening dress. The victim mewed unhappily, naked now except for her stockings and a pair of red high heels.

Although Phoebe had guesssed it was a performance she could sense the small blonde's growing excitement. The woman pushed her slave onto her knees and thrust her pelvis forward, one gloved finger easing into her own quim to hold the lips open.

The girl aped revulsion, whimpering a protest while Phoebe stared in disbelief, feeling the heat and shock building in her belly.

'No, no, please,' the girl sobbed but her leather-clad mistress was merciless. She wound her fingers into the girl's long hair and forced her face into her groin. The girl let out a stifled scream and then relented, her tongue working back and forth along the pink flushed lips of the dominatrix's open sex.

Even from where she was standing Phoebe could hear the wet sounds as the girl worked at the taller woman's quim and see the way her harnessed breasts flushed and swelled, nipples hardening as the blonde girl lapped and nibbled at her clitoris.

Phoebe was stunned; she could almost feel the web of pleasure seeping up through the woman in the harness, who was moving with the girl, rhythmically thrusting her hips forward in time with the girl's eager tongue. She snorted as the girl whined, dragging her closer and closer, trailing the end of the whip across the girl's delicate flesh.

Phoebe could sense the tall woman's orgasm approaching, a sparkling lightning flash. Between her own legs she could feel the same unnerving flickers of excitement and the wetness gathering.

At the last second, just as Phoebe felt sure the leather-clad woman could take no more, she leapt back and dragged the girl to her feet. In a single smooth movement the blonde straddled the chair and the woman snapped her wrists into a set of handcuffs, securing her to the bentwood frame.

The blonde girl could no longer keep up the pretence of fear; her eyes glittered with expectation, her skin glowing and alive with excitement. Behind her the leather-clad woman flexed the whip speculatively and let the end swish through the air in a practice swing.

The blonde girl shivered, eyes widening. The next blow was closer, a crueller stroke, scything through the air with a dramatic hiss. Phoebe could feel goose bumps lifting on her skin. She looked around; every eye in the room was concentrated on the stage.

The blonde girl tensed in the split second before the first blow struck her squarely across the back. She let out a desperate cry of pain, her breasts thrust forward, nipples darkening to scarlet – as if the blood had rushed into them to escape the whip's merciless kiss. Between the bent-wood frame of the chair it was possible to make out the open lips of her mink-trimmed quim. Open and pink, it glistened in the low stage lighting.

Phoebe could feel the colour rising in her face, a strange unnerving heat rushing through her, while on the platform the leather-clad woman stretched back to apply the next stroke.

Phoebe couldn't decide whether she was excited or horrified. This time the blow was lower, making the girl writhe against the chair. Her lips were drawn back in an ecstatic grimace, her eyes shut tight, her pelvis thrusting forwards so that the mouth of her sex gaped.

Phoebe swallowed hard, wishing she had the strength to look away. Instead she was mesmerised by the spectacle. Again the whip fell and the girl's head jerked back. Her torturer smiled beneath the mask and, leaning forward, planted a wet, sensual kiss on her victim's open mouth. Around her Phoebe could feel the erotic undercurrents rising, the room was working its way as a single body towards release.

Four, five – the whip head fell again and again. The blonde girl had given herself over entirely to the call of the explosive pain. Phoebe tried to imagine what it would feel like and shuddered as she pictured the raw sting of the whip across her back.

Six, seven – the blonde girl was grinding her pelvis into the chair, straining to press her quim against the smooth frame.

Eight, nine – Phoebe wondered how much longer the beating would continue. The tension in the room was almost unbearable.

Ten – the final blow cracked against the girl's pale flesh and she slumped forward, sobbing uncontrollably.

The leather-clad bitch threw down the whip and undid her victim's handcuffs. Then, dropping onto her hands and knees she crawled across the stage, her submissive pose at odds with the strange leather harness.

Phoebe thought the exhibition was over and looked away just as a man in a long dressing-gown stepped onto the stage beside the women. Phoebe looked back and realised with a jolt that it was the man she had been introduced to by Storm as their host. The leather-clad woman scuttled across the floor and rubbed against his legs like a huge exotic cat.

Their host smiled thinly and stroked her smooth black leather skull-cap. The wild woman purred with delight and lifted her hands to undo his robe. It opened to reveal that he was naked beneath, his cock arched and angry. The size of it made Phoebe gasp – he was huge.

The woman took his shaft in her hands and began to lap at the end where a single teardrop of excitement glistened. She sucked greedily, hungry to pleasure him, one hand lifting to cup and stroke his heavy scrotum.

The man's expression was impassive as the girl worked herself to a frenzy, fingers dipping down into the wet ripe confines of her own sex, then lifting to smear his shaft and balls with her thick glistening juices. Soft moans of pleasure trickled from between her lips.

Phoebe felt as if she had opened Pandora's box. She had no idea that things like this went on and the revelations made her shiver with a subtle mixture of excitement and astonishment.

The woman started to pull away, breathless, but the man caught hold of her head and pulled her further onto him. She snorted and writhed, saliva trickling down her chin as she fought to bring them both to release. Phoebe could sense their mutual excitement despite the man's deadpan expression. Suddenly he let out a single throaty gasp and jerked away from the leather woman's open mouth. An arc of semen flooded over her, splashing across her face and breasts. At almost the same instant the woman began to twitch and shudder, drowning in the great well of her own orgasm as her fingers worked in the sopping pit between her legs.

The room was silent except for the base beat of the

music and the sound of the performers' excited breaths.

The woman collapsed at the man's feet, his swollen cock, wet from her caresses, still jutted above her like a sword. Snake-like the blonde girl clambered off the chair and crept across the stage. Dropping onto all fours beside the prone body of her torturer she began to lick the silvery warm semen off her mistress's ripe breasts, lapping like a kitten, drinking it in. The spotlight picked out the criss-cross of raised livid weals across her narrow back.

Phoebe finally looked away, her senses totally overwhelmed. She felt dizzy and, even more unnerving, wildly excited. More than anything else she felt she needed air. Silently, trying to ignore the continuing passion on the stage she crept through the shadows towards the doors that led out into the entrance hall. With every step she felt the disturbing glow of excitement between her legs.

'Hello there,' said a familiar voice as she stepped out into the cool dark air. Joe Blenheim, standing in the shadow of the stairs, grinned at her. 'What did you think of Gordon's little exhibition?' he said darkly.

Phoebe glanced back towards the closed doors. 'How . . .?' she began.

Joe smiled and extended a hand towards her. Without thinking, she stepped into the shadows to join him. Under the stairs was a tiny control room, barely bigger than a cupboard, in which a bank of small TV screens flickered. One showed the antics on the stage; the blonde girl had now mounted the harnessed woman and was pressing her sopping quim to the leather-clad woman's enthusiastic tongue. Phoebe shuddered and looked at the other screens; a second camera showed the door through which she had just escaped.

Joe was close behind her, cutting off her retreat. He was so close she could smell his cologne and a delicate male musk that made her shiver. She didn't need to be told he was aroused, she could almost touch the tension in the air. She shivered. Between her legs, low in her belly, she felt the same enticing need.

Slowly, almost as if in a dream, she slid onto her knees and lifted her hands to his flies. Beneath the fabric she could feel the hard outline of his cock. Trying hard to quell the voice of reason that bubbled up in her mind, she slid down the zip and released him. His cock was meaty, thick, and the slightest touch of its intimidating contours made her quiver with expectation. Closing her eyes she guided him into her mouth and began to lap at the rigid shaft.

Above her, Joe let out a snort of delight and pulled her head closer. Her fingers fumbled to cup the heavy bulk of his balls, gently stroking and thumbing the delicate puckered skin. Joe groaned appreciatively as she ran her tongue around the end of his cock, across the raw angry glans, lapping eagerly.

'Oh yes,' he hissed.

She could taste his excitement, slick and salty on her tongue. He began to thrust forward rhythmically, driving his cock deeper and deeper into her mouth. She tried hard to stay in control, while deep inside she could feel her own pleasure growing, unsatisfied and compelling.

Beneath her fingertips she could feel his power building

– an instant later Joe's seed flooded her mouth. She gasped at the sheer power of it, afraid she would choke. He thrust forward again as if he wanted to be sure she had taken every last drop. Finally he pulled her up to kiss him.

His tongue opened her lips, eager and hungry, lapping up the remains of his own excitement while his hands slid between her thighs, bundling up the dark oily fabric of her evening dress. She was confused; her mind told her this was complete madness, while her body bayed for satisfaction.

Joe backed away, grinning. 'Take off your clothes,' he whispered.

Phoebe stared at him. For an instant she saw not Joe Blenheim but Gerrard Gottlieb, standing over her, his cock glowing ivory-white in the shadows.

'Take off your clothes,' he repeated, more firmly now.

Wordlessly she pushed the straps of her evening dress down over her shoulders revealing the black teddy beneath.

Joe grinned. 'Very nice,' he murmured. 'Take it off.'

Her eyes never leaving Joe's face, Phoebe eased the teddy down and let it drop to the floor. Standing in the little control room, naked except for black stockings and the ridiculous spiky high heels, Phoebe suddenly felt an overwhelming sense of panic.

As if sensing her fears Joe reached out and stroked her cheek. 'It's all right,' he hissed in an undertone. 'It's all right.'

Stepping closer, he slowly sank to his knees. She could feel the caress of his breath, and knew he was breathing in the smell of her excitement. His lips were warm and unnerving against her delicate flesh. He pressed a single kiss to her navel and she knew then that she was lost.

It felt as if she began to come even before he reached her sex. Great waves of pleasure coursed through her, drowning out reason and the tiny inner voice of fear. His tongue lapped and teased at the folds of her quim, drinking her in.

She heard a throaty moan of delight as the waves crashed through her mind and realised with a start that the voice was her own. Joe pulled her tighter against him, tongue and fingers driving into her. Her whole body seemed to be drowning in wave after wave of ecstasy. At the last second, when she thought she would faint, Joe got up and slowly turned her in his arms, bending her face down over the security console.

Without prelude, he guided his revived and straining cock between her legs and slid into the wet throbbing depths of her sex. With one hand he traced the delicate glittering ridge of her clitoris, while with the other he pulled her back onto him. She began to sob – whatever she had felt before, this drove her out on a final breathtaking journey. The pleasure built in spirals, going on and on until, finally, she felt a white-hot explosion deep in her mind and she floated, totally sated, back to reality.

Hunched over her, Joe Blenheim was gasping for breath.

'Jesus,' he whispered, slipping from her exhausted body. 'You're wasted as a student.'

It was after two when Storm Brooks pulled the little Stag

to a halt under the street light outside Phoebe's flat. When Phoebe had left Joe, head still reeling, she had returned to the party where the floor show had inexplicably moved onto the floor alongside the stage. The sedate audience had slowly thinned, disappearing Phoebe guessed, to relieve the tension the exhibition had sparked in all of them.

Storm had vanished and for the next hour or so Phoebe had consoled herself with champagne. Finally Storm had reappeared alone, her face glowing.

The journey home had been made in almost complete silence as Phoebe tried to make sense of what had happened.

Storm cut the engine and lit a cigarette.

Phoebe turned towards her. 'Would you like to come in and have coffee?'

Storm smiled and shook her head. 'Nope, I want to get home to bed, preferably alone. Did you have a good time?'

Phoebe laughed. 'I'm not sure that's how I would describe it.' She eased herself out of the low seat. Between her legs she could still feel the wet, glistening remnants of Joe Blenheim's excitement. 'What about your dress?' she said as she stood on the pavement.

Storm smiled. 'Drop it by the agency, I'm too bushed to worry about it tonight. Oh and don't forget your bag.'

When she had gone, red tail lights vanishing along the darkened avenue, Phoebe stood for a few seconds and wondered what on earth she had done.

In her bedroom she looked at her reflection in the dressing-table mirror. The elegant beautifully dressed young woman who stared back at her with knowing sensual eyes seemed to have very little to do with the Phoebe Williams she had known all her life.

Chapter Five

'I came round to see you last night,' said Shaun the following morning, as he and Phoebe walked across the green towards the main university buildings.

Phoebe smiled an apology. There had been a brief moment after she had woken up when she thought perhaps the night's events had been nothing more than a dream. The fleeting thoughts were followed an instant later by the stunning realisation that it had all been real. She'd glanced around the bedroom and seen the evidence; Storm's evening dress, the silk teddy, the dark sensuous curve of the black stockings lying discarded on the floor beside the bed.

Shaun slipped his arm through hers. 'So what did this Storm character have to say for herself? Did you go to her place? I was worried.'

Not wanting to be drawn into a conversation she wasn't ready for, Phoebe glanced down at her watch. 'I'm sorry, I should have rung you. Look, would you mind if we talked about this later? I've got a meeting with Gottlieb in about five minutes.'

Looking slightly bemused, Shaun said, 'How about if we meet up for lunch?'

Phoebe flashed him a reassuring smile. 'Great, about twelve?'

Shaun nodded. 'In the refectory. What had she got to say for herself?'

'Some interesting stuff,' Phoebe began. 'She'll be a great help with my paper. I'll tell you about it later. I've got to go.'

Phoebe hoisted the strap of her bag higher onto her shoulder and was about to hare off across the grass when Shaun caught hold of her. Eyes alight, he spun her into his arms and kissed her tenderly.

'I really missed you last night,' he whispered.

Phoebe felt her whole body respond instinctively to his sweet lips.

'Missed you too,' she said softly and realised it was true.

What Storm Brooks had shown her had nothing to do with real relationships, or emotion, it was purely business. She shivered – who was the fool who said you couldn't mix business with pleasure?

Shaun tightened his arms, making her giggle as he pressed the breath out of her. The heat from his body made her ache for him. Reluctantly, she disentangled herself from his arms.

'I really do have to go,' she said thickly.

Shaun grinned. 'Pity. My mind was working overtime.'

From the window of his office Gerrard Gottlieb watched Shaun Rees and Phoebe Williams making their way across the grass. The boy kissed Phoebe one more time before they parted and she hurried towards his office. He sensed their mutual desire as the young man brushed Phoebe's lips with his. Gottlieb smiled thinly.

Young love was so very touching. For an instant he imagined the young man's eager fumblings, their embarrassed innocence, raw desires laid bare. The thought of Phoebe Williams shimmying out of her sensible warm clothes for her young lover – in the dark, self-conscious and blushing madly – lit a tiny flare of desire in his belly.

What he would give to be privy to their first clumsy attempts at lovemaking. He could almost feel the sensual delights of her tight sex closing around Shaun Rees' shaft, her throaty whimpering in the darkness as Phoebe tried to find the passion that Gottlieb knew lurked within.

Poor, repressed Phoebe Williams, unaware of the addictive and compelling prize she nurtured between those long sensibly clad legs. He doubted Shaun Rees was man enough to discover the holy grail, to tame it, to both worship and control that scintillating beast. Gottlieb felt a familiar stirring in his groin and looked away from the window, trying to shake off the compelling images.

Phoebe Williams, head down, was now scurrying up the path. He settled himself behind his desk and opened the notebook in front of him.

Her knock was polite, tentative.

'Come in,' he called, buttoning his jacket over the discomforting bulge in the front of his trousers.

The door opened slowly and for a second Phoebe was framed in the doorway. The hungry wind had brought the colour to her cheeks, teasing a wisp or two from out of her ponytail. Her coat was open, revealing a pale grey sweater, pulled tight over her pert little breasts. The cold or perhaps the excitement of the embrace with her young lover had hardened her nipples and they pressed, erect and mouth-watering against thin fabric. Gottlieb smiled.

'Good morning, why don't you take off your coat, Miss Williams, and come inside. It's much warmer in here.'

Phoebe smiled and stepped into his lair.

Slipping off her heavy coat he noticed that a single button was undone at the neck of her sweater and shivered; an oversight without doubt. Girls like Phoebe Williams weren't aware of the subtle invitation of the single unfastened button, suggesting that more lurked beneath. She picked up a file from her bag and pressed it to her chest before sitting down; an instinctive protective gesture. He smiled at her provocative modesty and looked again at the notebook in front of him.

'Do take a seat,' he said. 'Have you given any more thought to what you might do for your final paper?'

To his surprise Phoebe looked him straight in the eye, the slightest of smiles playing on her full pink lips.

'Yes,' she said quietly and opened her file. 'I thought I would look at professional sexual services.' She paused, almost as if her courage was about to fail her.

Gottlieb leant forward. He could see a tiny rapid pulse fluttering in the pit of her throat.

'Really,' he said darkly. 'The oldest profession is a long way from nursery provision, Miss Williams. What has decided you on this course of action?'

He could sense her composure crumbling and felt a disproportionate sense of triumph.

'Well?' he pressed.

Phoebe's fingers curled around the edge of her file, tightening a little. For an instant he imagined her tensing in the split second before the whip bit into her narrow back, then the muscle spasm as the heat and the explosive charge roared through her slim body. It was tempting to open the drawer and remove the manacles just to see the expression on her face. She really was quite fascinating.

Phoebe took a deep breath. 'It interests me,' she said in a small voice.

Gottlieb grinned. '*Interest*, Miss Williams – do you think that will be enough?'

To his surprise she got to her feet and turned around to stare into the full-length mirror on his office wall. Her electric blue eyes reflected back at him. Her face was flushed, her nipples still peaked and hard, her pale skin glowing with something he had no problem in identifying as passion.

'Oh yes,' she said in a deep throaty voice. 'I think it will.'

Gottlieb was astonished, perhaps he had underestimated the effects of the young man on her, perhaps the boy was an earthy, debauched lover despite his appearance. Even as he thought it, Gottlieb doubted it was true. The boy was like a thousand others – safe and unschooled. But something had most definitely happened to the tight-lipped repressed Miss Phoebe Williams. Now all he had to do was endeavour to find out what.

He got to his feet and poured two mugs of coffee from the filter machine on a side table. 'Perhaps, Miss Williams, we ought to talk about this. I would hate to think of you taking on something that you couldn't manage. My position should be to guide you, to instruct you, to . . .'

Phoebe spun round, blue eyes ablaze. ' . . . To initiate me?' she hissed darkly.

Gottlieb stepped back as if she had struck him. 'What?' He fought to regain his normal sense of control. He handed her the mug of coffee. 'What an interesting choice of words. Why don't you sit down, Miss Williams? I'd like to hear what has brought about this change of heart.'

Phoebe crumbled into the chair, fingers laced tight around her mug.

'You have no idea what you've done to me, do you?' she said unevenly.

Gottlieb settled back behind his desk. 'No. Why don't you tell me, Miss Williams?'

Phoebe stared out of the office window at the wind-swept trees beyond. The silence hung between them like a veil. Gottlieb was tempted to prompt her to speak when suddenly Phoebe took a deep breath.

'You made me feel so dull,' she began unsteadily. 'You were right – I've played everything so safe until now.' Her voice trembled with emotion.

Gottlieb licked his lips. 'So what has happened since we last met?' he prompted in a low even tone.

Phoebe Williams swung round to stare at him. 'I did something about it,' she snapped.

Gottlieb nodded sagely, feeling his pulse quicken. 'And what was that?

Phoebe took another deep breath and began to speak in a quiet unhurried voice, so distant it was almost as if she were talking to herself. Gottlieb sat back and listened in enrapt silence.

'I went to supper with some of Shaun's friends. Tony, his friend, was drunk and he looked at me.' She shivered and stared up at Gottlieb with a mixture of confusion and elation. 'He wanted me, he was weighing me up, assessing his chances – in a way that had nothing to do with who I was as a person but purely because of my sex.' She paused. 'I suppose I must have seen that look before, but until you talked to me about passion I'd never thought about what it meant.

'Shaun looks at me in the same way; completely mesmerised, hypnotised by possibilities. When Tony looked at me, it was exciting. Not because it was Tony, he repulses me, but there was this sense of . . .' She paused, struggling to find the right words. 'It was like having this ancient power that I can't define. Magic. A sort of enchantment. And then when I was at work at the restaurant I saw these girls . . .' Her voice trailed off.

Suddenly she glanced up at Gottlieb, eyes flashing an accusation.

'You looked at me in the same way when I came here for the first time. Women have used that special addiction since time began, haven't they?' She stopped and took a mouthful of coffee. 'I wanted to understand what it was, so I rang up an escort agency.'

Gottlieb shook his head in disbelief but Phoebe was oblivious now, her thoughts turned inward. Slowly she began to tell him about meeting Storm Brooks, her transformation from student into siren; the party, the floorshow, Joe Blenheim, and her young lover, Shaun Rees, all plaited and twisted into an erotic narrative that shook Gottlieb to the core. Whatever he had expected her reaction to be, this certainly wasn't it. He was stunned. Finally she took a long slow breath and laid her file on his desk.

'So, Professor Gottlieb,' she said, 'is there enough passion for you in this?'

Gottlieb was almost too astounded to speak, but finally he said, 'And where do you plan to go from here, Miss Williams?'

Phoebe sighed, pushing a stray hair back behind her ears. 'Research. Isn't that the backbone of a good paper? I was introduced to several girls last night, and then there's Storm Brooks. I'm going to interview them, collect more information.' She paused and bit her lip.

Gottlieb leant closer. 'And what about you? What are you going to do?'

Phoebe shook her head. 'Nothing,' she said emphatically. 'My interest is going to be purely academic from now on. Because of you I've experienced things I never knew existed . . .' She stopped. 'It is an addiction, isn't it? This passion you hold so dear.'

Gottlied allowed himself a wry smile. 'Oh yes, Miss Williams,' he said quietly. 'Very much so.' And one, he thought, as Phoebe closed her notebook, that was not so easy to walk away from.

After she had gone, he took the photo album from his bookcase and opened it to the picture of the girl secured between the bedposts. Perhaps his fantasy wasn't as impossible as he had anticipated. He opened the telephone directory and found Bad Company's telephone number. He wouldn't ring today but he wanted the number at hand.

* * *

The refectory was bustling with life when Phoebe hurried in out of the cold. She was pleased to see that Shaun had already arrived and saved a table for them by the window. He saw her as she came in and raised a hand in greeting. Even across the crowded canteen she could see the expectation in his face and wondered why it was that the understanding had passed her by for so long. Everything about him exuded a quiet but inescapable invitation: he wanted her. If she walked over to him now and suggested they went back to her flat he would follow her without protest, eager and willingly ensnared.

She tried to shake the thoughts off. She hadn't really meant to tell Gottlieb about the weekend but in a strange way she was glad she had. It was as if she had left the events with him and walked away free and untouched.

Stepping into the queue for lunch and hooking a tray off the pile, Phoebe grinned. She had shocked Gottlieb to the core and it had given her a real sense of pleasure. Passion was not his exclusive province. Waiting to be served, she wondered what she should say to Shaun; she didn't want to lie to him but she could hardly tell him the whole truth. In the end she decided on economy – she would tell him nothing more than the bare bones, without telling any lies.

He smiled and stood up when she got to the table. 'How did it go with Gottlieb this morning?' he asked.

Phoebe slid her tray onto the table. 'Not too bad at all. Quite well, in fact,' she said guardedly. 'I just needed some time to adjust to his way of thinking.'

Shaun nodded. 'Great. I told you it was just a difference of style. And how did you get on with that woman?'

Phoebe waited, considering her answer.

'Last night?' he said lamely.

'She took me to meet some very interesting people. Like I said, they'll make great material for my paper. I'm going to work on an interview – maybe a questionnaire.'

Shaun nodded, he seemed unsatisfied but reluctant to push for a more detailed answer. 'You're not getting into anything you can't handle, are you? She seems like a bit of a character.'

Phoebe was about to agree when Nina King, huffing and puffing, appeared alongside their table.

'God, I'm so glad I've found you,' she hissed, dropping her books onto the table beside Phoebe's lunch. 'I've had one hell of a morning.'

Shaun who had been leaning across the table shuffled his chair over to let Nina sit down.

'I'll go and get us some coffee,' he said quietly to Phoebe.

Nina beamed at him. 'God, you're such a little treasure. Could you get me a sandwich while you're up there?'

Shaun nodded and wordlessly got to his feet.

'So what's the matter?' said Phoebe.

Nina rolled her eyes heavenwards. 'I got lousy marks for my last paper. The head of the department gave me a real dressing-down this morning and told me to pull my finger out.' Nina slipped the chewing gum out of her mouth and slid it under the table. 'I've spent the whole bloody morning in the library for God's sake. Unheard of!' She grinned. 'I did offer to bring the smile back to his face for a decent grade but he said we couldn't really get away with that in my final year.' She paused for an instant. 'Great pity, he's a lot of fun when you get to know him.'

Phoebe stared at her. 'What . . .' she began. 'Are you being serious?'

Nina snorted. 'For God's sake, Phoebe, how do you think I've managed to get this far? I've done an awful lot of practical work to get my credits.'

Phoebe leant closer and dropped her voice. 'Are you seriously telling me you've been sleeping your way to a degree?'

Nina opened another stick of gum and rolled it onto her tongue. 'Let me tell you, Phoebe Williams, there hasn't been an awful lot of sleeping. Besides, it's continuous assessment, I've had to work really hard to get this far.' She glanced left and right around the crowded room. 'Trouble is, I've still got to submit an extended essay – a project – to stand any chance of getting a degree, let alone a decent one.'

Phoebe stared at her incredulously. 'Why didn't you say anything before?' she hissed, watching for Shaun to return.

Nina shrugged. 'Don't know really,' she looked at Phoebe. 'I didn't think you'd understand, but you've changed, something is different about you.'

Phoebe reddened, wondering if it was so obvious to everyone else. She was about to ask, when Shaun re-appeared with a tray laden down with coffee and sandwiches. Nina wolfed hers down as if she hadn't eaten in a week, threw a handful of change onto the tray and then hastily said goodbye.

'Got to get back to the library,' she said with a wry grin. 'Oh, by the way, my head of department says he's going to see if Gottlieb will take me on for some extra study. Says he will be able to get the best out of me – what do you reckon?'

Phoebe stared at her, utterly speechless.

Nina shrugged. 'Anyway, got to go and hit the books. The library calls.' She grinned. 'Did I *really* say that?'

When she had gone Shaun shovelled up the change. 'That girl is totally off the wall,' he said with more than a hint of disapproval in his voice.

Phoebe's mind was elsewhere – Nina's college career was something else she hadn't considered until that moment. Nina and Phoebe's head of department was a distinguished, staid-looking man in his late fifties who, Phoebe had thought, was far too lofty to involve himself in the day-to-day lives of his students. Obviously she was wrong. Phoebe stared at the retreating form of Nina King as she manoeuvred between the groups of students. Nina had bought a passage to a degree with her body. Phoebe was stunned – did every woman use her body to get what she wanted? Stirring her coffee, she realised that Shaun was talking and quickly turned her attention back to him.

' . . . Tickets for the fourteenth. So what do you think?'

Phoebe stared blankly at him.

He looked up and grinned. 'I mean, I'm not banking on it, I'm sure Tony and Beth will sort everything out before then.'

'Sorry,' she said quickly. 'It's so noisy in here, I missed that.'

Shaun, to her surprise, laughed. 'Don't tell me, your mind was elsewhere. Mine too. Have you got any more classes this afternoon?' His voice dropped to a low purr and she realised with a jolt he was talking about sex. He had imagined she was thinking about being in bed with him. He leant across the table and ran a finger across her lips.

'I *really* missed you last night,' he said softly. 'I haven't thought about anything else since yesterday.'

Phoebe closed her lips around the tip of his finger and caressed it with her tongue.

Shaun shivered. 'My God,' he hissed, 'you really are something else.'

Phoebe grinned and sat back from the table. 'Tell me about Tony and Beth again.'

Shaun coughed as if to drag his thoughts back on track. 'They had a huge row the night we went over there for supper and Beth ended up throwing him out. He's staying over at our place for the moment – Mark doesn't mind. Anyway, Tony said he'd give me some concert tickets he'd bought as a surprise for Beth. Wembley Arena on the fourteenth of next month, some big benefit concert with loads of great names. The tickets cover the coach and everything.'

Phoebe nodded her approval. 'Sounds terrific, shame about Tony and Beth though. Maybe they'll sort it out.'

Shaun groaned. 'God, I wish. Tony's on a real bender – he's on a sandwich course sponsored by his firm, so he's got the money to do it in style. When I got back from yours yesterday he was sitting on my doorstep making out with a bottle of tequila. In the end I was glad to get out and walk round to see if you were in, just to escape him moaning and crying. I left him with Mark.' He reddened. 'Sorry, that doesn't sound very complimentary, does it? Using you to escape from Tony. I don't sound very sympathetic, do I?'

Phoebe laughed. 'Nothing worse than someone else's broken heart. Sorry I wasn't in.' She paused and noticed the way his eyes moved over her face, his gaze a caress.

'Did you know my flatmate, Mark, is going out with Nina?'

Phoebe laughed. 'I knew she had plans for him.' Her voice was low and teasing.

'And have you got any plans for me?' he said, his tone dropping to match hers.

Phoebe's eyes twinkled. 'I might have – after we finish eating.'

She moved fractionally closer and didn't resist as he brushed her lips with his. Under the table she felt the pressure of his fingers on her thighs and shivered.

Shaun's eyes darkened. 'So, have you got any lectures this afternoon?'

Phoebe shook her head. Without another word, Shaun offered her his hand.

'I never dreamt it would be like this in a million years,' Shaun hissed softly as Phoebe turned the shower onto full.

The warm water coursed over their bodies. She lathered the soap in her fingers, wiping the bubbles in thick glittering bands over Shaun's chest. He shivered, pulling her close, her breasts glittering and slick. Eagerly he kissed her, moaning with delight as she rubbed herself against him.

Against her belly she could feel the taut curve of his shaft, begging for attention, hungry for her touch. She hadn't imagined that it could be so good either. Fleetingly she thought of the unsatisfactory lovemaking in the few relationships she had had before Shaun – dark rooms and uneasy fumblings accompanied by an overwhelming sense of shame and unease. God, this was so much better.

She threw back her head and surrendered as Shaun drew a ripe nipple between his lips, tonguing fragments of sheer pleasure into its sensitive peak. She lifted one leg to encircle his waist, thrusting her pelvis forward, opening herself for his cock.

He grinned. 'And there was me thinking all this was just my torrid imagination.'

Phoebe giggled. 'Do you think I'm wanton?'

Shaun snorted. 'Oh my God, yes, I'm convinced you are.'

She lifted her pelvis, rubbing the lips of her quim against his thigh. 'And you don't mind?'

His reply was a throaty bark. With one hand he took her weight and thrust her back against the cold tiles, sliding into her, letting out a sobbing gasping cry of triumph as he found his mark. She gasped as she felt her body tighten around him, as hungry and as needy as his.

The water added a sensual, electrifying garnish, hot needle-points biting into their skin before running down over the junction of their bodies, adding a glistening sheen to the curves and plains of their flesh. The dark hair between her legs was festooned with diamond-bright droplets of water, which shimmered as she thrust forward again and again.

Phoebe was mesmerised; every thought and every sensation was absorbed in the compelling motion of their bodies. She kissed him as she never had before, grabbing wildly at his back, dragging him closer and closer, pressing her tongue deep into his mouth, seeking out the soft sensitive places. She stroked the roof of his mouth with the very tip of her tongue, making him shiver.

He moaned, hands moving down over the curve of her breasts, teasing at her erect nipples, lingering over the tight little dimple of her navel before a single finger parted the diamond-strewn lips of her sex and sought out the jewel within.

She moaned with sheer ecstasy as he stroked her clitoris, thrusting onto him, the waves of satisfaction crashing through her slender frame as if his caress had opened up a well-stream of pure platinum pleasure. She realised with stunning clarity that at that moment they could have been anyone – their personalities had faded away, their whole consciousness totally absorbed by their bodies' over-whelming struggle for release.

Deep inside her, she felt the first rhythmic throb of Shaun's cock as it surrendered its seed, his ragged earthy thrusts adding a final glittering thrill to her own orgasm. As her body began to shiver and twitch she gave up thinking, gave up the safe rationalisation of what was happening to her, and surrendered instead to a world of pure sensation.

When they were done, the only sound was of the torrent of cascading water, cooling now over their warm bodies.

Shaun pulled her to him.

'I love you,' he murmured thickly, pressing his lips to hers and for a split second Phoebe wondered if this was how the ancient trap of passion was always sprung.

Later, when they were dressed, they drank tea in the sitting room, curled up in front of the fire. Phoebe couldn't quite suppress a wry grin as she handed Shaun a mug. How very civilised, she thought mischievously, after an animalistic, invigorating fuck to sit and have tea.

She flushed. While Nina King wouldn't hesitate to call a spade a spade, Phoebe couldn't think of a time in her life when she'd ever thought of sex as anything other than making love. She rarely swore, had never used the f-word aloud and was stunned that she thought of what she and Shaun had done as fucking. She returned to the bedroom to fetch a towel for her hair – and also to disguise the fact that she was blushing furiously. Amongst the clothes on the chair by her bed was Storm Brooks' evening dress – a reminder of just what Phoebe was capable of.

She fingered the delicate shimmering fabric thoughtfully. On the floor, arranged in a neat pair were the spiky high-heeled court shoes. The stockings and silk teddy were washed and drying on the radiator – Phoebe shuddered – they would all have to go back. There was no way she wanted Shaun to see the evidence of the party. Quickly she scooped everything up and threw the bundle of clothes into a carrier-bag.

When she got back into the sitting room Shaun was laying at full stretch in the armchair, eyelids drooping. She smiled tenderly. He looked wonderfully pink and clean, his hair still hanging in damp dark curls.

'Hello,' he purred in a sleepy voice as she knelt down beside him and prised the cup out of his fingers.

She stroked his face. 'I've just got to pop out,' she said in a whisper. 'You can stay there. I won't be very long.'

Shaun's eyes were closing rapidly. 'Are you sure?' he said on a weary breath.

Phoebe didn't answer. Instead she went back into the
bedroom and picked up the bag with Storm's party clothes
in it. Bad Company's offices were not far away. It
shouldn't take her more than half an hour to get there and
back.

The offices were above a shoe shop in Dove Street.
Phoebe looked left and right before hurrying inside. Two
flights up the corridor opened into a wide waiting area,
painted in oyster pink and arranged with a comfortable
sofa, a coffee table and a wealth of artificial plants.
Opposite the stairwell was a door marked 'Reception'.
Phoebe took a deep breath and knocked.

'Come in,' said a cultured female voice. 'The door's
open.'

Behind a large desk sat a stately but quite elderly
woman, grey hair teased up into a sleek chignon. She
smiled at Phoebe. 'How can I help you?'

Phoebe felt the colour rising in her face and held the
bag out in front of her like a shield. 'I was with Storm
Brooks at the party last night,' she began.

The woman nodded and turned to open a filing cabinet.
'What's your name?' she said, pulling out a bundle of
papers.

Phoebe was a little nonplussed. 'Phoebe,' she said,
'Phoebe Williams.'

The woman turned to look at her more closely. 'You
haven't been here before, have you?'

'No, I haven't, but I did ring,' Phoebe began again. 'I
wanted to arrange an interview with . . .'

'No need,' said the woman, opening the bundle of

papers and peeling off a form. 'Consider yourself hired. If Storm recruited you, I've no doubt you'll do just fine.'

Before Phoebe could protest the woman cut her off and slid the form across the desk.

'Now, if you'd just like to sign this, down at the bottom there.' As she spoke, she opened her desk and produced an envelope which she handed to Phoebe. Phoebe stared at her in astonishment and then at the envelope; it was unsealed and as she turned it over in her fingers she realised it was full of money. 'There's been a mistake,' she started again.

The woman's expression hardened. 'I don't think so, my dear, that's the going rate for new girls. We offer the best rates locally and always in cash. Now, if you'd just like to sign at the bottom of the page.'

Phoebe took the pen and signed almost without thinking.

'Right,' said the woman, consulting a large book on her desk. 'I've got a real problem tonight. Can you cover for one of the other girls? She's off with the flu.' She ran her finger down the page. 'Dinner party at Lampeter Hall, the cars are booked to pick the girls up from here at seven-thirty. The host is called Lawrence Langman, he's an exporter. Black tie, eight for eight-thirty. Will you be able to do it?'

Phoebe stared at her blankly and found herself nodding. 'Yes,' she said in an undertone. 'Yes, I can.'

The woman smiled. 'Wonderful. Don't forget the cars will be here at half past seven. I'd appreciate it if next time you come in you give me a list of nights you're free to work and a phone number. Now what did you want me to do with that bag?'

Phoebe shook her head, folding the envelope of money into her handbag.

'Nothing,' she said unsteadily. 'Nothing at all.'

Before she went home Phoebe went into the shopping centre and bought herself an evening dress, a pair of high-heeled sandals and a selection of delicious frothy underwear. There was more money in the envelope than she normally spent all term.

When she unlocked the door to her flat, Shaun was still asleep, curled up in the soft glow of the fire. She slipped her shopping into the bedroom and made more tea.

He woke with a stretch and a wide shame-faced grin. 'Sorry,' he said, as she bent close to breathe in the sleepy warmth of his body. 'Not exactly very tactful of me. How long have I been asleep?'

'It's all right, I'm not mortally offended. I'm afraid though that I'm going to have to throw you out. I've got to work tonight.'

Shaun wrinkled up his nose. 'I thought you only did weekends?'

Phoebe was careful to avoid his eyes, she didn't want him to see the uncertainty or the lie lurking in them. 'I'm doing someone a favour,' she said casually. 'No big deal.'

'Ah well,' he sounded resigned. 'Never mind, do you want me to come by later when you've done?'

Phoebe snuggled up close to him and kissed him on the end of the nose. 'Not really, I'll be grouchy, tired and ready for bed.'

Shaun grinned. 'Really? Maybe I should drop in then.'

She pulled away and slapped his arm playfully. 'You're insatiable.'

Shaun's eyes clouded over with desire. 'Oh yes,' he whispered. 'I think I probably am where you're concerned.'

'You'd better go, I need to get ready.'

'You're always sending me away.' Shaun pantomimed a doleful face. 'It's early yet.'

Phoebe lifted her eyebrows. 'I know, but if you stay I know I'll be late. I need to have another shower, maybe snatch an hour's sleep. You're not the only one who'd like to curl up in front of the fire for a cat nap.'

Reluctantly Shaun got to his feet. His soft cotton shirt clung to his broad muscular chest, tight faded denims emphasising his long legs. Phoebe swallowed; he was hard to resist. Quickly, before she had a chance to reconsider, she picked up his jacket.

'If I'm back at a reasonable time I'll give you a ring,' she said. 'Now, clear off before I succumb to temptation and call in sick.'

Phoebe sat in front of her dressing-table. The transformation was almost complete. Unable to recreate Storm's tumble of curls she had twisted her shiny dark hair up into a sophisticated pleat, teasing out a few tendrils out around her face to soften the overall effect. She'd added long diamante earrings and make-up. She didn't look quite as sophisticated as when Storm had worked her particular brand of magic but, even so, Phoebe looked very different from the fresh-faced student who had sat down in front of the mirror an hour earlier.

She slipped off her robe and looked critically at her body. The new teddy was dove grey, with silk stockings to match. She turned to admire herself. The thin silken fabric emphasised every curve. A carefully cut bodice accentuated her small high breasts before easing over her flat stomach, the swell of her hips and the inviting rise of her sex.

For a few seconds Phoebe wondered if she really had the confidence to go through with it and then thought about Storm's advice; she could be anyone she wanted. There was no need to be Phoebe Williams, the nervous and uncertain student. In this stunning camouflage she could be whoever she wanted. Slipping on the chic blue silk evening-dress she had bought, Phoebe glanced at the clock. She had booked a taxi to take her to Bad Company's offices for seven-thirty – all she had to do now was wait.

She turned again in front of the mirror. Following Storm's example she had chosen an outfit that was stylish and sophisticated; the pale blue sheath complimented her colouring and accentuated the smooth slim lines of her body. On the dressing-table was the price tag – it was too expensive to bear looking at.

Despite her appearance, Phoebe's stomach was in knots, she'd already left it as long as she could before getting ready in case her courage failed her. Looking at the clock for what must have been the hundredth time, she wondered whether it was too late to cancel the taxi. In the mirror her eyes were glittering with nervous energy – she could ring up and make her apologies. Hadn't she told Gottlieb she wouldn't feed the addiction again? It wasn't too late. This was madness.

Snatching up her handbag, she was about to head out into the hall to use the communal phone when she heard the honk of a car horn outside the window. The taxi had arrived. Phoebe swallowed hard, choking back the nervous lump in her throat, picked up the leather coat she had borrowed from Storm and headed towards the door.

As she slid into the taxi, the driver eyed her speculatively in the rear view mirror.

'Where to?' he said, cigarette dangling from the corner of his mouth.

'Outside the shoe shop in Dove Street,' said Phoebe quietly. 'Number eighteen, near the lights.'

The driver nodded. 'Right you are,' he said and started the ignition. As the sound of the engine filled the car Phoebe was certain she heard him say, 'I might have guessed.'

She bit her lip. 'I can be anybody tonight,' she said under her breath. 'Absolutely anybody.'

Gerrard Gottlieb sat in his study and turned a pen thoughtfully between his fingers. Phoebe Williams had turned out to be something of a dark horse. In his fantasies he had encouraged her to be bolder, stirred the dark sexual chemistry of her hidden nature, encouraged her compliance in his games – but never in his wildest dreams had he considered that anything would come of it. He poured himself another glass of wine. What a find she had turned out to be. He smiled. Perhaps he might have the chance to enact his fantasy after all.

He didn't imagine for one second that she would repeat her experiences at the party, but the guilt . . . He picked up the pad on which he had written the telephone number of the escort agency. With the right encouragement, Phoebe might be persuaded to atone for her sins and he would be on hand to mete out that punishment.

He could see her now, tied between the posts of his bed, her perfect breasts shivering, anticipating her punishment. His little housekeeper, Maya, might enjoy it too. In his mind he visualised Maya creeping in to see what was going on. Phoebe would be flushed, straining against the manacles as she suddenly realised her helplessness. He could imagine Maya's dark bright eyes drinking in the scene, her taut little body quivering with excitement. She would beg him to allow her to join them. Crawling across the bed, she would cup Phoebe's breasts lovingly in her tiny hands, lapping at their erect pink nipples.

Phoebe Williams would gasp and try to pull away, her expression an intoxicating mixture of revulsion and curiosity. She would gasp as the little whore snaked her tongue lower, a wet trail of sensation and pleasure, lower and lower ... Gottlieb closed his eyes and let out a strangled breath.

He would have to find a way to arrange it – and he hadn't even got as far, in his mind's eyes, as flexing his wrist and watching Phoebe writhe, twist and beg for mercy in the split second before the pain coursed through her back.

He was trembling when Maya opened the door. Her bright feral eyes took in the details of his arousal in an instant. She pouted provocatively and slid the silk robe off her narrow shoulders. The lamplight threw her pert breasts into gold-kissed relief. Slowly she crossed the room, her fingers toying with the slick, almost hairless, lips of her quim.

Gottlieb watched her, spellbound, his own arousal like a hungry force in his gut that bayed for satisfaction. Maya sashayed closer, posing with every step. When she was alongside him she boosted herself up onto the desk, opening her legs, her hands lifting to tease her sumptuous breasts. Gottlieb, who hadn't moved until then, suddenly sprung to his feet making her cry out in fear. He grinned and, grabbing hold of her tiny frame, flipped her over onto her belly, forcing her down amongst the piles of books and notes.

She shrieked in protest, wriggling furiously in his huge hands. Her surprise delighted him. Securing her with one great paw, he opened his flies and pulled his engorged shaft free. She whimpered as she felt it brush against her thighs.

'Wait, Gerrard,' she hissed thickly. 'Let me . . .'

But Gottlieb didn't want to wait. Kicking her ankles apart, he plunged into her sex, nailing her like a butterfly to a pin board.

She shrieked again as he plunged deeper still, grinding his hips up against her. Fingers locked in her black hair he jerked her onto him, bowing her up in an arc. She wriggled helplessly; he was far too strong for her. On and on he pressed, oblivious to everything except the pursuit of his own pleasure and the enticing haunting features of Phoebe Williams. He would have her too – and he would have her soon.

Chapter Six

In Dove Street, Phoebe stepped out onto the pavement and pressed a ten-pound note into the cabby's hand. She tried hard to avoid his eyes, which moved across her with a mixture of contempt and curiosity. She wanted to be away from him as quickly as possible.

'Keep the change,' she said, pulling Storm's coat tight around her.

The driver laughed dryly. 'Cheers. Lotta money in your line of work, is there?'

She reddened. Phoebe Williams, student, would have run a mile. Phoebe Williams, professional escort, ought to be a very different kettle of fish. She made an effort to stand her ground and turned to smile at him. 'I'll ring you when I want you to pick me up. I've got your card.'

The man lifted a hand in salute. 'Right you are,' he said with a wink. 'See yer later. Don't work too hard.'

Phoebe smiled coolly and turned on her heel.

At the door to Bad Company's offices she hesitated for a second. A passing cab driver was one thing, how would she cope when she met the rest of the girls? She took a deep breath – there was only one way to find out. Making her way up the stairs, she could hear the subdued sound of voices and laughter. Her confidence ebbed with every step; what the hell was she doing?

By the time she got to the landing it was all Phoebe could do to stop from turning tail and running back down. Only the prospect of another cab ride or, worse still, a long cold walk home in high heels kept her going.

'Hiya,' said a bright voice, as she crested the stairs.

A petite blonde in a stunning black cocktail dress stood behind a small table holding wine bottles and glasses.

Phoebe swallowed nervously and put on a smile. Squeezed onto the landing was a small crowd of stunning, chic young women. Phoebe looked at the girl who had greeted her and, with a flash of astonishment, realised it was the little blonde who had received the dramatic whipping on the stage at the party.

The girl smiled again. 'You're Storm's friend, aren't you? The student. I met you last night? Would you like a glass of wine? I've just opened another bottle.' She pressed a glass into Phoebe's hands. 'I'm sorry. I can't remember your name.'

Phoebe struggled to find her voice. 'I'm Phoebe.'

The girl extended a hand. 'Oh yes, I remember now. I'm Daisy, Daisy Forbes.' She glanced at her watch. 'Storm should be here any minute. The cars are booked for half past.'

Phoebe felt uncomfortable; it hadn't occurred to her that Storm Brooks might be there as well. Around her the girls were talking, drinking and putting final touches to their make-up. Daisy drifted off to take a glass to another girl, leaving Phoebe standing uneasily at the top of the stairs. She heard footsteps and turned to glance into the stairwell.

Storm Brooks smiled up at her. 'Well, look at you,' she said, taking the stairs two at a time. 'All dressed up and ready to party. You look good. I thought maybe we'd seen the last of you. I should have known better.'

Phoebe blushed. 'I came round this afternoon to bring back the outfit you lent me,' she began, 'but the reception-ist misunderstood.'

Storm's eyes twinkled mischievously. 'Really?'

Phoebe flushed crimson. 'She hired me.'

Storm laughed. 'In that case, welcome aboard. I'd better introduce you to the rest of the girls if you're on the staff now. You've already met Daisy, this is Alice . . .'

By the time the cars turned up to collect them, Phoebe felt a little more at ease – not much – but enough to quell the sick feeling in her stomach. As they hurried downstairs Storm caught hold of her arm. 'You can travel with me in the last car. We'll have a chance to talk.'

Phoebe nodded. After the other girls had clambered into a fleet of expensive black cars, she slid into the dark confines of the last limo alongside Storm.

'A word of advice,' said Storm, folding her coat over her long legs. 'If you're serious about working for me, keep your hands off the hired help. You're paid to enter-tain the punters not the boys in the back room.'

Phoebe gasped. 'How did you know?' she spluttered.

Storm patted her thigh gently. 'Don't worry about it, it won't go any further and you wouldn't be the first to get hi-jacked by Joe Blenheim. He does a nice line in erotic movies if you're ever short of work. He's never been known to say no to a good-looking volunteer.'

Phoebe reddened. 'How did you find out?'

Storm laughed dryly. 'You underestimate yourself. Joe rang me up this morning to see if you would consider some film work and David – you remember David? – rang to see if he could get your number. He says he's been a terribly naughty boy and needs a good firm hand to get him back on the straight and narrow.'

Phoebe stared at her. 'Are you serious?'

Storm took a cigarette out of her bag. 'Never more so. Just watch out for Joe Blenheim. He's very well connected and it doesn't do to upset him but try to keep him at a distance. He's pushy and very manipulative. He can take you down pathways you don't want to go – David on the other hand is a total sweety. I'll give you his number.'

Phoebe sat back and watched the street lights pass by. That first phone call to Bad Company had opened the doors into a very different world.

'Where are we going tonight?' she said after a second or two.

Storm took a long pull on her cigarette. 'Dinner party at Lampeter Hall. The host is a guy called Lawrence Langman. Set himself up as a local squire.'

Phoebe glanced at her. 'You've been there before?'

Storm shook her head. 'No, I keep well in with Beatie, that's the woman on the reception desk at Bad Company.' She grinned, her teeth unnaturally white in the darkness. 'The one who interviewed you.'

'She rang you too, didn't she?' said Phoebe.

Storm leant closer. 'Oh yes, babe, she most certainly did. Said you'd been up to the office, something about an interview. She'd got no idea you were doing research and, as you agreed to do the number at Lampeter Hall, I assumed you didn't want me to tell her the truth.'

Phoebe stared at her thoughtfully. 'How was it you came to my flat the other day?'

Storm's eyes narrowed a little against a plume of cigarette smoke. 'You left a message on the answering machine, didn't you? I nipped in to see Beatie and played it back. No great mystery.'

Phoebe let the information sift through her mind for a second or two. 'Why did you listen to the machine? I mean, you're not a receptionist.'

Storm threw back her head and laughed. 'God save me from girls with an education. I'm a partner in Bad Company. Half of it belongs to me, although I'd appreciate if you didn't make that public knowledge. You can call me a recruiter if you like. A talent scout.'

Phoebe stared at her. 'A talent scout?'

Storm nodded. 'Yep, and I thought you had real talent, Miss Williams.' She stared at Phoebe, eyes reduced to bright pinpricks. 'I was right, wasn't I?'

Phoebe didn't reply, instead she turned her attention to the window and watched the night speeding past. In the distance she could see the lights of the campus where Shaun Rees was at home waiting for her to ring. She shivered.

Lampeter Hall was a few miles out of town. Set in its own grounds, well back from the main road amongst a floodlit formal garden, it was an impressive sight. Phoebe stared as the procession of cars made their way slowly up the winding driveway towards the house. She let out a low hiss of astonishment.

Storm poked her playfully. 'Whole new world eh, Miss Blue Stocking?'

Phoebe smiled. 'Certainly is, Dr Brooks. How did you get caught up in this?'

Storm shrugged. 'It's too long a story to go into, let's just say it pays an awful lot better than listening to people whining on a couch all day long. Not to mention being a helluva lot more fun.' She paused. 'It should be fun, you know, Phoebe. Relax, enjoy yourself. What you do, how much you do, is your choice. You can call the shots. Some of the girls always take a client to bed but it's not obligatory. If they do, the guest pays them directly in cash. Guys like Langman and his cronies pay well, they've got a lot more money than they know what to do with. Get them to talk about themselves, there's nothing a man loves more than a captive audience.'

The car crunched to a halt on the gravel outside the main doors. Phoebe's stomach did a back flip as the chauffeur opened the door for them.

Storm grinned. 'Relax.'

In the main entrance hall, their host, Lawrence Langman was welcoming the girls as they arrived. On his arm was a stunning blonde Amazon, dressed in a silver fishtail evening-gown.

The room was dimly lit, with a log fire burning in an inglenook fire place. The girls milled around amongst a group of well-heeled middle-aged men who – Phoebe suspected – had been there some time. Their eyes were already wine bright, their laughter a little too loud.

When Storm and Phoebe fronted the queue, the blonde woman kissed Storm warmly on both cheeks.

'Lovely to see you again,' she purred.

Storm smiled. 'You too, Caroline.'

The blonde woman turned to Lawrence, a distinguished, well-preserved businessman in a white dinner jacket and smiled enthusiastically. 'Lawrence, darling, this is my friend, Storm Brooks.'

Lawrence Langman eyed her avariciously. 'I've heard a great deal about you, Storm,' he said pleasantly, shaking her hand.

Beside her, Phoebe suppressed a shiver. Langman's eyes were as cold as those of a basking shark. He absorbed the details of Storm's body and soul in a single icy glance.

Storm didn't so much as falter. 'You too, Lawrence. I hope the girls are to your liking.'

Lawrence glanced into the main reception area where the men were already surreptitiously choosing partners. Waiters moved discreetly between the guests handing out cocktails from the bar.

Langman nodded noncommittally. 'Caroline assured me your agency was the best,' he said flatly. 'I only ever have the best.'

Storm smiled again. 'A nice compliment,' she said quietly, shooting an encouraging glance at Phoebe.

Caroline smiled and then clapped her hands. 'Shall we begin then, darling? I think everyone is here.'

Langman nodded. 'If you'll excuse me, ladies,' he said and moved into the crowd, Caroline close at his side.

When they had moved off, Phoebe let out a sigh of relief. 'He's frightening,' she said uneasily.

Storm took another cigarette out of her bag. 'Caroline says he's a pussycat. She used to work for us. Langman hired her to go with him to the Caribbean last winter and they've been together ever since, that's how we got this job,' she said quietly. 'This is a party for Langman's business cronies.' She nodded towards the crowd of men.

Phoebe shivered as she watched Langman move amongst the crowd. He was certainly like no pussycat Phoebe had ever encountered.

'What do we do now?' said Phoebe as a footman relieved them of their coats.

'Caroline's organised some sort of game to break the ice and pair people up,' said Storm, heading towards the rest of the girls and the trays of cocktails. 'Just follow me and remember you're supposed to be having fun.'

As they reached the main group, Caroline was clapping her hands for silence. She smiled and glanced around the party, her diamond necklace reflecting the lights from the chandeliers. Phoebe noticed that Langman stood at her shoulder, his face cold and impassive.

'Good evening,' she said warmly. 'I really hope everyone is going to have a super time tonight. We've organised a little game—' As she spoke two uniformed men came forward carrying silver punch bowls. 'I'd like everyone to take a card from one of the bowls. Ladies from the left, gentlemen from the right. You'll find it's half of a playing card. To find your partner for this evening, all you have to do is find the person with the matching half.' She giggled excitedly as she plucked half a card from her evening bag and held it up. It was half of the ace of hearts. Behind her, Langman slipped his hands into his jacket pocket and produced the other half. When they held them together there was a general chorus of approval and a few muted cheers from the men.

122

Caroline smiled and pressed her lips to Langman's cheek. Phoebe noticed their host slip a proprietorial hand around the blonde's waist, his fingertips lifting a fraction to brush the heavy curve of Caroline's breasts.

Two disorderly queues formed and, with much giggling and laughter, girls and men chose their cards. Phoebe was separated from Storm, carried along in the wave of party-goers. When she reached the front she took a card at random – the three of diamonds.

She looked around the room, couples were comparing cards and already pairing up. She wondered if she had the courage to make an approach when she felt a hand on her shoulder.

'Five of spades?' said a pleasant-looking sandy-haired man, cradling a glass of champagne.

Phoebe shook her head. 'Sorry. Three of diamonds.'

The man groaned theatrically. 'Shame.' He extended his hand. 'I'm Gary, pleased to meet you.'

Phoebe shook it firmly. 'Phoebe,' she said, as another man, a little the worse for wine appeared at his shoulder.

'Eight of clubs?' he said, eyeing Phoebe with enthusiasm.

Gratefully Phoebe shook her head, while the first man said, 'No, sadly old chap neither of us have been that lucky. She's got the three of diamonds. Damned shame—'

'Three of diamonds?' Phoebe looked up nervously as her card was called, straight into the eyes of a dark-haired man in his late thirties, holding half a card between thumb and forefinger. 'Did you say three of diamonds?'

The first man groaned. 'Baxter, trust you.' He turned back to Phoebe. 'My dear, may I introduce you to the lucky dog who's won your company during dinner? Phoebe, this is Baxter Hayes, entrepreneur and general lucky-bastard-about-town.'

Baxter smiled and took her hand, pressing it to his lips. 'Delighted,' he said in a low cultured voice. 'Would you like to join me for a drink?'

Phoebe nodded trying to get a grip on the fluttering feeling in her stomach. Baxter Hayes was tall, his dark hair greying at the temples. His dinner suit was beautifully cut to make the most of his broad shoulders and a slim well-honed body. Baxter slipped his arm through hers and guided her towards the bar.

'I'm usually not very lucky at cards,' he said, waving the barman over.

Phoebe smiled. 'Me neither,' she said, trying to keep the nervous tension under control. She could feel a little tic in her throat. She wondered what to say. Baxter smiled warmly.

'Do you do this kind of thing often?' he said, sliding a glass across the bar towards her. Phoebe could feel her colour rising. Phoebe Williams, sophisticated escort about town, was in imminent danger of sliding back into Phoebe Williams, gauche student.

Have fun, Storm had said. Nervously she scanned the room for Storm's familiar face; a touchstone to give her courage. Storm was in deep conversation with a small balding man by the fireplace. As Phoebe caught sight of her Storm smiled graciously at the man and effortlessly moved an inch or two closer.

Phoebe took a long pull on her glass and swallowed the nervousness back along with the alcohol. 'No,' she said painting on a radiant smile. 'Actually this is my first time.'

Baxter's eyes brightened. 'Really?' he said.

Phoebe nodded. 'I'm quite nervous.'

Baxter laughed and edged his stool a little closer. 'You don't look it, you look stunning.' He lifted a finger to trace the outline of her jaw. She shivered under his touch and fought the temptation to move away. Despite Storm's reassurances that she could call the shots, she felt that Baxter was in control. His eyes moved down over her face, her shoulders – it was all she could do to suppress a tremor of apprehension.

Baxter, by the choice of a card, had won her company for the evening and by coming to Lampeter Hall she had already agreed, at some level, to play any game he wanted.

She could sense the interest in his face and the way his eyes worked down the curve of her breasts. There was an uneasy tight pause when his fingers lingered in the pit of her throat.

What was it Storm had told her? Get them to talk about themselves – there's nothing a man loves more than a captive audience. She stirred the olive in her drink, tearing her attention away from the unspoken invitation of his caress.

'Do you do this kind of thing often?'

Baxter laughed, lowering his hand. 'No, I'm a bit like you really, first time for everything,' he said casually.

Across the room, double doors had been opened into a large candlelit dining room. Baxter offered her his arm. 'Why don't we beginners take it one step at a time and have

some dinner,' he said gallantly, standing his empty glass
back on the bar.

Phoebe nodded. 'Why not?' she said softly.

Dinner was wonderful, Phoebe had never tasted food
like it. Baxter was an interesting companion. As the wine
flowed, Phoebe gradually began to relax, enjoying course
after course of delicate gastronomic delights brought to
the tables by a bevy of uniformed attendants.

Remembering what Storm had said, she asked Baxter
about himself and listened in enrapt silence while he told
her about travelling the world, his business interests in
Hong Kong and the Far East. It could just be a friendly
dinner party, she thought fleetingly, as the waiters cleared
away another course. She took a deep breath. No, it
wasn't, she reminded herself, this wasn't just a dinner
party and these weren't guests in any true sense of the
word. Beneath the polite conversations and the bright,
light laughter was an implicit promise of sex.

Phoebe glanced around the beautifully decked tables,
trying to keep a grip on reality. The women were exquisite, radiant in the company of their partners, moving a
little closer than was normal, each a little more attentive
than any ordinary date. Phoebe took a deep breath and
turned her attention to Baxter. This was a job and however much she was enjoying it, she had to remember, she
was being paid to keep him company.

He smiled and refilled her glass. ' . . . after that we
went on to New York,' he continued. 'Are you sure I'm
not boring you?'

Phoebe shook her head emphatically. Baxter's life style
sounded unreal. He turned his wine glass thoughtfully

between his fingers. 'Actually, I've spent most of my life travelling. It doesn't give me a lot of time to spend on face-to-face relationships. Though I'm great on a lap-top.' He paused and stared into the candle on their table. 'What about you?' he said as the waiter poured their coffee. 'What do you do?'

Phoebe, finishing her sweet, pressed a napkin to her lips. 'My life is very dull by comparison to yours,' she began.

Baxter groaned. 'Oh, please, don't say that. I'd really like to hear. What do you do when you're not in places like this?'

The hubbub of noise in the dining room was being gently infiltrated by the sounds of a band playing close by. The dinner was almost at an end. Couples started to leave the tables and follow the sound of the music like children after the pied piper.

Phoebe watched as Storm made her way towards the door, arm in arm with her companion.

'What would you like me to say?' she said turning back to Baxter, whose eyes were glittering in the soft light. 'I'm not sure whether after all this wine I'm up to inventing a delicious specious history that would enthral you.'

Baxter grinned and moved a little closer. 'In that case, why don't we retain your air of mystery, then? Would you like to dance?' He indicated the stream of diners leaving the room.

Phoebe laughed. His expression suggested he had asked her reluctantly.

'They must all be mad. How can anyone dance after all this?' She indicated the remains of the meal on the table.

Baxter shrugged. 'Beats me, would you like to go for a walk instead?'

Phoebe nodded. 'Sounds like the perfect remedy to clear a fuzzy head. I'd be delighted.'

Baxter got to his feet and pulled out her chair, a hand catching hold of her arm. For a second they were totally still, so close that Phoebe could see the little flutter of the pulse in his muscular throat. His eyes glittered, wordlessly he moved closer and, without thinking, Phoebe returned the kiss he planted on her lips.

He moaned and closed his eyes, pulling her so close that she could barely breathe. She could feel the low rhythm of his excitement under her fingertips and a little shiver of anticipation as his tongue begged entry between her lips.

She knew she had to decide now how far this was going to go. This was the step she had wondered about. With Joe Blenheim at the party it had been sheer coincidence; a liaison that she hadn't engineered. With Baxter, she was being given the choice. He pulled away from her, pupils dilated with desire. She took a deep breath.

'Well,' he said softly. 'Where do we go from here? Would you like to spend the rest of the evening with me?'

'Yes,' she said quietly, barely able to control the tremor in her voice. 'I think I would.'

Baxter grinned triumphantly. 'Is that what you say to all your clients?'

The tension was momentarily broken. Phoebe laughed.

'I've got absolutely no idea what to say. I told you – I'm new to all this.'

Baxter stepped closer and slid his arms around her. 'In that case let me be gentlemanly about it and do the asking. Phoebe, will you let me make love to you? At this moment, I want to fuck you so much that I can barely think about anything else.' His eyes sparkled mischievously.

She nodded. The decision had been made.

Taking her hand, Baxter led her out into the main hall. It had been cleared while they had been at dinner. Under the chandeliers couples were moving elegantly to the strains of a soft smoochy tune. For a second Phoebe hesitated; maybe dancing wouldn't be such a bad idea after all, the bodies of the dancers were moving languidly, brushing against each other, the erotic overtones subtle and inviting.

As if Baxter could read her mind, he took her in his arms and guided her onto the dance floor. She shivered as his body pressed against hers. She could smell his cologne mingled with an inviting male scent that made her whole body glow with anticipation.

He seemed to overshadow her. Beneath her fingertips she could feel the heat of his skin, felt his impressive muscular frame. He could crush her if he wanted to. He tipped her face towards him and kissed her again, this time there was no veiled invitation but a sense of raw need. She felt her body responding, seconds before her mind had a chance to. Her nipples hardened to tight sensitive peaks as they brushed against Baxter's chest. Between her legs she could feel the first creamy wet heat of arousal. She moved closer, losing herself in Baxter's compelling embrace.

'Remember – have fun,' said a familiar voice.

Phoebe looked across into Storm Brooks's dark flashing eyes. She was dancing with her diminutive companion, who was resting his head between her breasts. His expression was ecstatic.

Baxter glanced at her questioningly.

Storm smiled up at him. 'I'm trusting you to take good care of our new girl,' she said. 'She's only here for the research.'

Baxter grinned. 'Don't worry, I intend to,' he said as Storm smooched off.

'My boss,' said Phoebe in answer to Baxter's unspoken question.

Baxter nodded. 'Are all these girls hers?'

Phoebe looked round the room. 'I think so, do all the men here work for Lawrence?'

Baxter snorted. 'No, this is one of his famous trade junkets. He's planning a big deal and wants us all involved. I think he's hoping to persuade us by fair means or foul.' He looked down into her eyes. 'I prefer fair, I think. What did your boss mean about research?'

The band's set had just come to an end and a flurry of polite applause rippled through the audience.

Phoebe smiled. 'Nothing really, it's just a private joke,' she said quietly. Before the band began again, Baxter guided her out from amongst the crowd into the shadows around the dance floor. He rested his hand on her back as she walked, kneading and stroking at the muscles along her spine. His touch made her shiver. In the shadows he pulled her into his arms, dragging her to him, his kisses hot and heady. Phoebe gasped as he lifted a finger to outline the swollen peaks of her nipples.

'Would you like another drink or should we go for our walk now?' he said in an undertone.

Phoebe looked around the hall, trying to get her bearings whilst Baxter's hands snaked over her, his knowing touch igniting glowing flares in her body. His touch was proprietorial, caressing something that he sensed was already his to explore. The hall was getting hot and stuffy, the air heavy with cigar smoke.

'A walk, I think,' said Phoebe unsteadily as his fingers stroked down her spine. 'Shall I fetch my coat?'

Baxter shook his head. 'No need, Lawrence has got the most amazing conservatory at the back of the house,' he paused thoughtfully. 'Do you like plants?'

Phoebe laughed nervously. 'Yes, but it wasn't exactly what I expected you to say.'

Baxter grinned. 'Nothing like a little surprise. Come on, we'll go through the dining room.'

The dining room was in almost total darkness – a few low lights had been left on to illuminate the tables, which were now cleared and set with ornate flower arrangements.

In the far wall, the curtains had been drawn to reveal French windows and an expanse of glass and lush tropical plants beyond.

'Over here,' Baxter whispered, leading her across the room.

'I'm following you,' Phoebe hissed and then giggled. 'Why are we talking in whispers?'

Baxter shrugged, eyes alight. 'Not sure. Come on.'

The wet heat of the conservatory hit Phoebe as Baxter pulled the doors open. The air was heavy with the earthy scent of loam and a rich tropical perfume.

'This is Lawrence's special baby,' said Baxter closing the doors behind them. 'He collects plants from all over the world.'

Phoebe looked around in astonishment; it was like a jungle. Creepers and vines reached up towards the glass roof, while curved brick paths led the eye away, through wrought-iron archways, into a mass of dense and subtly lit greenery. Somewhere close by she could hear the call of a parrot.

'This is unbelievable,' she whispered. Lawrence Langman's unnerving, impassive face was totally at odds with the image of the botanical collector who had created the exquisite conservatory. They walked in silence along the pathways into the heart of the indoor garden. Phoebe was completely entranced. Stepping between a tumble of vines they came across a huge shallow pool, underlit with silver spotlights that picked out a bubbling waterfall. On one side, on a broad paved area, was a heavy wooden bench and table on which stood a champagne cooler and glasses.

Baxter turned around to face her. 'I want to make love to you here,' he said softly.

Phoebe shivered. She hadn't expected him to be so forthright and had almost forgotten about their agreement as they had explored the magical garden.

'Here?' she repeated in surprise. 'What if someone finds us?'

Baxter laughed. 'They'll be coming in here for the same reason as we have. No one will take the slightest bit of notice.'

Phoebe stared at him. Something had subtly changed his expression. She stood very still, wondering what would come next. 'What are you waiting for?' he said quietly. 'This is what you're being paid for, isn't it?'

Phoebe nodded – she had already made the decision, hadn't she? Somehow it had seemed very much easier in the dining room.

Baxter stepped closer and took her evening bag from between her fingers and laid it on the bench, then lifted his hands to the neck of her dress, fingers sliding the zip down with practised ease. Slowly he peeled it over her slim shoulders, letting it drop to the floor. She shivered as the fabric slithered down over her bare skin.

'Very nice,' he whispered in a low voice, as he stepped back to admire her.

Phoebe stared at him. 'This isn't your first time at all, is it?' she said unsteadily.

Baxter, eyes never leaving hers, shook his head. 'With a whore? No, I'm afraid not. But then I doubt it's your first time either – very nice acting though. Why don't you turn round so that I can look at you?'

Phoebe felt her colour rising and was glad to break the eye contact. 'Whore' – was that what she had become under Gottlieb's influence? The word glowed in her mind like a firebrand. She turned slowly, feeling increasingly uncomfortable under Baxter's cool gaze. When she had turned full circle, Baxter took a fold of banknotes from his jacket pocket and tucked them into her evening bag.

'There we are,' he said pleasantly. 'That's the formalities out of the way. By the way, if this really is your first time, a little word of advice – make sure you always ask the client for the money first. It's very tempting to fuck and run. Now, would you like a glass of champagne?'

Phoebe nodded. He popped the cork from the bottle and handed her a glass; her fingers trembled as they touched his. He looked at her steadily. 'This really *is* your first time isn't it?'

Phoebe nodded.

Baxter smiled. 'How delicious,' he said, sipping his glass. 'Now drink your champagne while I tell you what I expect from a whore.'

Phoebe flinched but Baxter carried on regardless. She took a long draught of champagne but the alcohol did nothing to calm her nerves.

'Obedience, that's what I'm paying for,' said Baxter, refilling his own glass. 'I pay you to do exactly as I want, is that clear? It's my pleasure and I call the shots.'

Phoebe nodded.

Baxter raised his eyes heavenwards. 'That's not enough – I want you to tell me. Do you understand?'

'Yes,' said Phoebe unsteadily.

'Yes, what?' said Baxter firmly.

Phoebe's pulse was racing in her ears. Flushing crimson, she whispered, 'You're paying me to do exactly what you want.'

Baxter smiled. 'Right, that's very good.'

He sat down on the bench and let his eyes travel up over her slim body. She wanted to curl up and die under his undisguised inspection of her.

'Bax—' she began.

'Be quiet,' he said. 'I'm not paying you to talk to me. Put your champagne glass down and turn around again. More slowly this time.'

She did, feeling a raw sense of humiliation with every passing second. What she couldn't reconcile was that, amongst the feelings of surprise and shame, was a bright flare of expectation and excitement.

Baxter smiled narrowly. 'Now, come here.'

She walked over to the bench and didn't resist as his hands snaked around her waist. He stroked her stockinged thighs, opening her legs a little so that one hand could slip between them to cradle her sex. She trembled, tears unexpectedly pressing up behind her eyes, as with unhurried fingers he unfastened the crotch of the grey silk teddy.

A single invasive finger parted the lips of her sex. Phoebe closed her eyes, swallowing the tears back.

Baxter groaned softly. 'God, you're so tight,' he said on an outward breath, 'and so wet.'

She closed her eyes tighter still. He was right, while her mind might be stunned, even horrified, her body ached to be taken with a raw passion that shocked her. She could feel the soft silky flow of moisture trickling out onto her thighs. Baxter's probing fingers lit a million tiny flares somewhere deep inside her.

'Take this off,' Baxter said thickly, tugging at the teddy. Without opening her eyes, Phoebe complied, easing the delicate fabric up over her breasts, while all the time Baxter's fingers worked inside her. She couldn't see his face but heard him hiss in appreciation as she dropped the teddy to the floor.

135

He moaned softly, one hand lifting to cup the sensitive peaks of her breasts. She imagined what he could see; her naked body clad only in the grey silk hold-up stockings, her spiky heels accentuating the contours of her long legs and, between her thighs, his hand working into her sopping quim.

What she hadn't anticipated was the tip-tap-tip of high heels crossing the brick floor behind her. Phoebe stiffened. She could feel her colour rising dramatically; they weren't alone.

She desperately tried to shut out the sound but it got closer and closer and then there was a voice – Lawrence Langman's voice.

'So there you are, Baxter. Enjoying the party, I see. I thought I'd find you in here.'

Reluctantly Phoebe opened her eyes. Lawrence Langman slid onto the bench alongside Baxter and glanced up at her. Caroline, his girlfriend, stood beside him. Phoebe wanted to die.

Langman took a champagne glass from the table, eyes drinking in Phoebe's nakedness and Baxter's busy fingers still deep inside her.

'I'll help myself to champagne, I can see you've got your hands full,' he said wryly, glancing up at Phoebe's flushed face. 'Would you mind if we joined you?'

Baxter shook his head, sliding a wet glistening finger out of Phoebe's body. 'Not at all, what had you got in mind?'

Langman lifted his eyes thoughtfully. 'How about a little game of mixed doubles,' he said and smiled at his blonde companion. Phoebe noticed that Caroline didn't move. 'Come along, take your clothes off, my dear. Can't you see Baxter is waiting?' Langman said, waving a champagne glass in her direction.

Caroline smiled compliantly and shimmied out of her long silver evening-gown. Beneath, she was naked except for a diamante-studded G-string, tied with a leather thong on each hip. She giggled and posed for the men, her high breasts jiggling provocatively.

In spite of herself, Phoebe stared at the other woman's body in amazement. Caroline's breasts were heavy but uptilted, with huge, almost saucer-sized nipples. Below their stunning curves she had the tiniest waist Phoebe had ever seen and broad muscular hips that made her look like a stunning plastic doll.

Baxter grinned as his eyes moved over Caroline's heavy sensual curves. 'I see your tastes don't change, Lawrence.'

Langman laughed and drained his champagne glass. 'When you find what you like, stick with it. That's what I say.'

Langman looked Phoebe up and down. Baxter sat back as if he were her owner showing her with good grace to an interested party.

'She's new,' said Baxter flatly.

Lawrence nodded and waved Caroline closer. The blonde woman stepped over to him and settled herself on the floor at his feet like a pet dog. Phoebe was shocked. Caroline's stunning diamond necklace, which Phoebe had noticed earlier, now looked for all the world like a collar. Caroline rested her head on Lawrence's thigh, her breasts brushing lightly against his legs. Lawrence toyed with her hair, petting her casually, which added to the impression of her total and utter submission.

Langman grinned as Phoebe looked away. 'Your friend seems a little shy, Baxter. Why don't you tell her what's expected.'

As he spoke he got to his feet. Caroline crept after him, followed by Baxter, whose eyes never left Phoebe's.

'Lie down,' he said quietly, indicating the bench. 'Full length.'

Phoebe bit her lip, trying to imagine what was to follow. It almost felt as if this were a dream and she was watching someone else. Everything was tinged with a sense of unreality. Slowly she uncurled on the bench, conscious of her nakedness as the men watched her progress with interest.

Caroline, eyes bright, got to her feet and, before Phoebe could stop her, climbed onto the bench too, straddling her on all fours so that the blonde woman's glittering diamante-covered sex was no more than a few inches above her face.

Phoebe gasped in astonishment. 'No . . .' she spluttered.

Baxter laughed. 'Oh yes,' he said dryly. 'This is what you're being paid for.'

'It's all right,' whispered Caroline in an undertone, 'this will feel so good,' and as she spoke she planted a single kiss on the rise of Phoebe's quim. A split second later the quicksilver tip of Caroline's tongue slid effortlessly between the heavy outer lips, lapping at her clitoris.

Phoebe gasped, stiffening as a startling flash of pleasure surged through her. Revulsion fought with astonishment as the blonde woman sucked and nibbled playfully, rubbing her heavy breasts against Phoebe's prone body. Phoebe was so shocked she barely knew how to react. Above her she could see the men watching the spectacle with interest; eyes betraying their growing excitement.

The woman slid her hands over Phoebe's thighs, opening her up for her fingers and tongue. Phoebe, without thinking, instinctively lifted her hips to meet her and, as she did so, Langman undid the ties of the G-string, sliding the fabric away to reveal Caroline's naked, hairless quim, inches above Phoebe's face.

The smell of the blonde woman's arousal hit Phoebe like a body blow. Between the lips of Caroline's plump sex peeked the soft crimson inner folds, a slick trail of moisture adding a subtle highlight to the delicate opening.

Low in her belly Phoebe could feel Caroline's knowing kisses igniting a raging fire of excitement. She moaned, trying to avoid what she sensed was inevitable. She strained and wriggled which only seemed to drive Caroline on.

Suddenly, without warning, Caroline dropped her hips, lowering her sex a fraction of an inch above Phoebe's face. Almost without thinking Phoebe kissed it, her tongue running along the fragrant furrow between the hairless outer lips. Caroline let out an appreciative moan of delight and lapped at Phoebe's clitoris with renewed vigour.

The taste and smell of Caroline's sex made Phoebe's senses reel; so like her own but tantalisingly different. The taste stirred a compelling desire she had never so much as dreamed of.

She opened her mouth, tonguing the fragrant folds until her lips found the engorged bud of Caroline's clitoris. Caroline let out a throaty groan and pressed her body

closer. Every touch from Phoebe's tongue was echoed a
split second later between her legs by Caroline's skilled
mouth and lips. It was compulsive, terrifying in its intensity, the pleasure overriding all sense of revulsion and
fear. Phoebe closed her eyes, her reason overwhelmed by
the new sensations.

Eager hands opened her legs wider still, bending her
knees so that she was totally exposed and open to Caroline's insistent tongue. She gasped as something hard and
hot brushed against her thighs and then she felt a heady
rush of pleasure as a cock slid deep into her body. Her sex
closed around it like a hungry mouth, drawing it deeper
and deeper. Above her she sensed another body and,
when she opened her eyes, wasn't surprised to see
Lawrence Langman, guiding Caroline's hips towards him,
plunging his rigid shaft into her dripping quim.

His heavy balls brushed against Phoebe's face, making
her flinch. She tried to move lower so that her tongue only
touched Caroline but as he thrust deep into the blonde's
gaping sex she knew it was impossible. Phoebe's tongue
fluttered over him, smelling and tasting his ripe masculine
scent.

The contrast of his rock-hard cock and the soft crimson
recesses of Caroline's body was almost more than Phoebe
could bear. She felt pinned, trapped beneath them as
Langman's muscular body straddled her face.

She closed her eyes, struggling to breathe, fighting to
retain some sense of control. It was impossible to reconcile her sense of fear with the intense waves of pleasure
that glowed like fire in her belly.

Above her Caroline moaned enthusiastically, thrusting

her hips back, offering herself to both Langman and Phoebe; she drew Langman deeper still, before impaling herself again and again on his throbbing cock. She set the rhythm for them all. Moaning and writhing, she began to lap at Phoebe's sex again – now with almost frenzied intensity.

Her skilled tongue set off an avalanche of sensations, so strong and intense that Phoebe thought she might faint, while deep inside her she could feel the steady pulse of Baxter's cock as he drove himself towards release.

She imagined Caroline's tongue running over the junction of Baxter's shaft and her own excited quim, exploring the carnal contrast of hard and soft, coarse and delicate, rigid and yielding. She gasped, all fear receding as the images flooded her mind. Eagerly she opened her mouth, her tongue seeking out the slick curving shaft of Lawrence Langman's penis and the wet open folds of Caroline's excited body.

Every atom of her body was absorbed in its single-minded pursuit of pleasure.

She struggled for breath, lifting her hips again and again until suddenly she felt the rush of orgasm that crashed and ricocheted through them all, seemingly in the same instant. She flexed the tight muscles of her quim to drain every last drop from Baxter's body, while her tongue lapped at the lovers above her. She felt the astonishing throb of pleasure, deep in Lawrence Langman's cock echoed over and over in the undulating body of Caroline.

After the last shuddering thrusts, Langman slipped out of Caroline's quim, dripping a trail of mingled excitement onto Phoebe's lips. She shivered, fighting to grasp some ounce of control over the unstoppable passion they had awakened in her. She was shaking when Caroline climbed off her. Sweat – her own and Caroline's – trickled down over her belly.

Caroline grinned sheepishly and, without hesitation, planted a huge kiss on Phobe's lips. She tasted of sex – of Phoebe and Baxter. Phoebe gasped in surprise.

Caroline stretched to pick up her dress. With the silky garment carelessly bundled over her arm she poured them all a glass of champagne.

'See,' she purred, handing Phoebe a drink. 'I said it would be good, didn't I? You were *wonderful*.' She ran her tongue around her lips.

Phoebe, aware of her nakedness and the cold bite of the bench beneath her, flushed crimson. She got unsteadily to her feet, eager to retrieve her evening dress.

Baxter caught hold of her arm. He was still breathless, eyes dulled with satisfaction.

'You were great,' he said thickly and pressed his lips to hers, his hands lingering on her breasts.

Despite everything, she knew they were right, she had been good and – more disconcerting still – she had enjoyed it. The taste of Caroline's excitement lingered on her lips like a heady counterpoint to the champagne.

As the blonde slithered back into her gown, Langman turned to Baxter. 'There's a cabaret in the drawing room and we've opened up the games room as a casino,' he said evenly. 'Caroline and I have to circulate. See you later.'

Baxter shook his hand. 'It's been a great evening, Lawrie, but I've got to go soon. I've got a plane to catch tonight.'

Langman nodded. 'I'd forgotten. Look, ring me tomorrow first thing, will you? I'm very keen to get this deal up and running.'

Phoebe watched in amazement as, after a few warm farewells, Lawrence and Caroline disappeared. The encounter seemed to have meant little more to them than shaking hands. She stared at Baxter Hayes who was buttoning his shirt.

Good-looking in a worldly, rather careworn way, she wondered why he had to resort to liaisons with paid women. He was charming and charismatic enough to forge real relationships – or was he too addicted to the cutting edge of passion? Maybe he preferred the unfamiliar, with none of the possible pitfalls, rejections or responsibilities that accompanied real women in real life. She picked up her dress and pulled it over her shoulders.

Baxter smiled at her. 'Look, I really have got to go, I've got a car waiting. Is there anywhere you'd like me to drop you or are you staying for the cabaret?

Phoebe smiled, trying to hide her surprise at his rather formal good manners. 'It's OK,' she said, 'you go. Storm's made arrangements for us to be taken home.'

Baxter leant forward and kissed her gently. 'In that case, thanks for a great evening. I'll see you around some time,' he whispered. To her complete astonishment he then shook her hand and seconds later was gone.

Phoebe undid the door to her flat and kicked off her high heels. She was exhausted. She glanced at the clock – three fifteen – too late to ring Shaun Rees now even if she had wanted to. Carefully she folded the evening

143

clothes she'd worn into the linen basket and cleaned off her make-up.

From beneath the paint and the sophisticated hairstyle the familiar face of Phoebe Williams, student, reappeared, like an actress emerging from under heavy theatre make-up. The wanton character she had transformed herself into was discarded along with the tissues and cotton wool.

She blew out a thoughtful breath. Despite her reservations it had been a good evening. Phoebe shook her head in disbelief, was 'good' the right word? To her surprise there was no lingering sense of guilt or shame. Looking at her shiny, clean face it seemed as if the events at Lampeter Hall had happened to someone else. They seemed distant, removed, unreal. It was too late at night to fathom the workings of her mind, instead, eyes raw with tiredness she pulled on a crumpled tee-shirt and crept into bed. She wished she had the energy for a shower – she smelt of cigar smoke and the heady perfume of passion – but she was too tired. Gratefully Phoebe let sleep take her, her dreams haunted by images of strong powerful men and the ripe curves of Caroline moaning in a sea of pleasure.

Chapter Seven

Storm Brooks peered out of the window of her sports car towards the grim, dusty, student flats and then glanced down at her expensive gold watch. She'd been waiting almost half an hour, hoping to catch a glimpse of Phoebe Williams.

It was late in the week and Phoebe hadn't answered any of the messages she'd left, or been into the office to pick up her fee for Lawrence Langman's party. An envelope nestled in Storm's bag with Phoebe's wages in it. She could have put it through the letter box, sealed and addressed, but she had convinced herself it might get lost, which was as good an excuse as any. Besides, she was rather hoping that Phoebe would take another booking for Friday night.

She tapped her fingernails impatiently against the steering wheel; another ten minutes and then she'd leave. Her masseuse was due just before lunch.

Heading across the green, shoulders hunched against the wind, a familiar figure appeared in Storm's rearview mirror. She smiled triumphantly, buttoned her coat, slid out of the car and hurried across to meet him.

'Hello?'

Shaun Rees looked up blankly. 'Hi.'

He peered at her, his expression betraying the fact that he recognised her face but couldn't place where they had met or what her name was. She noticed there were dark smudges under his deep-set eyes – tell-tale signs of tiredness. Perhaps Phoebe had been passing on some of the new tricks she'd learnt.

Storm smiled and extended her hand. 'Storm Brooks, we met at Phoebe's flat the other day.'

Recollection split his face into a wide grin. 'Oh yes,' he said and then looked at her again. She sensed disapproval hot on the heels of the surfacing memory.

Storm pointed towards the flats. 'I was wondering if you'd seen Phoebe?'

Shaun eyed her more suspiciously. 'She's got a class this morning.'

Storm nodded. 'Oh, right. I was hoping to see her about her research,' she said. 'I've got some things she might be interested in.' She lied easily. By now they were almost on the doorstep and Shaun had pulled a bundle of keys on a leather fob out of his pocket.

'That's right. I remember now. You were going to help her with her final paper, weren't you?

Storm nodded as Shaun unlocked the door and, intent on getting inside, followed him quickly into the hallway. 'Have you got any idea how long she'll be? I just called on the off chance . . .'

He grinned. 'As long as she doesn't get side-tracked into the library she should be here in a few minutes.' He held up the key fob. 'She told me to get the kettle on.'

Storm laughed. 'I don't suppose there's any chance I

could wait in here for her, is there?'

Shaun considered it for a second or two. 'I don't see why not. Would you like a coffee?' Natural good manners were overcoming his reluctance.

Storm pressed home her advance. 'Sounds like a great idea, I'm frozen to the bone.'

Once inside, she slipped off her coat and settled herself in the armchair while Shaun busied himself in the kitchen. Phoebe's flat was small, with tiny rooms like a rabbit warren. Every surface seemed to be packed with books and files. Storm stared at the bowed bookshelves. It was not unlike the flat she had had while she was at university, though that seemed a life-time ago now.

Shaun reappeared with two mugs, stifling a yawn. He grinned an apology. 'Sorry, too many late nights. I've spent most of the week listening to my flatmate's sob story. I'm beginning to wonder if he ever sleeps.'

Storm arranged her carefully painted face into an expression of sympathy; listening to men came as second nature to her. 'Problems?' she asked encouragingly.

Shaun hunkered down on the hearth. 'You can say that again. His wife, Beth, has thrown him out. They've been together for years.' He groaned softly. 'We're all suffering for it. He goes over every word she said, again and again—' Shaun's face brightened. 'But not this weekend. He's going away with the firm that's sponsoring his degree, so we'll finally get some peace. I'm beginning to think it was a mistake to ask him to stay but you know what it's like with friends. I couldn't see him out on his ear with nowhere to go.'

Storm sipped her coffee thoughtfully. Shaun Rees was

very good-looking in a gentle, unthreatening way. His dark eyes sparkled with good humour and when he spoke he tipped his head to one side, revealing delicate laughter lines below thick black lashes. Watching him move she couldn't help wondering what he was like in bed. He had broad shoulders, his well-toned body accentuated by the open-necked shirt he was wearing. She imagined him leaning over her, watching her face with those enormous spaniel eyes of his as he guided his cock deep into her wet quim. She suppressed an excited shiver. He'd be good, she'd bet. Anyone with eyes like that would have a woman panting for more.

Bad Company had lots of female clients and male escorts were thin on the ground. Thoughtfully she slipped a cigarette out of her bag. Men often took a little more persuading than their female counterparts and Shaun Rees struck her as a man with a lot of misplaced scruples. She took a long pull on her cigarette. There were ways, however.

'Do you have a job?' she said pleasantly.

Shaun shook his head. 'No, not at the moment, that's the sod about this weekend. I'm finally free of Tony – that's this guy with the broken heart – and Phoebe's got to work at the restaurant.' He paused. 'She's a waitress at Don Giovanni's hotel.'

Storm smiled. 'Actually, I've got some work on offer at the moment, if you're interested. Do you drive?'

Phoebe scurried across the grey-green autumn grass to-wards the flats. Her last class had been with Dr Vine, who had an almost pathological aversion to the cold. The silly

148

old fool had had the heating up so high that everyone had stripped off their coats and jumpers. Coming back out into the bitter chill seemed like madness. As Phoebe turned the corner into her road, she saw the sensual outline of Storm Brooks' sports car crouched by the kerb and stopped mid-stride.

Since Lawrence Langman's party she had been wrestling with her conscience over the things she had experienced in the conservatory. It had felt as if Lampeter Hall was in a separate box from her real life but when Shaun had turned up the next morning, full of concern that she hadn't rung him and worried that something might have happened to her, she felt awful. She had kept him at arm's length, feeling completely unworthy of his undisguised adoration.

When she had stepped into the shower to wash away the last traces of Baxter Hayes' caresses and Caroline's stunning kisses she had decided there and then she wouldn't contact Bad Company again. Shaun was too special, too important in her life, to let their relationship be spoilt by Storm Brooks.

When, a few seconds later, Shaun had slipped off his clothes and stepped in beside her, it was a purified, clean Phoebe Williams that had welcomed him into her arms. As they had made love she had let his body drive away the remorse and the guilt she felt. Stroking his broad chest she had let the dark thoughts drain away with the tumbling water. The passion that burned inside her was better used on a man she loved and needed. As he whispered sweet tender words of affection she had almost felt as if her life was back on track.

Later, as they lay in bed together, she had thought about Gottlieb. His tutorial wasn't until Friday and, while Shaun dozed, his sleeping breath sweet and soft against her bare skin, she worked on a plan to head Gottlieb off. She needed to defuse Gottlieb's passion as much as her own. In the darkness, reassured by Shaun's familiar body, it had seemed so simple to get everything back under control. In the days since she had been to Lampeter Hall, she and Shaun had been inseparable.

Confronted with Storm's car, Phoebe's newfound self-assurance momentarily faltered. She took a deep breath and headed up the path. She would be polite but firm – decline any offers Storm made and then quickly send her on her way.

At the door to the flat she heard laughter and then Shaun's voice. The sound of them talking surprised her, seeing Storm's car had made her forget momentarily she'd given Shaun the keys.

She practically threw the door open. In the sitting room Shaun was sitting by the gas fire, completely at ease, with his long legs stretched out in front of him, while Storm sat in the armchair, cradling a mug of coffee. Although Phoebe convinced herself it was all totally innocent she felt a hot plume of anger low in her gut followed a split second later by a tiny flutter of panic – what had Storm Brooks told Shaun?

He looked up as she came in. 'Hi, I found Storm shivering on the doorstep when I arrived, I didn't think you'd mind if I let her wait inside. The kettle's just boiled.' He was already on his feet.

Storm smiled at Phoebe. 'Hello. I was passing and thought I'd see how your research was going,' she said pleasantly.

Phoebe stared at her as Shaun went into the kitchen. 'What are you really doing here?' she hissed in a low voice.

Storm slid an envelope out of her handbag. 'You hadn't been by the office to collect your wages, so I thought I'd drop them in.' She paused. 'I didn't really get a chance to talk to you after the party. How did you get on?'

Phoebe reddened, staring at the white envelope Storm had placed on the arm of the chair.

Storm picked it up and held it out to her. 'Here, I should take it, you've earned it.'

Phoebe's stomach knotted up into a tight unhappy ball. She was about to shake her head when Shaun reappeared in the doorway with a mug. Before Phoebe had time to think, she grabbed the envelope and folded it into the pocket of her coat.

Shaun grinned. 'You look frozen, come and sit by the fire. Did Storm tell you she's offered me a job?'

Phoebe stared at him and then glared at Storm, whose expression was open and relaxed.

'A job?' she repeated.

Shaun nodded. 'Yes, that's right. She wants a driver for some of her clients. What do you think? I told her you're working down at the restaurant. She said I can start this Friday and then organise it so that we're working the same nights.'

Phoebe took a deep breath and made an effort to smile. 'It's up to you,' she managed to say, her eyes fixed on Storm's impassive face.

Shaun carried on talking for a few minutes but Phoebe was oblivious. She couldn't quite believe what Storm was doing to them. Suddenly he sprung to his feet, making Phoebe painfully aware that she hadn't heard a word he'd said. He leant forward and kissed her. His gentle lips on hers made her stomach flutter, it was such a shame Storm had shown up. When he pulled away his eyes were glittering – he'd felt it too.

'Look, if you two have got work to do I'll come back later. I've got a class at two.' His voice was low and enticing. Phoebe nodded, still holding his hands after the embrace had broken.

Storm handed him a business card. 'Ring this number this afternoon and someone will explain the details to you,' she said warmly. 'We can always do with another reliable driver.'

When the door had closed behind him Phoebe rounded on Storm. 'What the hell are you playing at?' she snapped furiously.

Storm held up her hands in mock surrender. 'Stop it, you're over-reacting. It's only a driving job. He said he could use the money and we need another driver.' She shrugged as if that was answer enough.

Phoebe glared at her. 'What sort of job? Some rich businesswoman with raging hormones and an eye for something in a chauffeur's uniform?'

Storm lifted one perfectly plucked eyebrow. 'The green monster rears its ugly head,' she said calmly. 'Actually, you've got it wrong. It's completely legit. Bad Company runs an exclusive car service. If it makes you feel any better Shaun will be taking two very elderly businessmen down to Heathrow on Friday night. Which brings me to the other reason I came over to see you. I've got a booking on Friday and not enough girls to cover it. I wondered if you'd like a night's work at Cardene – the seaside resort up near Greys Point?'

'It won't take Shaun very long to work out what sort of agency you're running,' said Phoebe, ignoring Storm's question.

Storm shrugged. 'So? He's a big boy. I'm sure he can take care of himself. Now, about Friday night . . .'

Phoebe stared at her. 'I really don't believe you,' she said incredulously. As she spoke, mixed feelings bubbled up inside. Part of her wanted to throw Storm Brooks out on her ear, but another part was astonished and excited by the woman's sheer audacity. What harm would one more night do? said a little voice in her head. A graphic image of Caroline's body and Baxter Hayes' handsome face flashed through her mind. Firmly, resisting the compelling images, she shook her head.

'I'm supposed to be working at the restaurant.'

Storm snorted. 'Oh, for God's sake, what do you earn there? Three quid an hour plus tips? Ring them up and say you've found something else. Besides, Shaun's going to be busy Friday night.' She paused. 'You make a far better whore than you do a waitress. I can see it in your eyes.'

Phoebe flushed crimson. Who was it who said they could resist everything but temptation? She could feel her resolve wavering. One more night, said the compelling voice in her head.

Storm got slowly to her feet, uncurling with languid ease from the armchair. 'David, our submissive friend has rung me every day. Joe too, you remember Joe?' She lifted her hands in surrender. 'But, then again, maybe you prefer the safe options?' She looked steadily into Phoebe's eyes.

Phoebe stared at her. 'Who told you that?' she whispered. Gottlieb's words from the first morning they had met came back to her with stunning clarity. Even though she was certain now that she could cope with the man, his words still held a sting.

Storm shrugged. 'No-one.' She picked up her coat. 'So, are you on for Friday night?'

Phoebe looked at her. 'Will you tell Shaun?'

Storm laughed. 'For God's sake, what do you think I am? We're not the mafia. I'm not going to blackmail you into anything, if that's what you think. If you want the job, fine, if you don't . . .' She shrugged. 'No skin off my nose. I just thought you might like the extra money.'

Phoebe took a deep breath. 'What time are you leaving on Friday?'

Storm hesitated at the door. 'Be at the office around eight. Wear something less formal this time – a cocktail dress. I'll fill you and the rest of the girls in on the way.'

Before Phoebe could say anything else Storm Brooks had gone, leaving just the merest hint of tobacco smoke and perfume behind her.

Alone in the sitting room the sound of her heart beating echoed in Phoebe's ears. She sat down. Why the hell had she said yes? Hadn't she made up her mind that she wouldn't do it again? This was ridiculous – except – she paused, trying to steady her frantic heartbeat – except that some part of her craved the excitement she had felt as she had walked away on Baxter Hayes' arm, understanding the implicit invitation to join him in a sexual adventure. Even Joe Blenheim in his discreet security office had given her something, shown her a part of herself that she had never known existed.

She looked into the mirror above the fireplace. Steady blue eyes looked back at her, not for one instant betraying the turmoil that bubbled away inside. They sparkled with a promise of sensuality. She knew it had been this look that had given her true nature away to Gerrard Gottlieb and Storm Brooks. She stepped away from the mirror and went into the hallway. Slipping a handful of change from her purse she rang the restaurant and told them she was no longer available for work.

Later that afternoon, Phoebe was disturbed by frantic knocking. She wondered who on earth it could be – Shaun's knock was tentative and she imagined Storm Brooks' knock was much more refined. When she opened the door Nina King stood in the hallway, her face tight and pale.

Nina glared at her. 'Why the hell are you giving up on Giovanni's. The money's damned good *and* they pay in cash.' The words came out in an emotional jumble. 'This was waiting for me when I got in.' She waved a scrap of notepaper under Phoebe's nose. 'I thought you'd have come and told me yourself rather than ring and leave a message. I thought we were friends.'

Phoebe stared at her in surprise. She had no idea Nina would be so upset.

'I'm sorry,' she began. 'I didn't . . .'

155

Nina made a dark angry sound in the back of her throat but, in spite of her bluster, Phoebe could see tears forming in her friend's eyes.

'Why don't you come in?' she said, stepping aside. 'This isn't just about the job, is it?'

Dumbly Nina shook her head. 'No,' she snapped, her voice barely able to contain the threatened tears. 'No, it's not.'

Phoebe shepherded her in front of the fire hoping that Shaun would delay his return a little longer. 'What's the matter? This isn't like you at all.'

With the door closed, Nina took a wild gulp of air and burst into tears. 'It's that bastard Gottlieb,' she snorted miserably, dragging a soggy tissue out of her jacket pocket. 'Bastard.'

Phoebe put the kettle on, waiting for the first flood of tears to abate before she tried to find out what was the matter. Nina hunched unhappily in front of the fire, make-up running in thick mascara-tinged rivulets down her face.

'I had a tutorial this morning. When I got there he said the head of department had told him all about me.' She paused to blow her nose. 'I thought I was onto a good thing. Anyway, he said he thought he could help me to get my pass mark. He invited me back to his house and . . .' The tears changed to a thick miserable howl. 'Oh God,' she snuffled.

'What happened?' Phoebe encouraged gently.

Nina dragged the back of her hand across her face, trying to wipe away the grime and tears. 'He said he was certain that I understood what he wanted from me.' She paused, voice cracked and pitted with emotion. 'I thought he just wanted to screw me.' As she spoke she pulled up her sweater.

'Look,' she wailed unhappily, wriggling round in the chair. 'Look what he did to me. And he had that bastard – the head of the bloody department – in there to watch while he did it.'

Phoebe stared in astonishment. Criss-crossing Nina's narrow muscular back was a network of livid weals.

'He beat you?' she whispered in an undertone.

Nina nodded. 'Over a chair and when he'd finished they . . . they fucked me. Both of them,' she shivered.

Phoebe stared at her. 'What are you going to do?' she said lamely.

Nina sniffed. 'What can I do? I've used sex to get this far – how the hell can I complain now?'

Phoebe shook her head. 'Of course you can – he forced you into this.'

Nina let out a thin, miserable whine. 'No, that's the point, he didn't force me at all, he asked me over and over again if I was sure it was what I wanted. He said I had the choice. He wouldn't do it unless I agreed. In fact he offered me extra tuition instead if I wanted it . . .' She paused. 'But I said yes.' She burst into a renewed frenzy of sobbing. 'I said yes. I just don't want to fail now I've got this far.' She stopped and blew her nose again. 'And then there's you, working so bloody hard, you must think I'm dreadful. When I got your note I thought somehow you'd found out, I thought . . .' Her words broke up into an incomprehensible guttural sob.

Phoebe handed her a bundle of tissues and stroked the

wet, tear-stained blonde hair off Nina's face.

'Don't cry,' she said gently.

'But what am I going to do?' whispered Nina miserably. 'He says he wants to see me once a week until the end of the year.' She paused, struggling to get control of her quavering voice.

'To do this again?'

Nina nodded. 'I think so.'

Phoebe sat back on her heels. 'You could take the extra tuition instead,' she said slowly.

Nina forced a grin. 'Don't be daft,' she said flatly. 'It would take me forever to catch up on the work I've missed.' She shook her head. 'I shouldn't have come here.'

Phoebe put her arm around Nina's trembling shoulders. 'I'm glad you did,' she said softly. 'It's all right, really. Here, have your coffee. I'm sorry about packing in the restaurant job.'

Nina was beginning to get her emotions back under control. 'No, you're right. If I'd got an ounce of common sense I'd call Gottlieb's bluff and study...' She paused. 'Like you.'

Phoebe reddened and looked away. If only Nina knew.

When Nina had gone, Phoebe opened her notebooks and laid them out on her desk, trying hard to concentrate on the words – they eluded her, turning to meaningless hieroglyphics as she stared at them. Frantic images filled her mind; Gerrard Gottlieb's dark mesmerising face, Joe Blenheim, the party at Lampeter Hall, Storm Brooks, Nina King naked, Shaun Rees' beautiful willing body...

She shivered and rubbed her eyes. If she wasn't careful she might have to go and see Gottlieb with a proposition to ensure her success as well. Phoebe snorted. That was ridiculous, she was used to hard work, her grades had always been good, better than good. She picked up a pen and began to jot down a series of ideas, fighting her wandering mind with every pen stroke. She was relieved when she heard Shaun's tentative knock. His comforting familiar body would help her drive away all the confusion.

On Friday morning, Phoebe didn't wait for Gerrard Gottlieb to call her into his office before she opened the door. He smiled up at her from behind his desk and at once she saw the wolfish hunger in his eyes.

'Good morning,' he said, indicating a seat.

Phoebe complied wordlessly and opened her file pad.

Gottlieb stared at her. 'You're very quiet this morning, Miss Williams,' he said, getting to his feet. 'It's rather cold outside – perhaps I could interest you in a drink?' He pointed to the coffee machine.

Phoebe fixed a smile. 'No, thank you,' she said flatly. She had to maintain her composure. Gottlieb shrugged and poured himself a mug; the inviting smell permeated the room, making Phoebe's mouth water.

She glanced again at her notes.

'So what's it to be? More Marquis de Sade?' he said, waving a hand casually towards the bundle of notes on her lap. 'A very thought-provoking quote. I was going to ask you about it but, first of all, what else have you got for me?'

Phoebe coughed. 'I've been looking at contemporary accounts . . .' She stopped. Gottlieb's eyes were moving across her body. He was so close that she could smell him, his animal musk mingling with the scent of ground coffee.

He looked across at her. 'Why do women sell themselves, Miss Williams?' he said.

She shivered, trying to hold her mind on track. 'Economy, excitement,' she began haltingly. 'Fame or prestige by association with powerful men.' Gottlieb had moved closer still. She swallowed hard, focusing on the notes in front of her. 'The Cinderella syndrome, plucked from obscurity to a place of wealth and social position.' She stopped and looked up at him. 'To secure a degree . . .' she said slowly.

Gottlieb nodded, his face unchanging. 'Indeed, Miss Williams, and what about the men who indulge in this game. What is it they are looking for?'

Phoebe turned the page. 'Power,' she said quietly. 'They acquire scalps like collectors, or they indulge in passions that their partners wouldn't tolerate or they wouldn't choose to inflict on a permanent partner. They want control, power . . .' She stopped as Gottlieb stroked a single cool finger across her shoulders, delicately, his touch no more than the lightest of caresses. She held her breath, aware of the quickening pulse in her throat.

'We all make trade during our lives,' he said softly. 'Like your friend, Miss Nina King. Did she tell you she threw back her head and bayed for more while I beat her? She writhed and screamed when she came, sobbing and begging me not to stop. Did she tell you that? I don't suppose she did. The sweat stood out on her face and trickled down between her breasts. Did she tell you how she thrust back against me, while our illustrious head of department drove his cock in to her mouth so that she could suck him dry?'

Phoebe stared ahead, utterly speechless as Gottlieb's finger retraced its path. He idly stroked the curve of her ear lobe.

'Come, come, you aren't answering me, Miss Williams? What did she tell you? That I hurt her? Abused her?' He snorted. 'Nina King wasn't abused, Miss Williams – she is ashamed of herself, ashamed of what I made her feel. You're right though, it is a question of power. Your friend has had control for so long that she had forgotten it can be lost, relinquished, voluntarily surrendered. With our head of department, Nina King had all the power. As soon as he submitted to the demands of sex in return for good marks he lost any advantage he might have had. She called the shots. It caused him great pain to try and grab his power back from her. But not with me, Miss Williams. I pay the price, I call the shots. I will not relinquish my power.' He paused and took a sip of coffee. 'She found it liberating to surrender and hand over control. All women do.'

He turned so that their eyes met. 'Aren't you tempted to relinquish your power, Miss Williams?'

Slowly Phoebe got to her feet, putting space between them. She shook her head. 'No. Not yet,' she said softly. 'I've only just discovered that I have it. I'm reluctant to give away something that is so new to someone so...' She hesitated. 'So used to taking.'

Gottlieb grinned. 'Someone as experienced?' he said.

'If that's what you prefer to call it.'

He turned to the rolodex on his desk and spun the pages. 'What if I were to pick up the phone and ring Bad Company? Book your services for the evening.' He stared at her again, defying her to answer him.

Phoebe realised that he had assumed she was still working for Storm Brooks. How well he understood the compulsions of passion. She took a deep breath. 'It would still be my decision, wouldn't it?' She struggled to keep her voice even. 'My decision to say yes or no.' She paused, eyes firmly fixed on his. 'My power.'

To her total surprise, Gottlieb threw back his head and laughed uproariously.

'My God,' he gasped, the tension in the room dissipating like smoke. 'You really are astounding, sit down and let me get you that coffee. Let's get this bloody final paper thing sorted out. Tell me, what have you read so far?'

Chapter Eight

There was a coach parked outside Bad Company's offices when Phoebe arrived in Dove Street. Storm Brooks was standing at the door with a clipboard. She looked up and smiled as Phoebe approached.

'Glad to see you could make it,' she said, indicating the bus.

Phoebe looked at her in surprise. She hadn't expected girls to be shipped in by the coach load.

'Corporate junket,' said Storm flatly in answer to her unspoken question. 'We do this one every year. If you'd like to get on board, we're almost ready to leave. Just waiting for Daisy.'

As she spoke, a car screeched to a halt behind the bus and Daisy, the blonde from the first party that Phoebe had attended, clambered breathlessly out onto the pavement, and waved her driver off. She hurried across to them.

'Sorry I'm late,' she said, catching her breath. She grinned at Phoebe. 'Hi, nice to see you, are you sitting with anybody?'

Phoebe shook her head and followed Daisy up the steps of the coach.

Cardene was almost an hour's drive away. The bus took

the coast road so the first view Phoebe got of their destination was through the inky black night, the lights of the resort twinkling on the shore line, golden flashes mirrored in the sea.

Daisy grinned joyfully. 'I love the seaside,' she said with genuine enthusiasm. 'And the hotel we're going to, The Royal, is really lovely. I came to this do last year with Storm.'

Phoebe nodded. They had travelled most of the way without speaking while Daisy tinkered with her make-up and hair, transforming a pretty face into a stunning one. Phoebe, deep in thought, had watched Daisy without really seeing. She couldn't help wondering what Shaun was doing. She tried hard to keep her fears in check. Two businessmen Storm had said – why was it Phoebe had a problem believing it?

She glanced at her reflection in the coach windows. The dress she'd bought after going to Gottlieb's tutorial was black with a lace yoke, skilfully cut to accentuate her narrow waist and short enough to reveal a yard of slim leg. Beneath she was wearing a black silk teddy and black stockings – a black widow spider. She turned, her gold earrings catching the light. One more night, she said softly to the glittering eyes that reflected back at her in the windows, but realised even as she said it, it was probably not true.

'This conference,' Daisy said, fluffing her blonde curls into shape, 'is a bit more boisterous than the other night. More fun though.'

Phoebe glanced over her shoulder, the bus was full of girls. Storm sat staring out of the window, her face impassive.

Beside her, Daisy, now her make-up was complete, was hitting her stride. 'They had a really good comedian last year and strippers in the ballroom.' She stopped. 'The hotel bars are open all night.' Glancing into her compact Daisy opened her mouth into an exaggerated oval and added an arc of lip gloss. 'Not very classy, I suppose, and the guys . . .' She rolled her beautifully painted eyes heavenwards. 'By the time we got there, they were really well oiled, but it's much more relaxed – easier than the dinner parties.' She giggled again. 'I'm not very good at dinner parties. I'm always worried about which knife and fork to use while the guy with me is more interested in . . .' She stopped as if she expected to see disapproval in Phoebe's face. 'Well, you know.'

Phoebe nodded. The bus was driving slowly into a carpark. Even above the noise in the coach Phoebe could hear the low throb of disco music from the grand-looking, modern hotel. They pulled to a halt in the service carpark.

She shivered; they were part of the service, not guests. Around her the other girls were collecting their coats and bags. Phoebe felt the adrenaline course through her veins, the flutter of apprehension growing as the bus pulled to a halt by a set of double doors. Before they had a chance to get off the bus Phoebe spotted a group of men gathering inside. It felt like an auction. She kept her eyes lowered as she stepped into the foyer, while around her the men were pressing forward as if to get a better view of the lots on offer. Daisy immediately let out a whoop of delight as she recognised a familiar face and scurried towards a tall elderly man in a lounge suit. Other girls and men peeled off in small groups of two or three.

Phoebe blushed, feeling she couldn't take another step. When a man pushed forward and looked her over she hurried away from him. Far from taking offence he shrugged philosophically and turned his attention to a girl behind her.

To the right of the foyer was a darkened function room where disco music throbbed and lights glittered and pulsed in time with the music. She took a deep breath and clutched her bag tight against her stomach – at least the darkness would mask her discomfort.

Before she had time to step into the gloom Storm Brooks appeared at her shoulder.

'Let's get a drink,' Storm said flatly. 'The place is crawling with delegates; these are just the desperate ones. Come on.'

Phoebe stared at her. 'What?'

Storm pointed along the corridor past the press of men. 'We'll go to the bar down here.' As she spoke she nodded to another woman who Phoebe didn't recognise as one of their party.

'There are girls from two other agencies here tonight,' said Storm as they pushed their way through groups of people milling around the disco doors. 'It's all very democratic – there's at least one woman for every man here. They can take their pick, so no-one is going to bat an eyelid if we take our time.'

'Do you always take on big occasions? I thought escort agencies did personal dates?'

Storm nodded, guiding her up through the chrome and scarlet opulence of the hotel's ground floor towards a small bar overlooking a more sedate function room.

'We do that too but there's more money in corporate entertaining. It's safer for the girls this way.' She waved the barman over and ordered them both a cocktail before turning back to Phoebe. 'Why?' She grinned. 'Do you fancy a little one-on-one?'

Phoebe blushed. 'No, not really, I just ...' She stopped mid-sentence as two distinguished-looking businessmen slipped onto the stools alongside them. Storm immediately turned on her most radiant of smiles. The taller of the two men said, 'May we join you?'

Storm smiled again. 'We'd be delighted. Are you here with Starcor?'

The second man nodded and held out his hand. 'I'm Charlie Bryce,' he said with a soft American accent. 'And this is my friend, Gordon Hartley. We wondered if you ladies would care to join us for the evening?'

Storm's eyes glittered seductively. 'We'd be flattered,' she said, moving imperceptibly closer to the man Charlie had introduced as Gordon. As Storm introduced them, Phoebe sensed that an unspoken, mutually agreeable selection had been made, though she had missed the signals. Heat rose along with the nervousness in her stomach. She glanced around the almost empty room, trying hard to stay calm while Charlie moved his stool alongside hers.

'Have you had supper yet?' said Charlie, his arm sliding slowly along the bar behind her. 'There's a great buffet if you're hungry.'

Before Phoebe could speak Storm shook her head. 'Actually, we've already eaten,' she said. 'We thought we might go and join the dancers a little later.'

Charlie grinned, his face revealing a network of tiny smile lines. 'Sounds like a great idea as long as you don't want to hear yourself think.'

Storm teased the olive from her drink along the cocktail stick with her tongue. It was so provocative a gesture that Phoebe shivered; Storm Brooks exuded an unnerving sexuality that the men would have had to have been dead to have missed. Phoebe watched their faces. Charlie grinned, while Gordon's eyes narrowed, the colour rising in his plump rather unmemorable face. Storm leant back casually on her stool, her breasts thrust forward, hips tilted a little.

'I'm open to suggestions,' she purred and held the olive between her teeth before biting down on it with a sharp intimidating snap. Gordon swallowed nervously. Phoebe had to suppress a giggle. The businessman was putty in Storm's hands.

She turned her attention back to Charlie Bryce who was watching Storm's polished performance with some amusement.

'Are you also open to suggestions?' he said in an undertone, sipping his drink.

Phoebe smiled. 'I suppose am I,' she said. 'Why? What had you got in mind?'

'Do you swim?'

Phoebe laughed. 'You're joking?'

'Not at all,' said Charlie. 'They've got a really good pool here – spa and plunge pool. I thought maybe you'd like to go somewhere quiet.'

Alongside them Storm was executing a subtle dance of seduction. Phoebe knew she couldn't match Storm's game. Watching Storm in full flood was a breathtaking experience.

Her invitations and insinuations were faultless, though to anyone watching across the room her virtuoso performance would be all but invisible. As Storm talked to Gordon in a low intimate whisper Phoebe could almost feel the sexual temperature rising.

At her elbow Charlie Bryce moved a little closer. 'So what do you say?'

Phoebe slid her glass back onto the bar. 'Why not?' she said softly.

Charlie grinned. 'Why not indeed.' He got to his feet. 'I'll show you the way.'

The reception area outside the bar was hopping with activity, the bass beat of the disco a steady counterpoint to the hum of the voices. Couples were making assignations, others were drinking or huddled secretively in corners. It surprised Phoebe that there were so many people about.

'Are all the people here from Starcor?'

Charlie nodded. 'That's right, every last man jack of them. We take the place over once a year for our conference. Out of season it's a great place to be. I flew in from the States Wednesday just to be here—' He indicated a door. 'What do you do?'

Phoebe wondered if she should lie, wasn't fantasy the fuel that fired these liaisons? She hesitated then decided to try the truth. 'I'm a student.'

Charlie nodded appreciatively. 'At Fernhill?'

Phoebe felt uncomfortable – maybe the truth hadn't been such a good idea.

'Yes,' she said lightly. 'Do you know it?'

'Certainly do, that's one of the reasons we hold our conferences here. We're working with them on some of our projects. The truth is, lots of our best research and development men come from there,' he said, as he guided her down a carpeted corridor towards the distant sound of water. At the far end, the corridor branched left and right off a central sitting area.

'Here we are, what do you think?' Charlie lifted a hand to encompass the view beyond the seating.

Behind a screen of carefully manicured plants was a plexi-glass window overlooking a huge circular pool, ringed with metallic blue and gold tiles.

Phoebe laughed with genuine surprise. 'I have to admit I hadn't thought swimming was on the agenda this evening.'

Charlie shrugged. 'Why not? I'm not much good at all the social stuff. Can't dance, don't drink that much – come on, let me show you around.' He opened the door and Phoebe followed him inside.

Padded loungers were arranged around one side of the pool and spa, together with a rack of luxurious towels and thick cotton robes. Charlie began to unbutton his shirt. Phoebe felt a little rush of nerves.

'No swimming costume,' she said lamely when he looked up at her.

Charlie laughed. 'Come on, be brave. Don't tell me you've never been skinny-dipping.' As he spoke he slipped his trousers down over narrow hips. He seemed to be naked in seconds. With athletic ease he took a short run and a long faultless dive into the water. When he surfaced, sweeping hands back over his face and hair, he was grinning.

'Wow,' he said. 'It's beautiful, come on in.'

Phoebe shook her head in disbelief and then shrugged the little cocktail dress down over her shoulders. She could sense Charlie's eyes taking in the details of her body as she dropped the dress onto one of the loungers. Charlie's soft whisper of approval echoed around the deserted pool.

Suddenly what had been a casual undressing took on another dimension. His interest lit a tiny glow of expectation in Phoebe's belly. She turned to face him. Like exploratory kisses, his gaze moved slowly over the swell of her breasts, the flat plain of her belly, lower still to the curve of her hips and the inviting junction between her legs.

She laughed. 'You're making me nervous.'

Charlie snorted. 'No need, you look fantastic—'

She turned artfully in the spotlight of attention his excitement was creating. Very, very slowly she slipped off her stockings, lifting one leg onto the lounger so that she could roll the sheer silk down over her slim calves. The atmosphere in the pool was becoming electric with anticipation. She ran her hands up over her belly, then up to caress her breasts. Beneath her fingertips she could feel the puckered buds of her nipples as they hardened in expectation.

In the water Charlie Bryce was mesmerised, his eyes following every movement. She traced a finger up over her neck and undid the pins that held her sensible hair in its chic pleat, shaking her head, running her fingers through it.

Charlie shivered, his eyes darkening to intense waterlit orbs. She caressed her shoulders and slipped a long finger under the straps of her teddy.

171

Charlie shook his head, holding out a hand, inviting her to join him in the pool. 'Leave it on,' he said softly in a low, throaty voice. 'You look beautiful like that.'

Phoebe smiled. Under his undisguised approval she *felt* beautiful. Her whole body seemed to glitter with excitement, her mind raced with a thousand possibilities. Maybe it hadn't been such a strange idea after all, she thought ruefully. Charlie Bryce had managed to get her to take off her clothes well ahead of anyone else, managed to make her quake with desire without so much as lifting a finger and now she wanted nothing more than to join him in the water to explore the sensations that his eyes promised.

She stepped to the edge of the pool, knowing he was watching every step. She felt the tiles cool and slick beneath her feet, took a deep breath and dived in.

The water enveloped her like a warm embrace, stroking across her skin with bubble-strewn kisses. When she burst back up through the surface Charlie was close by, treading water.

He smiled. 'You look like a mermaid,' he whispered softly, his fingers caressing the curve of her breast where the wet silk clung to her pert nipples.

She laughed and ran her hand over the hair on his chest, slick now and pressed close to his body. 'And you look like a seal,' she purred, feeling the heady vibration of his heart beating frantically beneath her fingertips. He leant closer as if to kiss her.

Quick as a flash, she twisted away from his outstretched hand, turning in the water and striking off towards the shallow end. She heard Charlie laugh and then sensed him giving chase, the turbulence of his strokes disturbing the water around them. At the far end, barely a yard ahead of him, she surfaced, gasping for breath. Under the water, his fingers brushed the delicate sensitive skin of her inner thigh, making her shiver as he sought out the swell of her sex. He turned her effortlessly in the warm water, pulling her into his arms, lips seeking hers, while his fingers worked at the fastenings of the teddy between her legs.

Below the shimmering water she could see the impressive outline of his cock, hard and hungry amongst a tangle of dark hair; a great sea creature, nestling amongst a bed of seaweed. She sighed and opened her mouth to his tongue while her hand tracked down over his belly. When her fingers closed around his shaft he moaned with delight. His fingers struggled to find a way into her, fighting with the wet, clinging fabric. Phoebe held her breath. She knew she was wet, creamy moisture trickling into the folds of her sex.

When he found her quim, slick and open she gasped, her fingers tightening instinctively around his rampant cock. When his thumb lifted to trace the hardened ridge of her clitoris she let out a cry of pleasure, her own hands joining his to undo the teddy, to give him more access to the tight throbbing opening that she wanted him so desperately to fill. His eyes had worked as well as any kisses or caresses. She wanted him to take her, to fuck her, to fulfil the heady promise of his gaze.

He groaned and dragged the sodden straps of her teddy down over her body, unleashing her shimmering breasts. He cupped them, fingers teasing over her pert pink nipples. Phoebe felt her whole body flex hungrily around his touch. She strained back against the side of the pool, lifting her legs to encircle his waist, her hands guiding his cock closer and closer. When she felt the tip of his shaft nuzzling between the lips of her quim she called out in pure liquid pleasure and thrust her hips forward, driving his cock deep inside her.

Snorting frantically, Charlie threw back his head, eyes closed as the sensations swept through them both. The warm water lapped around them, echoing and repeating every thrust of their bodies. He kissed her lips, her neck, her shoulders, lapping at the liquid diamonds that clung to her nipples. Every touch sent her higher and higher. She thrust herself onto him again, lost in the purest sensations of pleasure.

She felt his sex pulse deep inside her body and – as if diving into the same raging torrent – allowed herself to be carried forward on the current. Their orgasm was breath-taking and she sobbed as she felt him buck and twist, filling her to the brim.

When they had done he slipped out of her glowing body, rolled over onto his back and slowly did a lap of the pool, turning like an otter in the water so that his eyes held hers. When he got alongside her he leant forward for a single kiss before lifting himself effortlessly out of the pool. Oblivious of his nakedness he padded across the poolside and pulled a robe from the rack.

'I've got a suite upstairs,' he said holding the robe out towards her. 'Why don't we go upstairs and crack the bottle of Krug I've got cooling?'

Phoebe grinned and slipped out of the water's embrace, dragging off the wet teddy.

'Sounds like a great idea.'

She didn't resist when he wrapped her in the soft towelling, nor when his hands slipped under the cotton to explore her. He nipped playfully at her shoulders and throat, excitement rekindling as they got dry.

Phoebe wriggled out of his arms to rescue her clothes.

Charlie laughed. 'Why bother with getting dressed,' he said in a low voice, scooping up his own clothes under one arm.

Phoebe glanced back over her shoulder. 'I'm not sure I'm ready to walk around the hotel in a bath robe.'

Charlie pulled a face. 'I shouldn't worry, no-one will notice. Besides,' he added, eyes twinkling with mischief, 'you'll only have to take them off again.'

'I might not get a chance to get them back,' she said with a wry grin.

Charlie snorted and started to dry his hair.

Phoebe dropped the robe onto the floor and instantly had Charlie's complete attention. 'On second thoughts,' he said, 'maybe it isn't such a bad idea. Let me take a look at you.'

She pulled on her stockings under his undisguised interest and shimmied the little black cocktail dress down over her shoulders. Her teddy was too wet to put on so she wrung it out, rolled it into a ball and slipped it into her bag.

Charlie laughed. 'I love the idea that you're completely naked under that dress. Maybe I'll take you back up to the bar, sit you on a stool and slip my hands, slowly, slowly up your skirt. Nice thought.'

Phoebe tucked her bag under her arm, eyes alight. 'Your choice,' she said softly.

* * *

175

After the glittering silence of the pool, the hotel foyer seemed to be incredibly busy. As they approached the reception desk Charlie hesitated.

'Would you mind waiting for me for a minute, I've just got to check if I've had any calls?'

Phoebe shook her head and turned her attention to the displays of luxury goods in the glass cases that lined one wall. She wasn't surprised a moment or two later when she felt a hand on her shoulder. She turned slowly.

'So are you going to take me upstairs or are we heading for the . . .' The words caught in her throat. She froze, staring into the all too familiar eyes of Tony Goodman, Shaun's room mate. He was very drunk, a trickle of saliva clinging to his chin, eyes so bright that they looked as if they had been painted on.

He grinned lasciviously, running his hand down over her hips. Phoebe shivered, rooted to the spot. Fragmented thoughts filled her head. There was a dark uneasy silence while Tony peered at her, blinking hard as if he were struggling to focus.

'Don't I know you?' His speech was slurred and guttural. 'Aren't you the girl I screwed in the lift? Where did you get to – I . . .' He snorted, struggling to stand, screwing up his face in an effort to remember where he'd seen her before.

From the corner of her eye Phoebe saw Charlie approaching and quickly stepped away from Tony, almost running across the foyer.

Charlie looked at her anxiously. 'All right?' He looked beyond her to where Tony was standing, still supporting himself against the display cases. 'Was he giving you any trouble?'

Phoebe shook her head emphatically, struggling to regain her composure. Shaun had said Tony would be away for the weekend with the firm that he worked for, the company who were sponsoring his degree. She felt the colour rising in her cheeks; it hadn't occurred to her in a million years that he might work for Starcor.

Charlie slipped his arm through hers. 'Come on,' he said softly.

Phoebe nodded, between her legs she could feel the remnants of Charlie's desire, a silvery trail that oozed out of her naked sex. She glanced back at Tony who was now bent double. She shuddered, praying he wouldn't look up.

Charlie sensed her discomfort. 'Do you know him?'

Phoebe gathered up her thoughts into a tight, controlled knot, turned to Charlie and forced a bright unnatural smile.

'No,' she lied. 'I was just a bit worried, he's had an awful lot to drink.'

Charlie snorted. 'By midnight they'll all be like that. Let's go upstairs.' From the pocket of his robe he produced a room key. 'The champagne will be just right.'

Phoebe fell into step beside him, while aross the foyer she was certain Tony Goodman was watching her.

Chapter Nine

Charlie Bryce unlocked the door of his suite. Phoebe waited behind him, one eye on the corridor, almost expecting that at any moment Tony Goodman would reappear. She was relieved when they were inside. The rooms were luxurious, the door opening into a large sitting room with a chesterfield suite, cocktail cabinet and television, beyond which was a bedroom – its double doors open to reveal an enormous bed.

Charlie rescued the champagne from its ice bucket and poured them both a glass, while Phoebe folded herself onto the settee.

Charlie eyed her speculatively. 'You don't strike me as the kind of girl who should be working as a hooker,' he said flatly, handing her a glass.

Phoebe reddened. 'Have I disappointed you?' she said unsteadily.

Charlie shook his head. 'No, far from it. But it means something to you, doesn't it? Most of the girls in this game are icy cold inside, outside they're all show. When you make love you mean it.'

Phoebe blushed, unable to answer. How could she explain she was tracing a path to discover her own passion?

She smiled. 'You're probably right,' she said with forced levity. She wished she had a pat answer, some subtle word play in the game Storm Brooks was so adept at.

Charlie sat down beside her. 'I know I'm right. I like the fact that you care,' he said. 'It turns me on to think that when I made love to you in the pool that look on your face was for real.'

His eyes darkened. Slowly he slid a hand up over her stockinged thigh, easing her dress higher and higher until the triangle of her sex peeked provocatively from amongst the lacy folds of her skirt. She shivered, his skilled touch lighting the first fires of excitement.

'You're very tempting,' he said in an undertone, sipping his champagne. Phoebe shivered under his examination.

'Open your legs a little more,' he said softly. 'I want to look at you.'

Reddening, Phoebe lay back, only aware of his curious gaze.

'My God,' he sighed, tracing the contours of her labia with his fingers. His touch was gentle as a breath but it didn't combat the self-consciousness Phoebe felt. Her colour deepened as he slid his fingers into the fur-trimmed folds, stroking back and forth, teasing in and out of her sopping quim. She moaned instinctively as he stroked the rise of her clitoris, fingers lingering provocatively at its peak until she couldn't hold back any more and lifted herself up, chasing his caress.

He smiled. 'Very nice,' he murmured. 'Why don't we go into the bedroom?'

Phoebe nodded. 'Why not? Shall I bring my champagne?'

'No, I don't think so, you can finish it later.' He got to his feet and Phoebe followed him.

In the bedroom he dimmed the lights until the whole room was suffused with a soft golden glow.

'I'd like you to lay down,' he said sitting down on the edge of the bed.

Phoebe thought about the way he had revelled in her stripping by the poolside. 'Would you like me to take off my dress?'

'No, just come over here and lay down beside me.' He patted the duvet.

She smiled and eased herself onto the bed, the soft quilt billowed up around her like a cloud. He looked down at her, eyes alight with desire. 'You look so beautiful,' he said. 'Lie still.' Slowly he leant forward and spread her hair out on the pillow.

She waited for what seemed like an eternity while he looked at her. It was so tempting to relax, the comfortable bed lulling her into sleep. Just when she felt her eyelids begin to droop Charlie stood up and opened the drawer of the bedside cabinet, teasing out a bundle of cord. Phoebe stared at him in horror, all thought of sleep vanishing in a millisecond.

'Charlie . . .' she began. 'I'm not sure—'

He lifted a finger to his lips. 'Sssh. Don't worry. It will be all right,' he purred. 'This will feel so good. I promise.'

She looked at him wide-eyed, caught in the compelling place between fear and fascination. With great care he looped the cord around the head of the bed and then gently around each of her wrists. She didn't resist him but lay still and tense, almost afraid to breath.

Charlie moved lower now, scrambling down over the bed to her feet. Delicately he slipped off her shoes, sliding his hands under her skirt so that he could roll down her stockings. She gasped as he eased her legs apart until she was spread-eagled, his cool fingers tightening a cord at each ankle. It suddenly struck her that she was totally helpless. She strained experimentally against the cords, feeling a surge of panic building in her chest, her heart-beat accelerating to a calypso beat.

Charlie stood back to admire his handiwork. 'There,' he purred. He pressed his lips to her toes, lapping at the sensitive spaces between them. She writhed back and forth, stunned that something so bizarre could feel so wonderful. He pressed wet kisses to her instep and calves, driving her wild as his tongue spiralled around the crease of her knees. While his lips explored he slowly pulled her dress up, exposing her quim. She writhed instinctively, adrenaline rushing through her veins – every touch of his fingertips and tongue felt so intense, like white fire.

'Relax,' he whispered softly, 'this will be so good.' His eyes lingered on the mound of her sex, open and still trickling with the remains of their mutual pleasure. She sensed he was talking to himself; he was fast becoming oblivious of who she was. Now, she knew, there was only the erotic image of her prone, tied body in his mind. He drank in her vulnerability like the champagne they had abandoned in the sitting room.

Dragging a cushion off one of the bedside chairs, he slipped it under her hips, tipping her pelvis so she was totally exposed. Again a finger traced along the sensitive folds of her outer lips, exploring the liquid heat of their mingled juices.

Phoebe whimpered. Every sensation was crystal sharp, almost painfully intense. He lowered his head, tongue lapping at her clitoris, while his fingers opened her and slid deep inside. She pressed herself against him, relishing his wanton expertise. He grinned at her from between her open thighs then sat up and slipped off the bed.

Phoebe turned in time to see him take a silk scarf from the dressing-table; her arousal grew more intense with every passing second. Gently lifting her head, he tied the scarf over her eyes cutting off her already limited view.

Now there was only sensation. She felt him working down over her body, teeth and tongue working across the fabric of her cocktail dress, lapping at her throbbing nipples, hands cupping and caressing, tightening and re-laxing, exploring every inch of her skin. When she felt his hands slip under the straps of her dress she froze, sensing what would follow. The delicate fabric ripped easily under his fingers and she gasped as he tore the top down over her breasts exposing her to his caresses.

'You look wonderful,' he murmured, tracing the outline of her areola. He moved lower, fingers, lips, tongue – they seemed to be everywhere at once. The compelling knot of excitement, gathering hot and damp in her belly and the sensitive folds between her legs, was unstoppable. When his tongue found her clitoris again, she snorted and bucked. Charlie moaned appreciatively. His fingers plunged into her, smearing her juices out over the curve of her thighs, the thick fragrant liquid cooling on contact, making her flesh tingle.

She held her breath as a finger tentatively traced the delicate bridge of flesh between the sopping open tunnel of her sex and the dark tight pucker behind. She stiffened as Charlie circled the rosebud of her anus, a shuddering sob of anxiety trembling through her.

'No, Charlie, please—' she whimpered, trying to move away from his touch. It was useless, she felt him teasing at the tight band of muscle, lubricating its gathered seal.

From behind the blindfold she heard his chuckle. 'Oh yes,' he said in a thick tone. 'I can do anything I want while you're like this. Anything at all. Don't worry, this will feel like nothing you've ever felt before.'

She lifted her hips again, trying to escape the touch that at once both repelled and excited her. He laughed, easing the finger deeper, opening her up for his explorations, while at the same time he renewed his attentions to her clitoris, nibbling and sucking with an expert touch. His tongue was unnervingly persuasive. Fear and pleasure mingled and almost before she knew what she was doing she began to move with him, lifting her hips up and down, chasing his teasing kisses. As she surrendered he slipped a wet finger into the tight forbidden closure.

She gasped in horror, while her body hungrily sucked him in. He murmured his approval, gently sliding in and out of the dark confines of her backside. She sobbed, caught up in a compelling, frightening web of sensations. Her body was baying for release. Her sex longed to be filled with his cock but instead there was only the heady rhythm of his finger in the frightening tightness and the electrifying caresses of his mouth and tongue.

Her body's needs seemed to be overcoming her mind, revulsion evaporating as his tongue wound the spirals of pleasure up and up until she was thrusting herself down onto his finger, impaling herself again and again. An orgasm hit her like a typhoon, driving her wild. She writhed madly, her secret places open and eager for more. At the very height of her pleasure he slipped the finger out from inside her, his other hand continuing the attentions to her clitoris.

She was lost in a sea of excitement until the instant she realised Charlie was guiding his cock into the place his finger had so recently left. Even amongst the overwhelming pleasure, she stiffened, instantly conscious, every nerve ending alight as he slowly, slowly inched his way into the forbidden orifice. The combination of tightness and sensation stunned her. She froze, all awareness returning. Charlie's reaction was to run a finger along the engorged ridge of her clitoris. She bucked again – an instinctive reflex – and his cock slid home, filling her to the very brim.

Phoebe screamed out in discomfort and fear but he was unstoppable. Close to the edge, Charlie took no more than seconds before his orgasm swept through her, the aftershocks of her own pleasure intensified by his ragged instinctive thrusts.

Gasping, he collapsed onto her, his breath like a blow torch against her skin. Phoebe lay motionless, terrified to move in case he hurt her. After a few moments he slithered out, leaving behind a sense of rawness and humiliation and – incredibly – a great wave of unexpected pleasure. The only sound Phoebe could hear now was

Charlie gasping for breath and the unsettling thump of her heart.

She felt Charlie moving. He undid her blindfold before untying her. Phoebe closed her eyes, the colour rising in her cheeks. She felt dirty, used – and yet at the same time strangely elated. Charlie stroked her cheek.

'Why don't we go and finish the champagne and then you can have a shower.'

She opened her eyes reluctantly. He was sitting beside the bed, wrapped in the towelling robe. He held out the glass towards her. 'I'm afraid I've ruined your dress,' he said, reddening slightly.

Phoebe glanced down. The little cocktail frock was in tatters, the top ripped to ribbons that even now added a certain erotic emphasis to her exposed breasts.

She took the glass and swallowed it down in one heady gulp. 'I think I'd like that shower now,' she said, getting unsteadily to her feet.

Charlie nodded. From the pocket of his robe he pulled a roll of notes which he threw casually onto the bedside table. 'I think this'll cover the dress and your time,' he said flatly. Phoebe flushed scarlet. In an instant all they had shared had been reduced to a business transaction.

He nodded towards a door. 'Bathroom's in there, I'll get room service to bring us up some supper.'

Phoebe travelled back to the campus in one of the hotel bathrobes. When Daisy clambered into the seat beside her Phoebe turned her attention to the ink black night and closed her eyes.

* * *

Phoebe was woken the next morning by the sound of Shaun's voice. Confused, she rubbed her eyes and then realised he was outside, calling through the letter box. Memories of the previous night came flooding back as she crossed the room. She could still feel the hot aching pathway that Charlie Bryce had opened. In the bedroom her ruined cocktail dress lay discarded in the bin, stockings, shoes and teddy bundled up near the linen basket.

Shaun grinned sheepisly when she opened the door. 'Hi, are you all right? I knocked but I couldn't make you hear.'

Phoebe managed an uneven smile. 'Fine,' she said, screwing up her face against the sunlight. 'I'm sorry, I must have overslept.' She stepped aside to let him in.

'You're not mad with me for waking you up?' Before she could answer he rounded on her, pulling her into his arms. 'God. You look almost edible, all warm and soft and sleepy.'

Phoebe tried hard not to wince as he pulled her closer; her whole body ached.

Shaun pulled away. 'Are you sure you're okay?'

Phoebe nodded and headed for the kitchen. 'Yes, I'm fine, really,' she repeated. 'Just a very late night.'

Shaun followed her with puppyish enthusiasm. 'Me too, I ran those two guys to Heathrow, remember? On top of my wages they gave me a twenty quid tip. Not bad, eh?'

Phoebe struggled to keep her expression impassive. 'So it went okay?'

Shaun nodded. 'Fine. The agency rang this morning to see if I wanted another job tonight.' Phoebe stared at him. She couldn't help but wonder what Storm Brooks had planned.

He continued, oblivious. 'You're at the restaurant till late tonight, aren't you? So I said yes. I should be done by midnight. Maybe I could come and pick you up in the limo—' He grinned. 'It's an amazing car, I've never driven anything like it.'

Phoebe turned her attentions to the kettle and said casually, 'Who's the fare tonight then?'

'No idea. They haven't given me any details yet. Just the route—' He slipped his arms around her waist. 'I thought we could go into town this morning, I'll take you out for breakfast.'

Phoebe felt the press of his familiar body against her back; he was such a sweet man. She giggled as he pressed nibbling, tickling kisses into the curve of her neck.

'Breakfast?' she said, wriggling away from him. Shaun held her tight, refusing to let go.

'Uh huh, it's nearly ten. I'll nip into the agency and pick up my wages for last night and then we can go and get something to eat.'

Phoebe tried hard to stay calm. The last place on earth she wanted to go was Bad Company's office in Dove Street. She turned in his arms, letting her robe fall open.

'Sounds like a great idea,' she said softly, not meeting his eyes. 'You can go to the agency while I go and pick up some shopping.'

Shaun nodded, his mind had swiftly moved from the prospect of food to the slim warm curves of her body. He ran his hands down over her chest, fingers seeking out the contours of her breasts. He made a soft appreciative noise as he found her rapidly hardening nipples.

'Maybe breakfast could wait for a while,' he said softly.

He kissed her, a tender lover's kiss that made her whole body tremble with pleasure. He tugged the robe back off her shoulders, his touch as gentle and kind as the man himself. His lips traced a ribbon of moist kisses over her neck, her shoulders. She didn't resist him, drinking in his love, his adoration. She shivered as he led her into the sitting room. He would take her into the bedroom but she wanted him now, here – wanted him to claim her back.

Turning round, working eagerly at his buttons, she dragged the shirt off his broad shoulders, her lips and tongue working on his chest, lapping at the fine covering of hair and the corona of soft down that surrounded his nipples. He needed no further invitation. Grinning, he pulled her down onto the hearth rug, a hand parting her thighs, his other hand lowering to undo his flies.

She was eager to help him, their hands working together to undress each other. Familiar and comfortable their coupling was seamless; she guided him into her, relishing the sensation of her body opening in his path.

Lifting her hips she sucked him deeper. Shaun moaned, eyes alight and glistening as she began to work against him, lifting her pelvis, brushing the swollen hungry bud of her clitoris. Her excitement was immediate, a flash flood of intense glowing heat, so raw and close to the surface that it astonished her.

Shaun matched her stroke for stroke, driving them both out towards an explosive all-engulfing release. It seemed to be timeless – and it wasn't until they lay, lovingly entwined in each others arms, that Phoebe realised she had no idea how long they had been together on the floor.

Shaun circled his body around hers, the damp kisses of

his exhausted cock pressing against her back – a final act
of love, a final caress, a final comfortable familiarity – that
made Phoebe want to cry. His lips nuzzled into her neck,
whispering soft messages of endearment and love.

They left the flat around midday. Outside in the street the
daylight seemed unnaturally bright after the comfortable
twilight of Phoebe's sitting room. Phoebe pulled her coat
tight around her and slipped gratefully into Shaun's car.

He gunned the engine, his expression elated. 'I've just
got to nip back to my place before we go into town. You
don't mind, do you?' he said.

Phoebe smiled and stroked his face. 'Not at all.'

'Good, I told Tony I'd give him a lift.'

Phoebe froze. 'Tony Goodman?' she said softly.

Shaun nodded. 'That's right. God, he's in a bad way.
He turned up at the flat first thing this morning. Looked as
if he hadn't slept all night.'

Phoebe fixed her eyes on the road ahead, staring unseeing at the rows of bare autumn trees. 'I thought you said
he was away for the weekend,' she said softly.

Easing the little VW out into the main road, Shaun
nodded. 'Me too, but apparently he decided to come
back. I think he's planning to go and see Beth this
morning. I told him to have a bath and clean himself up.'
He glanced at Phoebe and grimaced. 'He looked pretty
bloody rough when he got back.'

Phoebe tightened her hands around her bag; he had
looked pretty rough in the foyer of the hotel as well. She
could still see his drink-bright eyes and hear his slurred
voice. 'Don't I know you?'

She shivered wondering what on earth she could do. There was no plausible reason for her to suggest that they didn't pick Tony up. Her stomach contracted into a tight miserable knot as in the distance she saw the building where Shaun lived.

'Do you want to come up?' Shaun asked as he swung the car into one of the parking bays.

Phoebe shook her head, not trusting herself to speak.

Shaun grinned. 'Okay. Won't be a minute.'

Phoebe watched his retreating figure. He could take as long as he wanted. Her mind raced. She only hoped that Tony had been so drunk he wouldn't recognise her. She flipped down the sun visor and looked at her reflection in the vanity mirror. With no make-up, her hair brushed and pulled back into a ponytail, wasn't she a million light years away from the sophisticated girl he had encountered the previous evening? She bit her lip, she had to hope so.

Across the car park Shaun was returning, Tony sloping along beside him. She slid down, wishing that she was invisible. Shaun opened the door and flipped the seat forwards so that Tony could climb into the back. The smell of alcohol hit Phoebe as he slithered in. He barely looked at her, arranging his coat and rucksack beside him. He was obviously still drunk and murmured an incoherent hello.

Shaun glanced over his shoulder as he fastened his seat belt. 'Are you sure you want me to take you to Beth's, Tony? Maybe it would be better if you rang first and went over later when you're . . .' He paused, trying to find a reasonable excuse why Tony should wait.

191

Their inebriated passenger belched loudly. 'I want to go now. Take me now,' he said unhappily. 'I've got to see her this morning, need to see her now.'

Shaun shrugged. Tony leant between the seats and repeated his hello in Phoebe's ear. She winced; his breath would have cut sheet steel.

He leered at her, blinking, running a furred tongue around his lips. For an instant Phoebe was certain he recognised her; he seemed to be staring, his face contorted in thought. Then, quite suddenly he leant back and spread himself across the back seat.

'Beth's,' he snorted waving a finger at Shaun. 'I need to go to Beth's.'

Phoebe sighed.

They dropped Tony off first. He refused to let Shaun take him up to the house. Phoebe watched with relief as he shambled unsteadily along the path.

In town, Phoebe shopped while Shaun went to Bad Company's offices; they met up for brunch. The cafe in the high street was busy. When they'd ordered, Shaun surreptitiously slipped a white envelope out of his jacket pocket and thumbed through the money he had earned for his driving job. Phoebe looked away, trying to concentrate on the other diners. The envelope was the same kind Storm had given her with her fee for Langman's party. When he'd finished counting, Shaun grinned, screwed the envelope into a ball and pocketed the notes. 'Not bad for a night's work.'

Phoebe nodded. 'Did they tell you who you'd be driving tonight?'

Shaun sniffed. 'Some woman going to the theatre. I've

got to drop her off and then pick her up after the show. The receptionist said I might be late because the client wants to eat afterwards.' He looked at her unhappily. 'That means I probably won't be done in time to pick you up from work. I'm sorry.'

Phoebe forced a smile, trying to hold her mind in check. 'Don't worry,' she said with false good humour. 'Let's have lunch tomorrow.'

Shaun, relieved, nodded. 'Great—' He patted his pocket. 'My treat.'

At that moment the waitress arrived with their food and the conversation moved on. While she was eating, Phoebe wondered what she could do. A female client didn't necessarily mean that Storm Brooks had set Shaun up, but her instincts told her that was exactly what was happening. She ate without really noticing what was on the plate.

When they arrived back at Phoebe's flat one of the other students met her in the hall.

'Hi, I've just taken a message for you,' she said, handing Phoebe a slip of paper. 'Professor Gottlieb rang about ten minutes ago and asked if you could drop by his office, he's there until five if you want to ring him.'

Shaun read the note over Phoebe's shoulder. '"Gottlieb has something for you,"' he read. 'Do you want me to give you a lift round there?'

Phoebe stared blankly at him. What on earth could Gottlieb want?

'I was hoping you might come in,' she said softly.

Shaun grinned. 'I really ought to go and grab a couple of hours sleep if I'm working tonight. Anyway, aren't you the one who's always got a pile of work to do? If

Gottlieb's got something for your final paper it must be important for him to contact you at the weekend.' He paused. 'See, I told you it would work out with him. You've obviously made an impression.'

Phoebe didn't trust herself to comment, instead she smiled and folded the note into her pocket. She had no idea what Gottlieb might want, but it wouldn't be long before she found out.

Chapter Ten

Gottlieb was dressed casually in an open-neck shirt under a cashmere sweater, and faded cord trousers. He handed Phoebe a mug of coffee even before she had had a chance to sit down.

'You wanted to see me?' she said, folding her hands around the mug.

Gottlieb nodded. 'Indeed. Are you busy this evening?'

Phoebe stared at him. 'I'm sorry?'

Gottlieb waved her words away. 'Simple enough question. Are you free tonight?'

He stood with his back to the bay window, the sharp grey light accentuating the width of his shoulders. His sheer size was intimidating. Phoebe felt an unnerving ripple of something dark and magnetic.

'What had you got in mind?' she said, struggling to keep the tone light and conversational.

Gottlieb grinned wolfishly. 'A little trip out – a private educational visit.'

Phoebe shivered. 'Where?'

Gottlieb pulled his heavy features into an exaggerated expression of displeasure. 'Please, Miss Williams, so many questions. Why don't you just trust me? Eh?'

Phoebe took a pull on her coffee. 'I've told you already, Professor, my power isn't up for grabs,' she said quietly.

Gottlieb laughed. 'Who said anything about power? Think of this as an educational visit – a school trip for just the two of us.' He paused, eyes never leaving hers. 'Of course, unlike Bad Company I won't be able to pay you for your companionship.'

Phoebe struggled hard not to blush but even so felt the colour rising in her cheeks.

'What time?' she said.

Gottlieb broke his intimidating stare. 'Eight. I'll meet you here. It's a formal occasion so I'd appreciate it if your dress reflected that.'

Phoebe nodded and put her half-empty mug down on his desk. 'Eight, then,' she said softly and walked out of his office.

'Eight,' Gottlieb repeated into the empty room after she had left. He had already told Maya that he wouldn't be in for supper and not to wait up for him. He smiled. She would stay up nonetheless, she always did.

Phoebe locked the flat and glanced at her watch. She'd allowed ten minutes to get across the campus for her rendezvous with Gottlieb – and she was late. Outside wisps of fog hung in the autumn air, wreathing the yellow street lights like smoke.

Away from the main road the night seemed unnaturally dark, the thick undergrowth creeping towards the pathways that criss-crossed the college grounds. The night seemed to swallow the light up whole.

Phoebe felt nervous, trying hard not to let her mind linger on the evening that Gottlieb had planned for her. She was wearing the dress she had borrowed from Storm Brooks on that first night. It was hardly a warm choice – even with a coat, the chill air found its way in and nipped at her skin.

Through the gloom she could just about make out the lights of the main administration buildings amongst the trees. In the yellowing lamp light her breath came in dragons' curls of water vapour, her high heels tapping out a compelling rhythm.

The apprehension she had fought to control in Gott-lieb's office that afternoon was bubbling up inside her, making her shiver more effectively than even the bitter cold air. She dragged her collar up around her throat, hands tight around her clutch bag, wondering why she had accepted his invitation. Curiosity? Deep in thought she didn't see the movement in the bushes beyond the circles of light.

'Well, hello there. Cinderella, isn't it?' said a voice from the shadows. Phoebe let out a little shriek and froze. Tony Goodman stepped into the jaundiced arc of the street lamp. She took a deep breath, steadying herself as he looked her up and down.

'I've been watching your flat all afternoon,' he said darkly. 'Beth threw me back out on my ear, you know, wouldn't even listen to me.'

Phoebe took a step away from him. 'I'm really sorry to hear that, Tony,' she said quietly. 'But if you don't mind, I'm meeting someone. Why don't you come round to my place tomorrow if you want to talk. Shaun will be—'

Before she could finish the sentence Tony leapt forward and grabbed her wrists. 'I've been thinking about you all afternoon,' he said, his face just inches away from hers. 'I worked out where I'd seen you before.'

Phoebe felt an icy chill slice her to the core. Her confidence crumbled as Tony's hands snaked inside her coat, rubbing a lecherous hand over her belly.

'How much do you charge sweetheart?' he said with a snarl.

Phoebe pushed him back. 'Let go of me,' she said quickly.

Tony laughed. 'Oh, I don't think so. How much is it worth to make sure Shaun doesn't find out how his girlfriend makes her living?' His hands were working lower now, gathering up the thin material of her evening dress.

He grunted as he thrust his hand roughly between her thighs.

'Come on,' he said through gritted teeth. 'Let's see what I'm going to get for keeping my mouth shut. Maybe we could make it a regular thing. I'd like that—'

Tony leant forward to kiss her. His breath was foul, his tongue lapping at her closed lips like a filthy viper. Phoebe suddenly felt a flash of white hot fury. She tore herself away from him, anger raging in her gut like a clenched fist.

'You complete bastard,' she hissed, wiping her mouth with the back of her hand.

Tony grinned and cupped the intimidating bulge in the front of his jeans. 'Call me what you like. This is all for you. I like it when they fight a bit. I knew what you were like the first time Shaun brought you round.' He grinned and stepped nearer. Phoebe could smell his body, rancid with sweat and drink.

'Shaun doesn't know about it, does he? He thinks you're some sweet student princess. Quite the demure little blue stocking.' He let his eyes travel over her face. 'I'm going to fuck you so hard—'

Phoebe took a deep breath. She had to regain control. He was trying to frighten her, trying to force her. She squared her shoulders.

'Or what?' she snapped in a cold brittle voice.

Tony rubbed himself against her. 'I'd have thought you could work that out for yourself. Either you do what I want or I'm going to tell your precious Shaun everything, first thing tomorrow.'

Phoebe knew that if she once gave way to Tony she would never be free of him. She had to stay strong. 'He wouldn't believe you,' she said flatly, playing for time. She glanced over her shoulder – the main buildings seemed like miles.

He grinned. 'No?' he said. 'Want to try it, do you?'

Phoebe jerked away and rounded on him, harnessing the anger and frustration she felt deep inside. 'Why don't you tell him then?' she hissed, in a voice that was so vehement that it astounded her.

Tony smirked. 'I might have to.'

'You miserable blackmailing little bastard.' Before she had time to think what she was doing, she drew back her fist and hit him squarely in the face. The impact ricocheted up through her hand and arm, making them burn with pain. Tony snorted and crumpled, dropping to his knees.

'I wouldn't sleep with you if you were the last soul on earth,' she snorted, sweat breaking out on her face. 'And as for Shaun, tell him what you bloody well like. Where do you think he is tonight? Tucked up with a good book? Oh no, he's out screwing someone for money.' She was astonished by her outburst. The words came out in a furious tirade. She had no idea whether Shaun was being seduced by his fare but she realised, even as she let a stinging slap explode across the side of Tony's skull, that part of her fury was fuelled by the jealous certainty that he was.

Tony moaned and slid on his hands and knees, a trickle of blood rendered to glittering oily blackness by the street lights, dripping onto the path beside him. He looked up at her, ashen faced.

'You hurt me,' he whimpered, all his bluster gone, 'you've made my nose bleed.'

Phoebe looked down at him; he was pathetic. 'Go home and sober up,' she said slowly. 'Beth won't want you back like that.'

Tony snivelled. 'I only wanted to touch you,' he said miserably. 'I wouldn't really have told Shaun, honest . . .'

Phoebe stopped listening, instead she turned and headed towards the distant lights of Gottlieb's office, her whole hand still raw and humming, her mind racing.

Gottlieb had poured them both a glass of wine. When he opened the door Phoebe was flushed, her eyes bright and glittering. He eyed her appreciatively as she stood framed in the doorway. Her coat was open, revealing a superb evening dress which clung to every curve.

He lifted his glass in a toast. 'Good evening, my dear. I wondered whether perhaps you had changed your mind, or are you just being fashionably late?'

Phoebe accepted the glass without a word. Her perfume was exquisite; a subtle mixture of sandalwood and citrus, while beneath he could detect the compelling aroma of her body. There was a pulse beating in her throat. Was it excitement? Gottlieb hoped so.

'My car is outside. I hope you will join me for dinner as well.'

She looked up at him with those electric blue eyes, making a shiver ripple down his spine.

'Whatever you say,' she said flatly.

'Is there something the matter, Miss Williams?'

She smiled; it was a cool, professional smile that didn't quite reach her glittering, anxious eyes.

'No,' she whispered in a low voice. 'I'm fine, thank you.'

Whatever she said, her body said something else. She couldn't disguise the slight tremor in her hands. The lamps in his office refracted and reflected the crystal facets of her wine glass.

Gottlieb smiled. He had no intention of seducing her this evening. Let her wait. Let the expectation grow and build – for both of them. He took his coat from the hook and then drained his glass. 'Whenever you're ready, then, Miss Williams.'

She followed suit, swallowing her wine down in one. Gottlieb extended his arm. Dutch courage, he thought with a wry grin.

Of all the things Phoebe had been expecting, driving into

the underground car park of a huge modern office block on the far side of town was not amongst the possibilities. A uniformed doorman opened the lift doors for them, deferentially touching his cap as Gottlieb and Phoebe stepped inside.

'Penthouse, sir?' said the man.

Gottlieb nodded and then checked his bow tie in the stainless steel panelling before turning to smile at Phoebe. The lift climbed silently towards the top floor. The doorman stood by the control panel, his face a mask. He reminded Phoebe of Joe Blenheim – his impressive body at odds with his deferential manner.

'You look quite exquisite, my dear,' Gottlieb said, resting his hand casually on the small of her back. 'I'm sure you will find tonight's events entertaining.'

Phoebe glanced at him. He cut an imposing figure in his dinner suit, leonine hair swept back in waves onto his broad shoulders. Although relaxed and obviously at ease, his expression was expectant.

'Is this where we're going to have dinner?' she said, aware that they had barely spoken since she'd arrived at his office. She was beginning to recover from her encounter with Tony, though his face and slurred unnerving threats had astounded her. She could still smell him.

Gottlieb smiled. 'This is my club,' he said dryly. 'A meeting place for connoisseurs of a particular kind.' The lift slowed as they approached the penthouse. 'The food here is quite superb. I'm sure you will enjoy the evening.'

Silently the lift doors glided open into a large reception area, glass walls revealing the town below them. Lights twinkled like a cache of jewels in the darkness. The main road was picked out in a string of pearls, the river away to the left, glittering like jet. It looked quite beautiful.

Gottlieb caught hold of her arm. 'Spectacular, isn't it?' he said. 'Look, over there is the university. You can see as far as Fair Green on a clear night.'

Phoebe smiled, he seemed warmer – almost human.

'Do you come here often?' she said.

Gottlieb laughed. 'A little clichéd, but yes, as often as commitments allow. Actually, I was involved in setting the club up, several years ago now. I saw the need and made sure the right people, the men with the money and the influence, met each other under the right circumstances.' He paused and indicated a heavily panelled door. 'Why don't we go inside?'

Phoebe took a deep breath. The doorman was still standing outside the lift. He was a heavily set man. Phoebe wondered fleetingly what would happen if she declined Gottlieb's gentlemanly invitation.

She smiled. 'Why not?'

The door was opened by a uniformed waiter who directed them towards the maitre d', who stood by his lectern, dressed in an expensive tuxedo. Inside, a staircase circled down onto an elegant modern dining-area, with a dance floor beyond. A band was playing and half a dozen couples were circling arm in arm. Phoebe stared in disbelief. Elderly men sat around the tables drinking cocktails, deep in conversation with each other. She immediately recognised some of the faces from the university and the local papers. Women guests were sparse – for the fifty or so distinguished-looking men in the room there were no more than half a dozen women.

Phoebe had considered that perhaps the girls at Gottlieb's club might be provided by an agency like Bad Company but it appeared, with one or two exceptions, that the men who had brought women, had brought their wives.

At a table by the dance floor an elderly woman was picking at a steak, while her partner lovingly sniffed at his wine glass. Another heavily set woman in a stunning evening dress was holding a heated discussion with her equally well-heeled dining companion.

Gottlieb steered Phoebe down the stairs to a secluded table by the enormous picture windows. Attentive waiters lit the candles, shook linen napkins on their laps and brought them a menu. Phoebe felt the tension ease out of her shoulders. It really was a club and she began to wonder why Gottlieb had invited her, hadn't he promised her an educational visit?

As promised, dinner was superb. Gottlieb, to her amazement, was a relaxed and congenial host. He made her laugh, telling her appalling gossipy stories about the college staff. She almost forgot, as he raised his glass in a toast, that when they had first met he had terrified her – almost forgot that without his goading and derision she would have never rung Bad Company, never have met Storm Brooks, never chosen to relinquish all things safe.

Gottlieb ordered coffee and liqueurs.

The background noise in the club was intimate, conversations and laughter just audible above the strains of the dance music.

'So,' he said, watching the dancers slowly circling the floor. 'How do you like working for Bad Company?'

Phoebe smiled. 'It's well paid.'

Gottlieb snorted. 'You know I don't mean that. What have you learnt?'

Phoebe peered into the glittering amber of her brandy. 'Passion, sexual experience.' She paused. 'Desire.'

Gottlieb nodded. 'Do you like what you've discovered about yourself?'

'Like is a strange word,' she said. 'Last night a man told me that I cared too much to be a call-girl. I felt too much, didn't fake it.'

Gottlieb's eyes glittered. 'A perceptive soul obviously.'

The alcohol had lowered Phoebe's defences and loosened her tongue. 'I think he was right,' she said slowly. 'I now realise I'm not there for their benefit but mine. Some part of me enjoys what they make me feel.' She paused, the colour rising to her cheeks. 'I didn't imagine I would be telling you about this.'

Gottlieb leant a little closer. 'And what about your lover? Shaun, isn't it?' His voice was encouraging, gently cajoling.

Phoebe bit her lip. She didn't want to think about Shaun.

'Does he like the new you?' he said in a low voice. 'Do you share the things you have learnt with him?'

Phoebe looked away, breaking the spell of Gottlieb's dark eyes.

'How can I not share them?' she said in an undertone. 'I want him to feel what I've felt.' She stopped. On the dance floor the audience politely applauded the band and were returning to their seats.

Phoebe turned to look at Gottlieb. 'Why have you

brought me here? Are you hoping I'll tell you all about the men I've met through Bad Company?'

Gottlieb shook his head and indicated the dance floor. 'No, though I would consider that an added bonus. I brought you here to show you something. Look—'

Phoebe turned round and gasped. Heavy drapes were being pulled aside on silent runners to reveal an old-fashioned theatre stage, subtly lit by concealed spotlights. The lights in the dining area dimmed, concentrating everyone's attention on the stage set. It was dressed as if for a play, with Victorian furniture and fittings: a heavy mahogany bed, plants, rich brocade furniture, a panelled door to one side of an ornate hearth.

Sitting in an armchair by the empty fireplace was a girl in a cotton chemise and long drawers, her pert breasts barely covered by the drawstring top. She got up slowly to arrange her hair in the mirror. In the lamplight her sex was a dark shadow amongst the folds of thin cotton. Her breasts moved like liquid silk as she pulled the brush through her hair.

Gottlieb smiled as Phoebe realised with astonishment that the girl was Nina King.

'My God,' Phoebe hissed, almost leaping to her feet. Gottlieb caught hold of her arm.

'Watch,' he said softly. 'You aren't the only one who is discovering her true nature.'

Off stage there was a knock. A split second later a handsome young buck in frock coat and top hat stepped through the set door. He smiled artfully at Nina, drinking in her state of undress. She embraced him, their kisses real and electrifying. Phoebe felt a tiny flurry of excitement in the pit of her stomach as the man's hands lifted to caress Nina's breasts. Her nipples hardened, pressing through the thin cotton lace. Her lover moaned appreciatively.

Phoebe's body echoed Nina's pleasure, she felt her own breasts flush, nipples pressing against the soft bodice of her evening dress. She barely noticed Gottlieb sliding his chair closer to her.

On stage the young man fumbled with the drawstring that held the cotton top in place and, as he did so, Phoebe felt an icy chill. Into the open door on stage stepped an older, more muscular man, his face contorted in fury. In his right hand he held a short riding-whip.

Although it was playacting, Phoebe felt a genuine ripple of fear as the man strode into the room. The younger man leapt back, leaving Nina centre stage, her face white with what looked like genuine panic.

She looked so vulnerable; the shoulder of her chemise had slipped down, exposing the swell of one rounded breast, topped with an erect crimson nipple. Her eyes were bright with something that Phoebe sensed was both apprehension and excitement.

Nina looked into her master's eyes and then slowly dropped to her knees. The older man grabbed her, hauling her to her feet. As they struggled the little cotton chemise slipped down further, an erotic garnish to her ripe breasts.

'Vixen,' the man hissed, dragging her across the room. Nina let out a thin miserable sob as the man confronted her. His hands tugged and tore at her clothes, leaving them in shreds. She seemed to be fighting him in earnest, but Phoebe could sense Nina's excitement growing with every twist and turn of her body.

Phoebe didn't have to look around the club to know that every eye in the house was on the stage; she could feel it. The older man glared at the young lover in his frock coat, who was caught between fear and fascination as his supposed mistress was roughly manhandled in front of him.

'What were you going to do with her?' hissed the older man malevolently.

The young man reddened. 'I . . . I . . .'

'Speak up,' snapped the man.

The boy struggled to gather his wits. 'Make love to her,' he whispered in an undertone. 'Kiss her sweet breasts, tongue her . . .' His voice faded.

The older man's expression was triumphant. 'Then you shall,' he snorted melodramatically. 'Come here and undress the little bitch.'

With unsteady fingers the young man began to undo the ruins of Nina's chemise, fingers lingering on her ripe breasts. Slowly he moved lower, untying the waist string of her drawers and sliding them over her rounded hips.

Phoebe swallowed hard, she knew she was trembling. At her shoulder she could hear Gottlieb's breath quicken as the young man traced a finger slowly over the mound of Nina's quim.

The older man flexed the whip skilfully. Nina's eyes flashed. The young man's every move was being watched by his older companion. Naked now, Nina shivered under the eyes of the two men and those of the mesmerised audience. The older man waved the young buck on.

'Show me what you were going to do with her.'

The boy shivered, pressing nervous kisses to Nina's lips, hands cupping the orbs of her breasts, thumbs teasing across her nipples. She stood like a statue, eyes fixed on the middle distance.

The older man growled angrily, running the end of the whip across Nina's shoulders.

'Would you have been so unyielding if I hadn't been here? Is this the kind of obedience I have taught you?'

Nina shivered but still did not move under the caresses of her young lover.

The older man waved the boy away, his face darkening. 'Get on your hands and knees,' he snapped to Nina. 'Have you learnt nothing about pleasure or obedience?'

Nina sank slowly to her knees, moving so that her full buttocks were exposed to the audience. Phoebe knew what would follow and flinched as the first blow exploded across her friend's bottom, making her shriek with pain. As Nina's body contorted against the white hot pain, her sex gaped, a silvery trickle of moisture oozing from the scarlet slit.

Phoebe realised she had been holding her breath since Nina had crouched on the floor. She let out a long shuddering breath as the whip found its mark again.

'What do you think?' whispered Gottlieb in her ear, as the whip cracked again. Nina was writhing now, drinking in the compelling kiss of her punishment.

Phoebe shook her head. 'Who are they?'

Gottlieb grinned. 'The man with the whip is the deputy mayor. He's in the amateur dramatic society, adores Victorian melodrama, and the young buck is a local solicitor. Convincing, aren't they? It's something of an education.'

On the stage Nina was gasping with pleasure, her breasts flushed, her skin glowing. The whip cracked again and again until finally the deputy mayor threw it to one side and unbuttoned the flap of his jodhpurs. Without prelude, he fell to his knees and plunged his raging cock into Nina's waiting body.

The young buck followed his example, throwing back his head in delight as Nina's mouth closed hungrily around his shaft. They moved as one, groaning and straining and sweating their way towards ecstasy while a rapt crowd looked on.

Sitting beside Gottlieb, Phoebe felt wave after wave of pleasure echo through her body. She could almost taste the young man's growing excitement, salty and warm in her mouth. She could feel the tension and pleasure growing, no more than a breath away, until finally she sensed the change of pace, the rapid ragged spiral that signalled mutual release. As the players bucked and snorted the curtains slowly began to close until, finally, they framed the lovers in the spotlight for a scintillating instant – and then they were gone. There was a split second of complete silence and then a tumultuous burst of applause.

Gottlieb sat back and pulled a cigar from his pocket. 'At this rate, your friend, Miss King, may well be on the way to earning herself an honorary doctorate.'

Chapter Eleven

It was late when Gottlieb dropped Phoebe outside her flat. He didn't attempt to kiss her or even move closer when she climbed out of the car. In some ways his eyes were far more seductive than any caress.

Good manners compelled her to mumble a few words of thanks.

She could feel him watching intently as she walked up the path. At the door she stopped and turned back. In the gloom his eyes glittered, his expression wolfish. Gottlieb smiled, lifting his hand in a silent farewell and then drove away.

Phoebe let out a long shuddering breath as she watched the tail lights of his car vanish, wishing that Shaun had been there to meet her. The rest of the street was quiet and dark; there was no familiar VW, no outline of the imposing limousine that Shaun had taken to pick up his fare for Bad Company.

Once inside Phoebe slipped off her evening dress and wrapped herself in a bath robe. She pulled the armchair close to the fireplace and lit the gas. She hoped that Shaun might still call in on his way home. It would be bliss to fall into his arms and relieve the raw sense of need she felt deep inside. She fell asleep dreaming of Nina King's ripe vulnerable body.

When she woke again the first fingers of dawn were poking their way through the curtains. Stiff and aching Phoebe crept off to bed, trying hard not to let the intense images of Nina King's stage show and Gottlieb's educational trip drive away the sleepiness.

Sunday was very quiet. Phoebe made an effort to concentrate on her course notes but every noise made her look up in case it was Shaun. Every car, every male voice disturbed her train of thought.

Hadn't they arranged to meet for lunch? She was surprised he didn't arrive early. At half past eleven she started to get ready, showering, doing her make-up, watching the minutes tick past. Maybe he had arrived home late, slept in. Innocent explanations fought with a darker possibility that kept bubbling up alongside every excuse she made for his tardiness; Tony Goodman had told Shaun about her. When she called his flat the phone just rang and rang.

Finally, after lunchtime had come and gone, she decided she'd had enough. Surely Shaun had to be home by now? Her first instinct was to walk over to the flat on the far side of the campus but the prospect of meeting Tony Goodman quickly dissuaded her.

By six o'clock she began to seriously worry about him. When, at just after seven, there was a knock on the door she practically leapt to her feet.

'Coming,' she called. 'I wondered where you'd—' The words dried in her throat as she opened the door. One of the other students held out a sheet of paper.

'Message for you. Shaun Rees just rang, said he wouldn't be round tonight.'

Phoebe smiled unsteadily, feeling a sting of disappointment and hurt. 'Did he say anything else?'

The girl pulled a face and then shook her head. 'No, nothing else.'

Phoebe thanked her and closed the door, pressing her face to the wood. Tony had carried out his threat after all. She shivered, imagining his bright malevolent eyes. If Tony had told Shaun . . . she felt a lump rising in her throat. She went in to the hall and tapped in Shaun's phone number.

'Hi, I wonder if Shaun Rees is in?'

She could hear voices in the background, almost certain that one of them was Shaun's and was disappointed when the disembodied male voice told her he wasn't at home.

'Sorry, he's not here at the moment. Would you like me to give him a message?'

'Can you please tell him Phoebe called?'

It didn't ring true. She thanked the man and lowered the phone back into its cradle. It rang again before she had time to make it back to the flat.

A familiar voice asked for her by name – Storm Brooks.

Phoebe took a deep breath. 'Hello,' she said guardedly.

Storm laughed. 'Hanging around by the phone these days? Either you're desperate or you've started taking jobs on the side.'

Phoebe snorted. 'I was waiting for Shaun to ring,' she snapped.

Storm made an exaggerated sound of pain. 'Steady, no need to bite,' she said with humour. 'Did he tell you how he got on last night?'

Phoebe could sense the mischief in her voice and said nothing.

Storm continued undeterred. 'Anyway, I rang to see what nights you're free next week. We've got a lot of bookings.'

Phoebe gripped the receiver. 'I'm not certain yet,' she said hesitantly. 'I've got a lot of work to catch up on.'

Storm laughed. 'I'd forgotten, your final paper. How's it going?' She didn't wait for a reply. 'By the way, you haven't pick up the fee for the Starcor party yet, do you want me to call by and drop it in?'

'No,' said Phoebe quickly. 'I'll be in during the week. I'll tell you when I'm free then.'

'Okay, we've got bookings for the weekend and a couple of individual bookings midweek.' Storm paused. 'Didn't you say you were interested in a little one-on-one?'

Phoebe reddened. 'I'll call in the office,' she said and hastily added her goodbyes. Leaning back against the wall of the phone booth she tried to gather her thoughts. She didn't need Bad Company, what she wanted was Shaun Rees.

Monday morning was wet and overcast. Phoebe tried to fill the confused spaces in her head with work. Gottlieb's project notes haunted her; on her desk were a pile of jottings and a stack of books to read. She longed for Shaun to ring, but by mid-morning nothing seemed to be able to fill the tight unhappy space in her mind. Abandoning her work she headed off across the campus.

* * *

Gerrard Gottlieb sat in his office watching the wind blowing through the bare trees. He re-read the memo on his desk and then folded it into his pocket. He might go home for lunch; Maya would be waiting for him as always. His maverick mind refused to settle on the dull collection of notes on his desk. He closed the book and picked up the phone. The memo confirmed what he had been told by the head of department at their early morning meeting. Dr Audrey Manley, the lecturer he had replaced, had unexpectedly decided to come back before the end of term. By the end of the month he would be free to go back to Morrahills and his research.

He leant back and blew a stream of breath thoughtfully between his long fingers. Such a shame, just when he had begun to enjoy his new role as mentor and guide. Grinning, he thumbed through the telephone book on his desk and dialled Bad Company's number.

'Phoebe! Hang on, wait for me.' Phoebe swung round at the foot of the stairs to the library. Nina King hurried over towards her. Phoebe felt her colour rising and then thought how ridiculous it was. It was Nina who should be blushing, not her.

'Hi,' said Nina, breathlessly. 'What are you doing?'

Phoebe held out the books she was carrying. 'Library.'

Nina nodded. 'Right.' There was a slightly uneasy pause. Nina grinned. 'I wanted to say I'm really sorry about the other day. I shouldn't have cried all over your shoulder.'

Phoebe smiled. 'Don't mention it.'

Nina shuffled uneasily from foot to foot. 'I was upset

about Gottlieb,' she said flatly. 'But things have changed now.' She stopped and ran her tongue around her perfectly painted lips. 'I just wanted to say thanks for being so kind to me.'

'Don't worry about it. Look, I've really got to go.'

Still Nina didn't move. Phoebe didn't want to talk to her, she didn't want to hear about Gottlieb's club, the stage show or the pleasure she had seen on Nina's face as she and her lovers had reached their stunning, terrifying climax.

Nina grinned and pointed towards the refectory. 'I don't suppose you've got time for a coffee have you?'

Phoebe shook her head. 'Not at the moment, maybe later.'

The atmosphere between them was uncomfortable. Phoebe was relieved when Nina said her goodbyes, and hurried away.

Even in the quiet of the library Phoebe couldn't concentrate. She realised how much she had come to rely on Shaun being around and she hated the fact that whatever they had had been ruined by a little weasel like Tony Goodman. She stared out of the window. She wanted Shaun to think of her as special. She shivered, God knows what he thought of her now that Tony had had his say.

The university wasn't large, they were bound to bump into each other eventually. She reddened; she was making all kinds of assumptions. Maybe Tony hadn't said anything, maybe Shaun really had been out when she'd called, maybe he was tired, maybe . . . She ran her fingers back through her hair; this was ridiculous. Tony or no Tony she had to go and find Shaun.

216

She stuffed her books into her bag and hurried downstairs. The foyer was busy and to her surprise Shaun and Tony were standing by the soft drinks machine in the entrance hall.

'Shaun,' she said without thinking and she pushed towards him through the other students. For an instant he didn't see her.

He looked gorgeous, the winter sun catching his shoulder-length hair, spinning it into a halo. He leant casually against the wall listening to Tony, his face handsome in respose. Phoebe felt a tiny flurry of desire in her stomach.

He looked up and, to her horror, instantly reddened and looked away. Beside him, Tony watched her approach with ratty little eyes and grinned salaciously. His nose was noticeably red, a navy bruise staining the skin under one eye. Phoebe felt a surge of pain and anger.

Tony lifted a can of drink in salute and moved away, while Shaun lingered uncomfortably.

Phoebe couldn't bring herself to ask him what the matter was – she was convinced she knew. Shaun grinned nervously.

'I thought you'd be round yesterday. You asked me out to lunch—' she began tentatively.

He nodded. 'Sorry, I ... I was really tired,' he said, without meeting her eyes. The atmosphere was so strained between them that Phoebe struggled to take another breath.

Tiny dark curls of hair peeped out from the open neck of his shirt, and instantly she imagined the smell of his body as he bent to kiss her. She bit her lip, longing for him to move closer and take her in his arms.

'I waited up for you on Saturday night. I thought you might drop in on your way home—' She wanted him to say anything, to tell her something, she couldn't bear the strange taut feeling in her stomach. 'How did the job go?'

Shaun sighed and looked across the busy foyer. 'Look, Phoebe, I'm really sorry, I've got to go, I've got a lecture.'

Phoebe wanted to touch him. What was the spell she had used before to make him follow her blindly without question? The power Gottlieb had shown her? Was it so fleeting, so easily broken? She shivered.

'Are you going to come round later?'

Shaun looked uncomfortable. 'I'm not sure. I've got a lot of work to do at the moment,' he said lamely. 'I'll give you a ring.'

Phoebe felt hot. Around them other students were heading towards the lecture theatre, swirling around them like a river. By the doors Phoebe could see Tony and wished she had the courage to confront him with what he'd done. Shaun looked away.

'I'll see you around,' he said flatly and hurried off towards Tony.

Tears pressed up hot and angry behind Phoebe's eyes. She sniffed miserably. How could Tony be so vindictive, so bloody cruel? She wiped away a scalding tear with the back of her hand and hurried outside.

The day echoed her mood perfectly; freezing bitter rain nipped maliciously at her face and hands. She walked without being conscious of where she was going and was surprised to find herself outside Gottlieb's office.

It looked empty. She sniffed, tears falling unnoticed. Even Gottlieb wasn't there when she needed him.

'Are you looking for me, Miss Williams?'

Phoebe spun round. Gottlieb was standing by his car, wrapped up in a huge coat, collar turned up against the wind. She bit her lips, eyes bright from crying.

'I don't really know,' she said miserably.

Gottlieb looked her up and down.

'I was just about to have some lunch,' he said. 'I'd planned to go home but...' He stopped and extended his arm. 'Let's go and find a quiet place to talk, shall we?'

Phoebe nodded and said nothing when Gottlieb slipped his arm through hers.

'I know a very nice little pub down by the river,' he said warmly. 'You look as if you could do with a drink.'

Phoebe took a long pull on the wine glass and didn't resist when Gottlieb refilled it to the brim.

'... And then I hit Tony Goodman,' she said flatly.

Gottlieb's eyes twinkled. 'You hit him?'

Phoebe nodded, turning her hand over so that he could inspect it; her knuckles were still red.

'I punched him on the nose.'

Gottlieb laughed. 'Bravo, my dear. And there was me thinking the prospect of our little trip had filled you with all manner of excited expectation.' He paused, his expression becoming serious. 'And so he has now told Shaun?'

Phoebe sniffed. 'Yes. He must have.'

Gottlieb pulled a face. 'Are you ashamed of your involvement with Bad Company?'

Phoebe sighed. 'No... yes. Oh, I don't know. It's a totally different world, away from reality. I'm different when I'm working for them.' She paused. 'I suppose it was naive of me to assume that anyone else might see it that way.'

Gottlieb nodded thoughtfully. 'You mean Shaun.'

Phoebe wiped away what promised to be a tear. 'I thought I'd found someone really special, you know? The magical right one we're all supposed to be looking for.'

Gottlieb snorted. 'You believe that nonsense, do you?'

'I really don't know.'

Gottlieb waved the waiter over to bring their coffee.

'Would you like me to talk to Shaun for you?'

Phoebe stared at him incredulously. 'You?'

Gottlieb aped offence. 'Don't sound so astonished. Why not? I can tell him this was all my fault.' He struck a pose. 'Tell him I led you astray, corrupted you.'

In spite of herself Phoebe laughed. 'Don't be so ridiculous.'

Gottlieb groaned theatrically. 'You cut me to the quick, young lady. I do feel a degree of responsibility.'

Phoebe stared at him. 'And what will your advice cost me?'

Gottlieb grinned, lifting his wine glass in a silent toast. 'I'm sure I can come up with something, my dear.' His eyes sparkled mischievously.

Phoebe shook her head. 'You are incorrigible.'

Gottlieb sat back so the waiter could pour their coffee.

'How very nice of you to notice,' he said darkly. 'What are your plans for the rest of the day?'

Phoebe lifted an eyebrow. The wine had relaxed her and in the warm comfortable pub she began to feel better, though the pain was only numbed not gone.

'I thought I'd do some more work, maybe call in at Bad Company and pick up my money.'

Gottlieb nodded. 'By the way, you may be relieved to hear that you won't be having the pleasure of my company for too much longer.'

Phoebe stared at him. 'Sorry?'

'Your beloved Dr Manley is coming back at the beginning of next month.'

'I thought she'd had a breakdown.'

Gottlieb snorted. 'My, how rumours spread. Actually she has been suffering from some kind of virus. So, Miss Williams, you may relax now.' He sipped his coffee. 'Look on this episode as an interesting interlude in your academic career. The status quo will be restored very soon.'

Phoebe could sense the regret in his voice.

'What will you do?'

Gottlieb lifted his hands in resignation. 'I shall go back to my research. It will be a return to familiar ground for us both.' He paused. 'And I'll have a word with young Mr Rees to see if we can't even the balance there too.'

Phoebe forced a smile; she doubted there was anything Gottlieb could say to Shaun that would make things right.

Gottlieb dropped her off in town. Phoebe walked slowly along the road towards Bad Company's offices. In daylight it looked shabby. Phoebe climbed the stairs. The receptionist took her name and handed her an envelope containing her wages from Starcor.

'By the way I had a client ring up this morning and ask for

you by name,' she said as Phoebe signed for her money.

Phoebe stiffened, names crowding her mind: Joe Blenheim, Charlie Bryce, Baxter Hayes – Tony? A cold chill trickled down her spine.

'Who was it?' she asked softly.

The woman shook her head. 'No name. He said he'd ring back to confirm at the end of the week. He wants to book you for dinner on Friday evening. Storm's in her office, if you'd like to see her.'

Phoebe shook her head. 'No thanks,' she said, folding the money into her handbag.

The woman nodded. 'Shall I book you out for Friday night?'

Phoebe hesitated for a few seconds. Charlie and Baxter held no fears. Joe Blenheim's interest was professional. If it was Tony she would have her revenge. She took a deep breath; what would she do if it was Shaun checking up on Tony's story? Finally she nodded.

'All right,' she said softly. At least if it was Shaun they would have a chance to talk alone with no pretence between them.

The door to the inner office opened. Storm Brooks grinned at her. 'Hi, I thought I heard your voice. You decided to come in then?'

Phoebe nodded.

'I hear you're getting asked for by name. I knew I'd got you sussed when I first saw you. By the way have you rung David yet?'

Phoebe pulled a face. 'David?'

'Our submissive friend. He rings in every day, ten thirty, regular as clockwork.'

Phoebe reddened. 'I don't think . . .' she began.

Storm lifted a hand to silence her. 'I told you before, you can be anything you like. David is desperate.'

'But I've got no idea how to . . .' She stopped. 'You know what I'm saying don't you?'

Storm nodded. 'Don't worry. He likes to be caned. He lives in the most beautiful house, he's unnaturally rich, everyone else kowtows to him.' She smiled wolfishly. 'Why don't you give it a try, you might like it.'

Phoebe hesitated and then nodded. 'All right,' she said in an undertone. In her mind she saw Shaun's unhappy tight face – the damage was done now, whatever she did she couldn't wind back the clock.

Storm waved her into her office. 'You can ring from here. Don't haggle about time or price. Remember, you're in control.'

Nervously Phoebe tapped in the phone number from the card Storm handed her and waited to be connected with David.

'Hello.' Phoebe recognised David's cultured tones. She took a deep breath.

'Good afternoon,' she said briskly. 'This is Phoebe.' She glanced at Storm who gave her an encouraging look. 'Miss Phoebe.'

She heard David suck in a breath. 'Oh right,' he said happily.

Storm handed her a piece of paper on which she had hastily scribbled a few words.

Phoebe read the words aloud. 'Six this evening.'

'Six,' repeated David.

'At Storm's house.'

Storm leant forward and cut Phoebe off. Phoebe looked at her in astonishment. 'He didn't have a chance to reply,' she said.

Storm grinned. 'He'll be there. I've just got a couple of phone calls to make and then we'll go to my house and find you something to wear. Why don't you wait outside? I'll get the receptionist to make you a cup of coffee.'

Gottlieb had given himself the afternoon off. For a while he sat in his office, soon to be returned to the inimitable Audrey Manley. His presence there was barely more than an illusion; her possessions were neatly stacked away in a cupboard, it would take no more than an hour or so to return the room to its feminine glory. He would bring Maya over to help him move his things out. Maya: the image of her soft compliant body floated momentarily in front of his eyes. He finally had to admit to himself he was bored with her, or he wouldn't have been so determined in his pursuit of Phoebe – or Nina King.

He toyed thoughtfully with his pen. Pastures new, he thought philosophically. He felt an unfamiliar sense of responsibility. Without him, where would Maya go? What would she do? He could hardly just turn her lose. And then there was Phoebe Williams. Nina King, he knew would find her own way through life without help or hindrance from him. But Phoebe? He grimaced – he'd promised to have a word with Shaun Rees though he really had no idea what he would say. Gottlieb picked up his coat. He would go home to Maya, her uncomplicated obedience and her simple sexual prowess would clear his head. Bored or not Maya knew the ways to drive away all thoughts except the pursuit of pleasure. All those elegant little pleasures he had taught her. He sighed. What a shame to waste such a prodigious talent.

Chapter Twelve

Phoebe had an uncanny sense of *déjà vu*. Sitting in the understated elegance of Storm Brook's dressing room at her parkside house, Phoebe was painfully aware that this was how it had all begun. Storm lit a cigarette before she opened up a closet. Her expression was thoughtful.

'David likes leather,' she said almost to herself, ferreting amongst the hangers. Phoebe watched her in a distracted way; her mind was elsewhere.

Storm emerged triumphantly from the cupboard clutching a pair of leather thigh-boots and a heavily seamed leather body. '*Voilà*,' she grinned.

Phoebe lifted an eyebrow. '*Voilà*?' she repeated.

Storm arranged the clothes on the dressing-table. 'The perfect ensemble. Somewhere I've got a ... oh, here we are.' She grinned and plucked a leather cat mask from a drawer. 'Perfect. All you need are a pair of fishnet tights. Red lipstick, hair back in a bun. Perfect.'

Phoebe stroked the fine leather. Despite its intimidating appearance it was as soft as kid.

'David will adore this outfit,' said Storm. 'Here are the finishing touches.'

Phoebe looked uncertainly at the cane and mortar

board Storm produced from the cupboard. 'I've never caned anyone before,' she said nervously, fingering the smooth cool wood.

Storm laughed. 'Try the outfit on, you'll find it comes naturally when you're dressed for the part. Isn't there anyone you'd like to give a good thrashing to?'

Her eyes sparkled mischievously as Phoebe slipped off her sweater. Phoebe was aware that Storm was watching her.

'How hard do I hit him?' Phoebe said lamely as she slithered out of her leggings.

'As hard as you like, he likes six of the best. No holds barred, but still very civilised. Over and done with in next-to-no-time.'

Phoebe was very conscious of her body as she slipped off her panties and bra. From her perch on the dressing-table, Storm's eyes moved over her like a delicate touch, taking in the curves and plains, eyes lingering on the soft uptilt of her breast. Phoebe shivered.

Storm handed her the leather body. 'Relax,' she said softly. 'It's purely professional interest.'

The leather body fitted like a second skin, squeezing Phoebe's slim body into a stunning hour-glass. The seams make it look almost sculptural, as if she had been hewn from some kind of exotic wood. She eased it down over her hips and did up the fasteners between her legs. Wordlessly Storm handed her the boots and mask.

When Phoebe turned to look into the mirror she was stunned by what she saw – a chilling erotic masterpiece. The mask accentuated her piercing eyes and fine bone structure. In the mirror Phoebe watched Storm step

behind her and pull her hair back into a tight unforgiving
bun, topped by the mortar board. The transformation
was complete. Phoebe felt a peculiar sense of anonymity;
she really could have been anyone. She turned, looking
at her body with new eyes.

Storm reached out and drew a finger thoughtfully over
the triangle of Phoebe's sex. On either side of the leather
crotch, wisps of dark hair curled delicately into Phoebe's
groin. Phoebe was so surprised by the intimate nature of
the woman's touch that she froze and blushed furiously.

'You really ought to trim your pussy,' Storm said,
casting a professional eye over the rest of Phoebe's body.
'The clients like to see what they're getting. It turns them
on to see those luscious lips close around their cocks.
And in this outfit it looks tidier.' She grinned. 'Not to
mention how infuriating it is to pick pubic hair out of
your teeth.'

Phoebe was speechless. Storm swung round and took a
tiny pair of scissors out of a basket on the dressing-table.

'Why don't you lay down on the couch? I'll give you a
trim.'

Phoebe stiffened. 'I don't think . . .' she started. What
was it she was going to say in protest? Without Shaun
there was nothing to stop her carrying on working for
Bad Company. Nothing to hold her back from experienc-
ing everything Storm Brooks had to offer. And wasn't
there some part of her that relished the challenge? That
fed on the wild experiences?

Wordlessly she climbed up onto the massage couch
that stood in one corner of the room and closed her eyes
as Storm ran a hand over her leather-clad belly.

229

'Relax,' Storm said in an amused undertone. 'This won't hurt a bit.'

Phoebe felt her colour rising as Storm gently parted her thighs and unfastened the leather body. She felt the cool intimidating brush of the metal. Snip, snip. She flinched as the scissors moved closer and closer to the tender skin of her sex. Her embarrassment was replaced by a sense of nervousness and expectation as the blades skimmed her cool flesh.

Storm made a soft noise of approval and opened Phoebe's legs a little wider, teasing one finger into the moist confines of her quim, holding the lips apart so that she could trim away the hair. 'Next time we ought to use a razor to get rid of this, scissors aren't really the tool for the job.'

Phoebe held herself taut as Storm slipped the finger over the rise of her clitoris – almost casually, as if by accident. Storm giggled as Phoebe flinched.

'Relax,' she purred. 'You have to let go and learn to enjoy the sensations your body gives you. Christ, you're so tense. Don't tell me this doesn't feel good? Don't answer that, I know it does.'

Back went the finger, teasing now, a sweet caress. In spite of herself Phoebe moaned, perturbed by the demands of her body, which ached for fulfilment. She felt a tiny flurry of excitement low in her belly. Storm's fingers were lighting a spark that threatened to burst into a raging fire.

Storm laughed. 'See,' she whispered, fingers circling deftly.

Phoebe's eyes snapped open. 'Why are you doing this?'

she said in a tight uneven voice.

Storm's pupils were dilated, her huge eyes deep hypnotic pools. She smiled. 'Why do you always have to ask why? Isn't what you feel answer enough?'

Phoebe said nothing, frozen in the bizarre pose: her body constrained by the leather suit, legs open, Storm Brook's painted fingernail resting on the hard hungry bud of her sex.

Storm shrugged. 'Since you insist on explanations – what David wants won't satisfy you. You're not naturally dominant, you won't get off on seeing him squirm.' She paused and slid her finger into the tight confines of Phoebe's sex. Phoebe reddened, knowing that she was wet, her body unconsciously hungry; a reflex action, an intriguing compelling response that had been triggered by the other woman's attentions.

Storm bent closer, her tongue winding slow disturbing kisses over Phoebe's leather clad belly. Phoebe could feel the heat of her kisses even through the thin hide.

'But afterwards—' She paused, glancing up at her, letting Phoebe's mind fill in the possibilities.

Phoebe rolled away from Storm's kisses, trying to regain her composure. She struggled to her feet and crossed her arms over her body, aware that far from covering her it actually added to her appearance of sensual vulnerability. She caught sight of herself in the mirrors; the leather suit, her eyes glittering from behind the cat mask, the shell-like excited lips of her quim peeking provocatively from her newly trimmed pussy.

Storm shook her head. 'What's the matter?'

Phoebe shivered, confused, bemused, muddled. She

picked up her clothes. 'It's getting late. I ought to be getting ready.'

Storm smiled. 'David wouldn't mind waiting, but if you insist—'

'Miss Phoebe is ready for you now,' said Storm.

Phoebe could hear her from the hall, as she waited in the upstairs sitting room for David's arrival. She flexed the cane to steady her nerves, holding onto it like a talisman. Her hands still trembled as she heard them climbing the stairs. In the mirror that filled one wall she stared at her reflection. The image of the stunning leather-clad dominatrix who prowled around the expensively furnished room seemed totally at odds with the nervous expectation Phoebe felt inside.

David stood framed in the doorway, dark eyes betraying his obvious anticipation. Behind him Storm Brooks stood with her arms folded across her chest. 'Get inside, David,' she snapped. 'It really doesn't do to keep Miss Phoebe waiting.'

David glanced nervously over his shoulder. 'Will you be staying Miss Brooks?' he said in a voice barely above a whisper.

Storm gave him a withering look. 'Yes,' she snapped.

David smiled. 'Oh good,' he said in an undertone.

Phoebe took a deep breath. She could be anyone, couldn't she? She stared coldly at David. 'You're late,' she said in a low aggressive voice.

David swallowed nervously. 'I don't think I am,' he said. 'The traffic was—'

'Be quiet,' Phoebe said. 'Are you arguing with me?'

David shook his head. 'Oh no, Miss Phoebe, not at all, I—'

She brought the cane down with an intimidating crack on the arm of the sofa. 'I should hope not,' she said in an icy voice and turned her back on him, watching her own reflection.

By the door Storm smiled her approval.

'First you are late and then you argue with me. I really do think you need to be punished for being so badly behaved.'

David shivered, eyes alight. 'Yes, I do,' he purred. 'I really do.'

Phoebe bit her lip, wondering how they got to the next stage. David was wearing an expensive suit, a camel coat folded over his arm. He was hardly dressed for a caning. She tapped the cane thoughtfully against her boots.

To her surprise David instantly fell to his knees and crawled over to her, pressing his lips to her toes.

'I'm so sorry for being so naughty,' he mumbled. His kisses worked tentatively up over her calves, knees, thighs, until he was nosing at the tightly confined leather-clad triangle of her crotch.

She shivered and glanced quickly at Storm, who shook her head. David was sniffing at her like a dog at a bitch.

'Stop it,' she snapped, trying to hold onto her sense of balance. She was supposed to be in control. Slowly she stroked the whip across his cheek as he pulled away. 'Did I give you permission to touch me?'

David coloured dramatically. 'I'm so sorry. I thought—'

'Don't think.' Phoebe stepped away from him, the sensation of his breath on her legs was disturbing.

'I didn't mean to offend you, I—'

'That's not good enough,' she snapped, before David had a chance to finish his grovelling apology. 'You deserve to be punished for all the wicked things you've done. Don't you think so, Miss Brooks?'

Storm nodded, her face now an impassive mask. 'I do, Miss Phoebe, severely punished.'

Phoebe strode around the room while her heart beat nervously in her chest. On his knees, David was almost unable to contain his excitement. Beads of sweat were breaking out on his top lip.

She turned to Storm. 'And what do you suggest, Miss Brooks?'

Storm appeared to deliberate for a few seconds and then said flatly, 'I think the cane, Miss Phoebe. What did you do with disobedient boys at prep school?'

Phoebe bent the cane into a dramatic arc. 'I gave them six of the best, Miss Brooks, six of the best across their naughty little bottoms.'

David shivered. 'Six of the best,' he repeated in a tight, excited voice.

Phoebe nodded. Despite the ridiculous pantomime she could feel David's excitement rising like heat from his body. It was almost impossible not to be touched by it and, in spite of her nervousness, she felt a shiver of expectation.

Storm carried a piano stool across the room. David's eyes widened dramatically.

Phoebe made an effort to stay in control. 'Now, David, I think you know what I expect next.'

She prayed he did, she wasn't sure what to do, and even

with Storm there, she knew that she had to at least appear to be in control of the situation.

David scrambled to his feet. 'Yes, Miss Phoebe,' he said in a thick voice. 'Of course.'

With ungainly speed he threw his coat onto the sofa, undid his trousers and bent over the piano stool, resting his weight on his arms. Tipping forward he presented his large, fish-white backside to Phoebe. His excitement was obvious; his pale, scrawny cock was as stiff as a board. Phoebe took a deep breath and drew the cane back.

Storm lifted a hand to stop her for an instant. 'Miss Phoebe wants to know if you're sorry for being so naughty, David.'

David, who had been bracing himself for the first stroke, swallowed hard. 'Oh yes,' he gasped. 'I'm very, very sorry. I couldn't be more sorry—'

As he spoke Storm waved Phoebe on, and with a great sweeping arm movement Phoebe brought the cane down with a resounding crack across David's backside.

He yelped and then snorted. Across his pale flesh a great weal lifted almost instantaneously. Phoebe was shocked and fought the compulsion to apologise.

'And?' continued Storm.

David had barely had chance to catch his breath. 'I'll never ever be late again, Miss Phoebe,' he gasped, a split second before Phoebe brought the cane down again.

She felt hot, astonished that she could inflict pain on someone so deliberately, and equally astonished by her victim's obvious relish of the sensations. As David squirmed from side to side, she tried to imagine what the heat and pain might feel like across her own buttocks. It would be explosive, like liquid fire.

She shivered as David groaned with sheer pleasure. Between his legs his cock strained and thrust forward dramatically. He snorted, reddening violently as she laid on the third and fourth strokes. She could sense that he wasn't far from the point of release, a dew drop of excitement trembling on the end of his cock.

She swung the cane back again. Storm held up a hand to stop her.

'You have been very, very wicked, David,' she said in a menacing voice. 'Perhaps caning isn't the appropriate punishment for such a bad boy, Miss Phoebe.'

Phoebe saw David stiffen and then, as the impact of Storm's words dawned on him, he moaned in bitter frustration. Anticipating the twist in the plot, Phoebe nodded and lay the cane down where, from the corner of his eye, David could see it.

'Perhaps you're right, Miss Brooks. What else do you suggest?'

Before Storm could answer, David made an odd strangled sound deep in his throat. 'No, please,' he stammered, 'please, Miss Phoebe, I promise I've learnt my lesson, honestly I have.'

Phoebe picked up the cane and flexed it thoughtfully. 'I'm not so certain. What do you think, Miss Brooks?'

With passion-bright eyes David looked from one woman to the other.

Storm shook her head dismissively. 'Lines perhaps. Or no weekend privileges.'

'Oh no,' implored David. 'No honestly, I promise, I'm very, very sorry.'

Phoebe took a deep breath. 'If you're lying,' she said softly, tracing the curve of his hip with the metal tip of the cane, 'I will be so cross with you, David. I expect you not to let me down.' As she spoke she brought the cane down with a wild crack that exploded across his backside like a pistol shot.

David gasped, a great tear rolling out onto his flushed cheek. 'I promise I'll try and be good, Miss Phoebe, you have my word,' he snorted on a desperate outward breath.

'I do hope so,' said Phoebe coldly. 'If not then I will have to cane you again, David, or find some other way to teach you a lesson.'

'Oh yes,' hissed David, 'I do understand.'

Phoebe swept back the cane for the final stroke. Even before she began the descent that would sear another blistering stroke across his buttocks, she could see the contraction in David's pendulous distended balls.

The cane struck him across the rump – in the same instant a huge spurt of semen landed squarely on the piano stool. Gasping, David collapsed down onto the floor, his face florid, his breath coming in excited, sated bursts.

Storm beckoned to Phoebe and then stared down at David, whose eyes were glazed and unfocused as he relished the after-shocks of his passion.

'I hope you have learnt your lesson, David,' she said in a cool professional tone. 'I don't expect to see you in here again.'

Before he had a chance to reply she turned smartly on her heel and Phoebe followed.

'Don't we stay in there with him?' Phoebe whispered, as they headed across the landing.

Storm shook her head. 'He'll let himself out.' She stopped and turned to Phoebe. 'How did it feel?'

Phoebe grinned. 'Very, very strange.' She placed the cane and the mortar board down on the table in the dressing room. 'I'm not sure I understand. Why does he want to be humiliated like that?'

Storm smiled. 'It's a sense of release. He can be free to enjoy what he feels – you took control of him. He was helpless.'

Phoebe snorted. 'That's ridiculous. He could have turned the tables any time he wanted to.'

Storm shrugged. 'He needs to let go.' Her eyes were darkening. She stroked a long, painted fingernail across Phoebe's carmine red lips. 'I highly recommend it.'

Phoebe shivered. 'You sound uncannily like Gottlieb,' she said, hands lifting to undo her mask.

'Don't take it off,' said Storm quickly. 'It suits you.'

Storm smiled her bright predatory smile; the same one Phoebe had seen her use on the clients of Bad Company. There was something compelling about it.

Storm leant back against the door frame. 'Why don't you let me show you the pleasures of letting go?' she said softly. Her fingers traced a line down over her own breasts, circling the soft swell of her belly.

Phoebe felt her pulse quicken. She had never felt drawn to a woman sexually. Even at Langman's party, when she had found herself trapped into making love to Caroline, she had been fighting against revulsion mixed with desire. But Storm – she shivered. Storm Brooks radiated sex like a star gave off light. It was a strange unnerving sexual quality, almost as if she were without gender.

Storm beckoned to her. In the distance Phoebe was aware of the sounds of David leaving, his footsteps on the stairs heard unconsciously as if she were in a dream.

'Let go,' said Storm, in her low voice. 'Just let go, let me lead you and see how it feels.'

She took Phoebe's hand and lifted it to her breast, slipping it under the silk folds of her blouse. Phoebe gasped. Storm's flesh was so soft and warm, a total contrast to the men she had touched.

Storm stroked her face. 'Can you feel my heart beating?'

Phoebe nodded, the steady pulse beneath her fingertips was as engaging and exciting as the softness of Storm's fragrant skin. Storm eased closer and planted a tiny rosebud kiss on her lips, delicate and inviting.

'Why don't we go into my bedroom?'

Phoebe felt powerless to resist.

Storm led the way. The room was huge, dominated by an enormous bed draped with muslin curtains. One wall was completely mirrored and, as Phoebe reached the bed, she realised the ceiling above it was also covered in one vast mirror. Storm stood in the centre of the dimly lit room.

'Come here,' she commanded in a low voice. 'Wouldn't you like to undress me.' Storm lifted her hands above her head, undulating her hips in a heady invitation.

Phoebe swallowed hard. 'I . . .' The words stuck firmly in her throat.

Storm began to undo her blouse, every movement, every sensual gesture designed to ensnare her audience. There was no disputing Storm Brooks was a natural. Storm rolled her blouse down over her softly tanned shoulders, eyelids dropping provocatively so that every sinew of her body invited Phoebe to touch her.

Phoebe tried to hold back; she didn't naturally desire women. 'I can't,' she stammered unhappily while her body bayed to accept Storm's offer.

Storm pouted. 'I don't think that's true, I know you can,' she purred. 'Perhaps you'd prefer a man instead. Or maybe, as well?'

Phoebe coloured. Her excitement was rising in spite of her reservations. Storm's sexuality was all-pervading like a heavy perfume, it was impossible not to be affected by it.

Storm lifted an eyebrow. 'Well?' she said.

Phoebe shook her head to clear it. 'I think I really ought to go.'

'What? Leave before the fun begins?' A man's voice from behind Storm made Phoebe look up in astonishment.

Joe Blenheim, the security man from the first party, stepped out from a concealed door in the mirrored wall.

Phoebe gasped in horror. 'How long have you been here?' she managed to stammer.

Blenheim shrugged. 'Long enough to see you with David. Storm rang me when you agreed to meet him.'

Phoebe, rooted to the spot, thought about the long mirrors along the wall of the sitting room. She reddened. 'You saw me?'

Joe nodded. 'I had to fight the urge to come and join you then.' He smiled. 'You look good dressed up like that. The mask makes it.' He walked around her, eyes travelling up and down her body. 'And I know about the trip you took to the club the other night.'

Phoebe gasped in complete surprise. 'What? How on earth did you know about that?' she managed to hiss.

Blenheim laughed. 'Don't look so surprised. It's a very, very small town, news of a new girl travels fast.' He paused. 'Why don't you take Storm up on her offer. Wouldn't you like to undress her? Feel those soft, soft places of hers.' He looked appreciatively at Storm who was watching them both. 'She feels wonderful and the way she smells and moves—' He paused, eyes alight. He held out his hand. 'Why don't you let me show you?'

Holding her wrist, he pressed her fingers to Storm's ripe body. Phoebe shivered. Joe grinned and pulled her into his arms, his fingers tracing the seams of her leather suit. 'You feel good too.'

Breathlessly Phoebe jerked away from him. 'You set me up, didn't you?' she said to Storm.

Storm shrugged, discarding her blouse on the bedroom floor. Beneath, her heavy breasts were naked, their nipples erect and ripe, tinged with magenta. 'You're too good a prize to let slip through our fingers. A natural. I knew that from the minute I set eyes on you.' She teased a scarlet painted nail across one nipple, the tiny cone stiffening even further under her caress. 'You just need to learn how to let go.' She slid the zipper of her skirt down over her plump rounded hips. The expensive sheath slithered to the floor. Beneath she wore a tiny scrap of white lace, which barely covered the triangle of her sex.

Phoebe could see the distinct contours of her quim where it pressed against the thin fabric. Storm traced a finger along the junction of her outer lips, teasing at the place where her clitoris nestled. Phoebe shivered, imagining the sensation Storm was creating.

Joe, arm still around Phoebe's leather-clad waist grinned. 'Come with me,' he murmured. Phoebe felt powerless to resist. He glanced at Storm. 'Why don't you lie down on the bed, babe,' he whispered.

Storm lay back, spreading her long tanned legs, the lacy triangle an exciting contrast to her soft flesh.

Joe took Phoebe's hand and guided it between Storm's legs. Beneath her fingers Phoebe could feel an astounding pool of heat and moisture. Storm wriggled against her, spreading her thighs so all that divided Phoebe from entry was the scrap of lacy fabric. Storm moaned softly, lifting herself onto Phoebe's uneasy and inexpert touch. Joe's hands worked around her, tugging Storm's panties off. Her quim was ripe and full, the lips like a hungry mouth.

Blenheim grinned. 'She wants you,' he said softly. 'Wants to feel your tongue up inside her, lapping at that little bud, making her call out for more.'

Phoebe's heart was racing, reluctance and revulsion giving way to an urge to surrender. Blenheim cupped her breasts, stroking through the leather at her tight peaked nipples.

'I know you're excited,' he murmured, one hand sliding lower to the fastenings of her crotch. 'I've seen you before, remember. I know you. I know how good you feel, how sweet that tongue of yours can be.'

Phoebe felt as if she was drowning. She sank lower, drawn by the magnetic richness of Storm's body. Blenheim caught hold of her waist, pulling her hips up towards him so that, in the instant she planted a single kiss onto the depression of Storm's navel, his fingers slid into her quim, his thumb lifting to brush the swollen glowing bud of her clitoris. She let out a long throaty sob. Why not surrender – why not?

'Kiss her breasts,' Blenheim whispered. 'Let me see that tongue of yours working on them.'

Phoebe groaned and lifted her lips to take one of the cherry-sweet nipples into her mouth. Pressing back against Joe's fingers, he circled her clit again and again making her writhe with sheer delight. Beneath her, Storm murmured appreciatively and Phoebe knew it was too late. Every fibre of her body demanded release, her excitement growing with every passing second and every compelling sensation.

Storm's hands on her shoulders gently guided her lower. Phoebe lapped again at the rounded curve of the other woman's belly, the fragrance of Storm's sex rising up to fill her senses. She was astonished to realise her mouth was watering. Behind her, Blenheim's fingers worked their magic, gliding in and out of her sopping quim, the other hand lifting to tease and stroke her breasts.

At the point when she finally slid her tongue into the

salty depths of Storm's sex, she felt Blenheim shift position and a second or two later gasped as he slipped his cock deep inside her. Her body bucked, her tongue, no longer tentative, began to lap and dip into the gaping crimson ocean, her kisses satisfying Storm's hunger.

Phoebe felt as if each sensation was both crystal clear and at the same time shared between them all. Every thrust from Blenheim she mirrored with her tongue, every touch, every caress doubled and trebled until she could think of nothing but their mutual journey towards release. She could sense Joe on the brink, while beneath her Storm lifted her hips and pulled Phoebe closer still, flooding her mouth with fragrant moisture that drove her wild.

Orgasm roared through them like a hurricane wind. Phoebe let out a thin choking howl of joy, finally relinquishing control as the sensations drove away every thought but the crystal shards of pleasure that exploded in her mind.

She felt Joe thrust instinctively, riding out the last of the ripples, while Storm sobbed, writhing away from Phoebe's tongue as the pleasure became too intense to prolong. Exhausted, Phoebe slid down onto her knees, Joe slithering out of her engorged and throbbing quim. She rested her head on the end of the bed, struggling to catch her breath.

Storm rolled over slowly, dragging the bedclothes with her. With sleepy, sated eyes she smiled at Phoebe. 'Come to bed,' she murmured. 'Let's sleep.'

Phoebe crept alongside her, followed an instant later by Joe, who wriggled between the two women. Gently he encircled them both with his arms. Phoebe curled up against him, relishing the heat and strength of his body. Within seconds she was sound asleep.

Chapter Thirteen

When Phoebe woke she was totally confused for a few seconds. She glanced up and saw the reflection of herself and her two companions in the huge bed. Memories came flooding back.

Slowly, so that she didn't disturb Storm and Joe, she crept out from under the duvet. The leather body-suit felt hot and tight, its stark outlines a sharp contrast to her pale skin. It struck her as bizarre that she was still wearing the cat mask.

Joe snuffled contentedly like a well-fed puppy and rolled over into the warm space she had so recently left. His dark curly hair fell forward, softening the brutal contours of his face. She paused for a few seconds to look at the two lovers. Storm's long lashes shadowed her cheek bones, accentuating her fine bone structure, heavy breasts rising and falling in peaceful undisturbed sleep. Even unconscious, her body exuded a sexual promise. She moaned softly and curled up against Joe's broad back, an arm draped casually across his muscular torso.

Phoebe found it hard to imagine that she had savoured both of them. In sleep they looked beautiful, a perfectly matched, exquisitely handsome couple.

Stirring towards wakefulness, Joe caught hold of Storm's hand and pulled her closer, a simple gesture of affection that brought tears to Phoebe's eyes. She ached for Shaun's loving familiar touch; the reassuring intimacy of true lovers.

Her things were still in the dressing room. Phoebe showered and slipped back into her college clothes. Less than half an hour later, Phoebe Williams, final year university student, looked back at her from the misted mirror. Thoughtfully she laid the leather outfit back on the dressing-table. There was no way she could be considered safe any more, no longer predictable or repressed. Gottlieb and Bad Company had seen to that. She didn't feel any regret for the things she had discovered, her only sadness was that in becoming free she had lost Shaun.

Storm, wrapped in a white towelling robe peeped round the dressing room door.

'Hi, I'm just going to put some coffee on downstairs, if you want some,' she said. 'You look like Cinderella.'

Phoebe smiled, pulling a brush through her hair.

'Well, I've certainly been to the ball, haven't I?' Something else crossed her mind. 'Joe said that he knew I'd been to the club? How? Does he know Gottlieb?'

Storm pulled a face. 'Gottlieb? I've really got no idea. Who is he anyway?'

'My course tutor, or at least he is until the end of the month. It was him—' She paused, toying with the leather mask. Without Gottlieb none of this would have happened, but far from resenting him she realised with a start that she was grateful. 'If it hadn't been for Gottlieb I wouldn't have rung you in the first place.'

'In that case I owe him a favour.' Storm grinned and turned away, tightening the belt of her robe. 'Don't be too long.'

Phoebe nodded and picked up her bag, wondering why it was she felt no shame with the woman whom she had touched so intimately. All that was left was a soft glow of satisfaction, low in her belly, where she could also feel the memory of Joe's caress.

Downstairs Joe was already dressed and exploring the fridge. He looked up as Phoebe came in and grinned a welcome.

'Hello,' he said, waving a packet of bacon in her direction. 'Sleep well?' he joked and stepped forward to kiss her softly.

Phoebe shook her head in disbelief.

Storm snorted. 'Take no notice of him.'

Joe pulled a hurt face. 'I've been thinking about you since we met at the party,' he said, teasing rashers out of the packet. 'Have you ever thought about a film career? I can help you . . .' His expression was expectant.

Phoebe pulled out a chair and gratefully accepted the coffee mug Storm pushed in her direction. 'No,' she said firmly. 'Do you know Gerrard Gottlieb?'

For an instant Joe looked slightly ill at ease. 'Might do, why? I get to know a lot of people in my line of work.'

Phoebe took a pull on her coffee. 'You said yourself it was a small town. I didn't realise you lived here as well.'

Joe grinned. 'Me and Storm go back a long way, don't we?'

Storm pulled a face. 'What Joe means is that he and I

used to be in business a long time ago. He's staying here with me for a few days.'

'It wasn't so long ago, babe, not so long.' He turned to Phoebe. 'You could say I'm here on a working holiday. Anyway, about this Gottlieb – what did you want to know?'

Phoebe shrugged. It was too improbable a coincidence to think her meeting Storm and Joe had anything to do with Gottlieb. 'I just wondered, that's all.'

Joe pouted. 'He's a bit of a dark horse.' He paused. 'Likes it rough. I've sent the odd girl his way in the past. And we're members of the same club.'

Comprehension dawned. 'The one in the penthouse at the office block?'

Joe nodded. 'Nathan Street, that's right. I sometimes arrange the cabaret over there. My company supplies security for them, that kind of thing.' He grinned. 'Why? Fancy yourself up on the stage, do you?'

Phoebe blushed. 'No,' she said, 'No, I don't.'

'No need to be so coy,' he said and pulled a pan off the rack above the stove. 'I was in the security office when you turned up on Saturday. I was going to come over and renew our acquaintance until I saw who you were with. I didn't think your friend Gottlieb would be too impressed.' He glanced back over his shoulder at her. 'Mind you, if you're up for Gottlieb's games maybe you aren't so naive as you make out.' He stepped closer, tracing the outline of her cheek bones with his fingertips. 'Enjoy being tied up, do you? I thought today when Storm said you were going to sort David out, that maybe you'd prefer to be on the receiving end.' His hand dropped to her shoulder and for an instant Phoebe remembered the look of ecstasy on David's face as the cane had exploded across his backside. The images were overlaid with others of Nina King's lush body, gasping and writhing as the riding crop found its mark. To her surprise Phoebe felt an electric pulse of pleasure ripple through her and she flushed scarlet as she realised Joe was still watching her face.

He smiled, ruffling her hair playfully. 'Relax, it's all the same to me.'

Phoebe struggled to control the tight feeling in her stomach. 'Nina King,' she said slowly. 'Have you got anything to do with her?'

Joe looked blank. 'The name doesn't ring a bell. Who's she – another convert?'

'She was the girl on stage on Saturday night.'

'Oh her, right.' Joe's eyes lit up. 'Nothing to do with me, I'm afraid. Although I did think about making a few discreet enquiries.' He grinned. 'She was good. But a lot of the members are involved in arranging the entertainment. New girlfriends, contacts they've made in other venues—' He paused. 'Is she a friend of yours too?'

Phoebe nodded.

'And Gottlieb's?'

Phoebe nodded again.

Joe turned to Storm, expression alight with humour. 'This girl's better connected than we thought,' he said. 'Maybe she could teach us a thing or two.'

Storm screwed up a napkin and threw it at him. 'Just shut up and cook yourself some supper, Joe. I'm going to drink this and then take Phoebe home.' She glanced at Phoebe. 'Can't have too many late nights with all your

college work to keep up, can you? And then of course
there's your friend – what's his name? Shaun. How did he
get on with his fare on Saturday night?' Her eyes twinkled
mischievously.

Phoebe felt the pain returning, tears gathering in her
eyes. She looked away. 'Actually I haven't seen him for a
day or two,' she said carefully. 'If you'll excuse me, I think
I'll just nip upstairs and get the rest of my things.'

'So what nights are you free this week?' said Storm as they
climbed into her sports car. Phoebe threw her bag into the
back.

'None that I know of,' she said crisply. 'Like you said,
I've got a lot of work to catch up on.'

Storm laughed. 'Joe thinks you should leave university
and work for Bad Company full-time. I told him you've
only got another few months to go. Plenty of time to make
up your mind. I presume you'll be free for your Friday
night booking?'

Phoebe stared at her, trying not to think about the man
who had asked for her by name. 'I thought you told me
Joe was dangerous and that I had to be careful of him?'

'It's true. I certainly wasn't lying but he's a good friend
to have on your side.'

'What's he doing here?'

Storm eased the car out into the evening traffic. 'Business,' she said coolly. 'A security check at your friend
Gottlieb's club.'

'And?'

'My, aren't we the suspicious one?' grinned Storm. 'All
right, if you must know, he rang me up a couple of times

after the party. He was very curious about you after that first night – I mentioned you had decided to work for us. He was hoping you'd change your mind about doing some film work for him.'

Phoebe sat back. 'He came here to see me?'

Storm dropped the car down a gear and pulled out to overtake. 'New flesh always attracts. He thinks you've got just the right mix of innocence and sensuality – the something special that sells. But don't get too carried away, you aren't the only reason he's in town.' She smiled, her teeth sharp and bright in the oncoming headlights. 'I'm a shrewd judge of what makes a good girl. You've got it and Joe Blenheim would like to cash in on it.' As she spoke her hand brushed gently against Phoebe's thigh. Her touch was feather light, a gesture of both invitation and reassurance. Storm glanced across at her. 'I've told him I'd prefer you to stay with Bad Company – for a while.'

Phoebe stared ahead, mind in turmoil.

In the dining room of his house, Gerrard Gottlieb was staring at Maya across the supper table. Although he was looking at her, his mind was drifting free, without any real concentration.

Her delicate features were picked out by the candlelight. Tonight she had tied a belt around her robe so the silky fabric clung to the curve of her breasts, dark nipples shadowing through the material. A curtain of glittering raven-black hair framed her features making her look like a sleek wild animal.

He sighed. How was it possible to become bored with

something so exquisite, so perfect? She smiled, revealing tiny white teeth in her generous mouth.

'Don't look so sad,' she said in her low musical voice.

Her voice dragged him back. 'Sorry,' he said flatly.

Maya rolled her eyes heavenwards. 'This is not like you at all, Gerrard,' she said with a perception that surprised him.

She got up to get another bottle of wine. The silk robe fluttered open, revealing long thighs, the soft swell of her belly. Gottlieb shivered. Maybe he was being foolish. The light from the fire, glowing through the silk, carved her small frame into an erotic masterpiece.

'What would you do if you could do anything?' he said.

Maya turned. 'Don't do this to yourself or me.' Her voice was carefully controlled, each word enunciated with sharp almost unnerving clarity. Tonight the pretence of slave girl and master had completely evaporated. He looked up into her eyes, attention diverted from the contours of her willing body.

'What do you mean?'

Maya refilled his glass; the subtle fragrance of her perfume made his throat contract sharply.

'I know what's going on,' she said softly. 'I've known for months. It's time for us both to move on, isn't it?'

Gottlieb couldn't disguise his astonishment. 'I don't want to hurt you,' he said lamely.

Maya smiled, though he noticed her eyes were bright with unshed tears. 'Of course you don't,' she said carefully. 'And so far you haven't.' She paused and bit her lip as if struggling to keep control of her emotions. 'Let me ask you the same question. What would you do if you could do anything?'

Gottlieb shook his head. 'I really don't know.'

She smiled benevolently and curled onto his lap, light as thistle down, her arms linking around his broad neck. 'Then let me tell you. You would like to go back to the States, travel some more, sample some more of the delights that tempt you so much.' She nestled close to him, so close that he could smell the heady oceanic fragrance of the sex which had served him so faithfully. 'You really want to be free again. You're growing tired of me. Tired of all this—' She lifted her hand to encompass the elegant dining room with the fire light and candles throwing the corners into flickering shadows.

He was about to protest but she pressed a finger to his lips. 'Please, don't lie to me Gerrard, we both know it's true. When you touch me these days it's someone else you see.'

He shivered. How could she see so clearly inside his mind?

She slid her hand up under his shirt, teasing at the broad muscular plains of his chest. 'You are so distant, distracted—' She paused. 'It's time to move on, for both of us.'

He stared at her, wondering how she could be so calm, so matter of fact about something which had perturbed him since he had first met Phoebe Williams. He took a deep breath.

'What will you do?'

Maya smiled, pressing herself close to him. 'What I've always done,' she purred. 'Sex and food.' She grinned, and ran her fingers lower, brushing the sensitive hair over his belly. 'Let's have the courage to end it, before it goes dark and cruel.'

Gottlieb felt a familiar ache in his groin. 'What made you say something now?'

Maya's hands began to work at the button of his fly. She opened her legs so that she was straddling him.

'You hardly ever seem to be home, all those nights out, even when you are here your mind is somethere else . . .' She eased the zip lower, cool knowing hands slipping around the engorged contours of his shaft. 'And Bad Company.'

He froze. 'What?'

'They rang today to confirm your booking on Friday night with Phoebe Williams.'

Gottlieb felt his colour rising but before he could speak Maya smiled. Her fingers were working on his shaft, a sure teasing touch that was guaranteed to drive him wild.

'Don't say anything. They were extremely discreet, they left a number and so I rang back to check. I told them I was your secretary.' She eased his foreskin back, a long nail fluttering across the sensitive flesh of his glans. 'She's one of your students, isn't she?'

Gottlieb was speechless.

'I've seen her name on your tutorial list.' Her fingers tightened, making him gasp. Maya continued. 'I do know she isn't the only reason. She's a symptom not the cause.' She slithered down off his lap, hand still tightly clasped around his cock. He stared down at her, as she opened her beautifully painted mouth and ran her snake-point tongue along his rigid shaft.

'Give me a little time to find somewhere else to live,' she said as she reached the top of the wet compelling caress. 'I've got an interview on Friday afternoon.'

He couldn't take his eyes off her. In the candlelight her eyes were reduced to twinkling crystal orbs. 'Who with?' he managed to splutter, trying to regain some sense of control.

Her sharp little teeth glittered, feral and dangerous. 'Bad Company. Who else?' she purred, as she dipped again to take him between her lips. Her tongue wound around him, her fingers moving lower to cup his throbbing balls.

'Who else,' he sighed. She drew him deeper, her hands working in perfect harmony with her wet eager mouth. He stretched back, relinquishing his mind and his body to the girl who he had dismissed almost casually as a subservient mannequin. She stopped and drew back a little. He could see her fingers already working in the familiar slick confines of her own sex, seeking out the tiny glowing bud that nestled there.

'Let's share the power you talk so much about, shall we?' she murmured.

He nodded and slipped out of the chair, guiding her down onto the floor. 'Why not?' he whispered, pushing the robe back off her shoulders. Her pert breasts brushed his chest, the explosive dark peaks of her nipples making his mind reel. He suckled like a baby, drawing one and then the other into his mouth.

She moaned and threw back her head. 'Oh, Gottlieb,' she hissed and opened her legs, encircling his waist, hands moving to guide the crown of his cock into the hot, engorged folds of her quim. As he drove home she lifted her hips to ensnare him, her eyes wide and bright.

'I'm really going to miss you,' she purred.

Gottlieb felt a momentary unnerving sense of regret and unfathomable loss and then plunged deeper. 'I can always ring up and book you if I get lonely,' he hissed as the muscles deep inside Maya's succulent body closed tightly around him, as compelling and controlled as those in her mouth.

Maya threw back her head and laughed. 'Why not? You've already got the number.'

Gottlieb held her tight against him. He closed his eyes and surrendered to the sensations; for once it was her face he saw as he headed out towards oblivion.

Phoebe checked the noticeboard for messages when she got in. Nothing from Shaun. She glanced at the telephone booth wondering whether to have another go at ringing him.

If she continued to work for Storm Brooks and Bad Company her life would be reduced to a series of cold and meaningless sexual encounters. Though she would be well paid, ultimately the things she had discovered – the passion and the power – would be lost in a repetitious pantomime. She shivered.

Storm Brooks and Joe Blenheim could offer her a life of sensual indulgence, without feeling, without remorse or regret. She could explore every avenue of human sexuality. With Shaun – she stopped – what was the point of thinking about it? It was over between them. He knew all about her now, there was no going back, no undoing what had already been done.

She slipped the key into the lock. Gottlieb had promised her an education – and she had certainly had one. The priorities and goals she had held so dear had almost crumbled away. She swallowed back the tears that threatened. Gottlieb had unleashed a part of her nature she never knew existed but he couldn't help her sift through the pieces to help create something new. She had to find the strength to do that for herself.

Inside, in her wardrobe, were the outfits she had bought to wear for Bad Company; they were like costumes. She fingered the liquid silk evening-dress Storm had loaned her and struggled to get hold of her thoughts. One more night – Friday – and then she had to stop. If she didn't there was no telling where this strange odyssey would end. It might be too late to reclaim Shaun but it wasn't too late to reclaim herself. At the end of the month Gottlieb would be gone, Audrey Manley would be back. There was the prospect of end-of-term exams, which for the first time in her college career she knew she wasn't ready for. What was it Gottlieb had said in the pub? His sonorous voice filled her head:

'So, Miss Williams, you may relax now. Look on this episode as an interesting interlude in your academic career. The status quo will be restored very soon.'

He had said he would go back to his research – a return to familiar ground for them both. She closed the wardrobe door. He was right. She could get back to how she had been before, at least on the surface. She paused. One more night and she would find the strength and resolve to walk away.

She left her clothes where they fell and climbed into bed. Her dreams were full of random unconnected images: Gottlieb's dark eyes, Shaun, naked and sweating, arching above her as he drove home, bringing her to a breath-stopping orgasm, Nina King, on stage . . . All night long her lovers pursued her through her dreams – Storm and Joe, Charlie Bryce and Baxter Hayes – an erotic disturbing amalgam that left her exhausted.

When Phoebe woke the bedclothes were plaited and twisted into a tangled knot, and a glisten of sweat ran down between her breasts. She crawled out of bed and stared into the mirror; her eyes were ringed with dark shadows, her skin pale and feverish. She groaned.

'Just this week,' she murmured under her breath. 'Just this week and it will all be over.'

She glanced at the pile of text books beside the bed, they seemed unfamiliar and alien.

The old Phoebe Williams had been working single-mindedly towards getting a good degree and a good job, somewhere inside her that Phoebe Williams still existed. She pulled the first book off the pile. It was a dry dog-eared text book from Dr Dart's course on infrastructure and social development. Making herself a cup of tea, Phoebe picked up her notebook and curled up in the arm-chair by the fire, forcing her mind back on track.

Scanning the first page of notes, she realised that she didn't even know what day it was or what lectures she had. The handwriting in the notebook sharpened into focus; she couldn't remember taking the notes. They seemed to belong to a completely different world – and a completely different person. Phoebe took a deep steadying breath; she had to grab her life back and get on with the things that had been so important before she had met Gerrard Gottlieb.

Outside the new day was grey and windswept again: maybe it wasn't such a bad thing not to know which day it was. It looked too uninspiring to have a name.

Chapter Fourteen

Joe Blenheim parked his metallic gold Jaguar under the shelter of the main administration block and stretched. The car radio informed him that it was almost a quarter to eleven and – Joe thought cheerfully – about time he got himself into Gottlieb's office. The blonde girl in reception had been most helpful in directing him. Nice tits too.

He glanced out of the window. Very few people were out and about on the campus. He couldn't say he blamed them, it was too bloody cold. Those who were out were hunched forward, wrapped up against the bitter wind. Under those shapeless duffel coats and scarves it was hard to tell men from women – which was a great shame. Joe spent a lot of time and energy talent-spotting for his various interests. He had a nice line in persuasion and was prepared to dedicate quite a lot of his resources to developing a good lead.

Phoebe Williams was a girl with great potential. He grinned. She had all the qualities that appealed to him – a slightly unworldly air, an unselfconscious college-girl walk and those innocent blue eyes that promised so much. She had a guileless, natural sensuality. He had been delighted by her performance with Storm, in fact he could hardly believe his luck. The way she had moved, her tongue lapping, fingers exploring – her slim frame encased in that tight little leather body. Delicious. He adjusted his trousers ruefully. She was quite a find.

Phoebe's real talent might lie in obedience. He'd had the security camera move in closer when she had been watching the stage performance at the S&M club. Unaware that she was being watched Phoebe made no effort to disguise her excitement as her friend had taken such a delicious whipping. He had seen the expression on her face, the way her eyes had darkened in expectation. He wasn't into S&M himself but he knew an awful lot of men who were. His membership of the club was strictly business; not only did he provide the security but he also made sure he cashed in on the connections it offered him. The club brought him an awful lot of work.

Joe closed his eyes and shifted his attention back to Phoebe Williams. He had always possessed a vivid imagination, which helped him visualise the contents of his exclusive films. His mind shifted and overlaid images of Storm and Phoebe and Phoebe's friend, Nina King. He imagined Phoebe's wet hungry sex, dripping, eager, longing to be taken in the same way as her friend. He could see her pale slim frame writhing under the kiss of the whip. He presumed Gerrard Gottlieb had taken full advantage of her eagerness and wondered fleetingly if Gottlieb had had the foresight to set up a video to record the event. That was a tape Joe wouldn't mind seeing.

He would like to take Phoebe on as one of the girls in his stable. She would be most presentable in a normal social setting – bright, intelligent, the perfect companion.

He could think of at least half a dozen eminent, well-connected men who might be interested in taking her on on a long term basis. The thought made him smile. There was a judge, whose good books he wouldn't mind being in, who preferred to whip his female companions while dressed in his gown and wig – and for whom Joe had recently had a pair of stocks made.

Phoebe was wasted at Bad Company. Storm's escort agency was profitable and discreet but, really, it was just small time. Storm didn't have his connections – and Phoebe had the potential to go far with the right business management. Of course, Storm was a bit over-protective of her new protégée, but when wasn't she? Phoebe Williams was hardly a child—

Joe slipped the bulky envelope he had brought for Gottlieb into his jacket pocket and made his way up the path. After the warmth of the car, the wind cut into him like a knife. He shivered as he rang the bell and turned his back to the door.

Gottlieb looked at Joe Blenheim with barely concealed disdain. The handsome young man was a viper. His sun-tanned muscular body was honed in the gym. He could have been taken for a weight-lifter or a rugby player by the uninitiated – but Gottlieb knew him better. Joe lingered in the hallway, running his long fingers through his curly hair. Gottlieb motioned him inside and shut the door.

'Hello, Joe,' he said, indicating a chair. 'To what do I owe the pleasure of this visit?'

Joe smiled and extended his hand. 'Long time, no see,

Gerrard. I thought I might have bumped into you in
Thailand this year. Hot nights in Bangkok.' He grinned
salaciously and eased himself into the chair. 'How is the
little woman?'

Gottlieb stiffened. He had almost forgotten it had been
Blenheim who had arranged for Maya to be allowed into
the country. His influence was remarkably wide-ranging.
Gottlieb shrugged, determined not to let Joe detect any
surprise.

'Fine – how about yours? What was her name?'

Joe shrugged. 'It's a long time ago now. She was a
passing fancy, Gerrard. You know how these things are. I
moved her on to one of my clients. She was in New York
last time I heard. Doing very well for herself.'

Gottlieb paused, wondering why Joe had contacted him
after so long – it was ironic really, now that Maya was in
the process of leaving him. He couldn't imagine that there
would be any problems with her residency agreement
after all this time. He had certainly paid enough to ensure
everything went smoothly.

Joe pushed back the sleeves of his expensive suit to
reveal immaculate linen cuffs and gold identity bracelet.
He grinned and leant forward. 'I saw you at the club on
Saturday night. I thought while I was in town I'd renew
our acquaintance. For old time's sake.'

Gottlieb pulled a face, wondering where this was leading. He certainly didn't believe Joe's visit was purely
social. He knew him too well to relax his guard. 'Really? I
didn't see you there.'

'Security check,' said Joe casually. 'I was on duty in the
office. I usually drop in once every couple of months or so

to make sure everything is running smoothly.'

Gottlieb sighed. 'Yes. Look, shall we cut to the chase, Joe? You're not here on a social call so, what can I do for you?'

Joe looked pained. 'Gerrard, really,' he said, with mock indignation. As he spoke he pulled a padded envelope out from inside his jacket. 'It seems we have a mutual acquaintance.'

Gottlieb stared at him. Where was this leading?

'I'm sure we do. We often move in the same circles – what else do you expect?'

Joe grinned. 'Phoebe Williams.' He leant forward and slid the package on Gerrard's desk.

Gottlieb's eyes widened in genuine astonishment. 'You know Phoebe?' he hissed.

'You could say that. I thought you might be interested in a little souvenir of her extra curricular activities. Help yourself.'

Gottlieb stared at the package. 'How?' he managed to stammer. He knew what the package contained, he'd seen them often enough before to recognise one of Joe Blenheim's infamous videos.

'Storm Brooks.'

The name meant very little to Gottlieb, which must have showed in his face.

Joe pulled out a little cigar and lit it. 'Bad Company.'

Gottlieb took deep breath. 'You run Bad Company?'

Joe shook his head. 'No, not exactly but a friend of mine does. Storm. I'm surprised you haven't come across her. She's a *very* interesting woman. I'm certain you'd know her by sight.'

Gottlieb picked up the package. 'And what has this got on it?'

'A fascinating little *ménage à trois* with your new friend, but I'm sure you already know her tastes.' Joe pulled a face. 'The quality is a bit rough for general distribution. My clients are used to better stuff. I'm hoping for a more saleable film next time around.'

Gottlieb turned the package in his fingers. 'I can't believe Phoebe Williams agreed to this,' he said coldly.

Joe grinned. 'She didn't, that's why the quality is so bad. The camera wasn't in the right place to capture the full – what should we say? – flavour of the moment.' He indicated the TV in the corner of Gottlieb's office. 'Perhaps you'd like to take a look and judge for yourself. Unfortunately she's masked in this one but I'm sure you'll recognise her. Storm's on there too, maybe you'll be able to place her face once you've seen the film.'

Gottlieb felt a tight hot plume of fury rising low in his belly. He stared at Joe. 'How many copies are there of this?'

Joe shrugged. 'Just the one, it's not close up enough for my more discerning customers. You're welcome to it.' He got to his feet. 'At a price, of course.'

Gottlieb opened the drawer of his desk. 'How much?'

Joe grinned. 'Shall we say five hundred?'

Gottlieb pulled out his cheque book. 'Why did you come here?' he said coldly.

Joe sniffed. 'Just to let you know I've got my eye on your latest little friend, Gerrard. She'll be worth a lot of money to me when I've persuaded her that working for Bad Company is a dead end.' He smiled wolfishly. 'I'll see to it that she's public domain. Maybe you'd like to come along to the auction?'

Gottlieb stiffened.

'I'm planning to get her face on camera, next time. A little insurance to ensure she understands how difficult life could become if she tries to break our arrangement.' He took the cheque from Gottlieb and blew the ink dry. 'I just wanted to let you know, Gerrard, that you've still got an eye for a real winner.'

Without another word Joe turned on his heel and was gone, leaving Gottlieb holding the video tape. He stared at the package, his hand betraying the slighest tremor. He waited until he heard Joe Blenheim's car start up, turning the tape over and over until he was certain that Blenheim had gone.

With quiet deliberation Gottlieb undid the package, crossed the room, and locked the door. He slipped the cassette into the video machine. He'd paid dearly for the privilege of owning the only copy.

The machine whirred into life, the TV screen instantly blurred with a drift of white noise. The images flickered and then cleared. Gottlieb took a deep breath, pulled up a chair and sat down. He stared at the screen, his stomach tight with expectation.

The camera had been set up to one side of a huge canopied bed. A tall handsome woman dominated the centre of the room. She was dressed in a sheer blouse and tiny skirt, one hand cupping her breasts, fingers working at the tight dark peaks of her nipples where they pressed against the thin fabric. She began to undo the buttons, one at a time, sensuously, slowly revealing more and more . . .

Gottlieb stared, feeling his mouth begin to water.

Out in the shadows, beyond the subtle arc of light, he saw a flicker of movement and groaned aloud. He didn't need to be told the girl standing watching the slow provocative strip was Phoebe Williams.

She was masked, dressed in a leather suit, which accentuated every sinew and curve of her slim frame. She moved tentatively, mesmerised by the other woman's movements. Gottlieb could almost taste the mixture of fear mingled with desire.

'Come here,' commanded the woman.

She had to be Storm Brooks, the woman Joe had insisted Gottlieb knew. She peeled her blouse down over her shoulders as Phoebe, powerless to resist, moved closer. Phoebe's body appeared to be responding with a will of its own, as if Storm were a magnet, drawing the girl towards her.

Gottlieb heard Phoebe murmur that she had to leave but he knew she wouldn't. She had been ensnared by Storm's raw sensuality.

When Joe Blenheim stepped into the frame Gottlieb's surprise was almost as great as Phoebe's. Even behind the little leather mask he saw her eyes flash bright with astonishment. Blenheim took charge without waiting for Phoebe's reaction. Catching hold of her wrists, he guided her reluctant fingers onto Storm's magnificent body.

Gottlieb shivered, torn between anger at the way Phoebe had been manipulated and the overwhelming regret that it hadn't been him there instead of Joe. He wanted to be the one showing her, feeling those subtle plains and curves pressed against him as he held her wrists. He could imagine the smell of the women, mixed with the hot animal musk of the leather where it clung to Phoebe's body.

On screen, Storm stepped back, slithering out of her blouse, teasing a fingertip around the stiff peaks of her nipples before sliding her tiny skirt to the floor.

Joe orchestrated Phoebe's seduction like a grand master. At his request, Storm, her sex covered by a tiny triangle of lace, uncurled herself on the bed, legs open. She stretched out, looking like a succulent ripe fruit – good enough to eat.

Blenheim caressed Phoebe as she stared at Storm. He stroked her neck, cupped her breasts and caressed her belly – within seconds Gottlieb could see her excitement rising. Blenheim's hands moved lower, rubbing at the seam of the body suit where it brushed against Phoebe's clitoris. Gently he guided Phoebe between the other woman's legs.

Gottlieb shuddered, his own cock straining for a caress, for the touch of a lover's lips, for a quim to close tightly around him. Moaning with pure frustration he threw back his head, imagining every taste, every subtle scent as Storm offered her sex to Phoebe.

Joe slipped off Storm's panties, all the time guiding his protégée nearer, talking to her, touching her, making her feel that there was nothing she wanted more in the world than to slide her tongue into that honeyed slit.

Phoebe overcame her apprehension, bending to place a wet kiss on Storm's fragrant sex. Gottlieb was barely aware of Blenheim moving behind Phoebe until he saw the other man's hand working at the fastenings of the body-suit, opening her, seeking entry into the secret depths of her body.

He saw the look of delight on Joe's face as the sensation drove away every thought but the pursuit of pleasure. Phoebe began to move against Blenheim's fingers, holding back her satisfaction as the woman beneath her writhed with delight.

Gottlieb strained forward, trying to suppress his own need, as, on screen, Blenheim guided his cock into Phoebe's trembling body. Their pleasure-filled faces were almost more than Gottlieb could bear. Joe was plunging deeper and deeper. Phoebe, her tongue lapping and kissing Storm's sex, was writhing and bucking, and Storm's head was thrown back, lost in pure ecstasy.

Gottlieb felt the first shuddering vibration of orgasm in the lovers on the screen. Desperately he freed his own cock, cupping it in his hands, imaginging it sliding into Phoebe's compliant quim. Wave after wave of sensation echoed through the bodies on the video, each one echoed stroke for stroke in Gerrard Gottlieb.

Finally, exhausted, he slumped forward in his chair. On screen the lovers collapsed onto the bed. After a few minutes Gottlieb got to his feet and wiped away the glittering evidence of his excitement.

Breathing heavily, his mind still full of images of Phoebe's body, he ejected the video from the machine, folded back the tape cover and began to pull the film off the spools, yards and yards of crisp shimmering images. When it was completely unwound he scooped the whole lot, case and all, into a metal waste paper basket and took it outside. If anyone saw him lighting the small bonfire nobody came to stop him.

Staring through the flames, Gottlieb wondered how he could possibly put right the things he had started with the least amount of pain to everyone concerned. First of all he had to try and find a way to talk to Shaun Rees and then he would talk to Phoebe. Whatever the pleasures, Phoebe had to realise what a potentially dangerous game she had become involved in.

In Lecture Theatre Three Phoebe was looking for a seat close to the front. Books tucked under her arm, face scrubbed pink, hair scraped back into a severe ponytail, she looked the epitome of a studious young woman – only her eyes betrayed the fact that her thoughts were elsewhere. Dr Dart mounted the stage and flicked on an over-head projector.

'Good afternoon, ladies and gentlemen,' he said, adjusting his bow-tie. 'This morning we will be continuing our discussion on infrastructure and its impact on society.' He slid the first picture into the projector. 'Fowler's socio-economic study, conducted in the 1920s tells us . . .' His voice was low and even, imparting facts and opinions with measured grace. Phoebe stared at the blurred images of the national rail network above his balding head and forced herself to concentrate, her hand hovering above her notepad. There was a sign on the easel beside him. 'Students are reminded that Autumn Term exams being a fortnight today.' Phoebe shivered, wondering what her life would be like in a fortnight.

Dart's voice failed to hold her attention, instead she glanced round the tiers of seats, seeking out familiar faces amongst the crowd. Nina King was sitting by the door chewing gum, staring blankly into space. Other students from Phoebe's year were busy taking notes or looking at the changing images on Dart's overhead projector. A wave of tears threatened. Phoebe felt totally removed from what was going on and wondered if there was any chance that she could ever recapture the sense of belonging.

The week passed slowly. Phoebe made a conscious effort to work hard, struggling to make sense of what just a short while ago, before Gottlieb's arrival, had come as second nature. Diligently she got her notes up to date and revised – the only thing she neglected was the stack of research material she had collected for Gottlieb's final paper. She took no calls and made only one – to confirm that she would be accepting the Bad Company booking for Friday night. One last night and it would all be over. She repeated the sentence to herself again and again.

When, on Thursday morning, she saw Shaun and Tony wandering towards her across the campus she deliberately walked the other way – suppressing the hurt alongside the other mixed muddled emotions.

On Friday afternoon Phoebe flitted restlessly around the flat, glancing every few minutes at the clock above the mantelpiece. She kept catching sight of herself in the mirror. Amongst the apprehension and nerves was a sense that tonight represented one glorious finale – a last night of passion before life returned to normal. The receptionist had said a car would be sent for her. Her date preferred to remain anonymous but Phoebe wasn't to worry – a lot of clients were reluctant to reveal their names. The receptionist reassured her that her date was perfectly respectable. Phoebe had smiled wryly as she laid the phone back in its cradle – she doubted it very much.

Late afternoon there was a knock on the door. She prayed it wasn't Storm or Joe and opened it with some hesitancy. Nina King stood in the hall, grinning like a cat who'd got the cream, all her former confidence returned. She held her left hand out in front of her and wriggled her fingers.

'Well, what do you think?' she said with a grin.

Phoebe stared at her. 'Sorry?'

'The ring, you fool,' she said, her mouth still working on the ever-present stick of gum as she twisted her hand round to display a glitzy solitaire diamond on the third finger of her left hand.

Phoebe stared at it. 'You're engaged?' she said in surprise.

Nina nodded and teetered into the flat on impossibly high heels.

'Absolutely,' she said, grinning still. 'I wanted you to be among the first to know. I'm leaving college at Christmas.' She wriggled her fingers again as if she couldn't quite believe her eyes. 'We're going to have a winter wedding, I've already seen this beautiful fur-trimmed cape—'

'Who's the lucky man?' said Phoebe, still in a state of shock.

Nina slumped in the easy chair. 'His name's Gareth, you haven't met him yet, but he's really, really lovely. You'll like him.' Her eyes glittered. 'He's a solicitor.'

Phoebe's mind raced back to the stage show at the club. Hadn't Gottlieb said that the young buck, Nina's supposed lover, was a local solicitor? She wondered if either of them had considered how Nina would fit into Gareth's social circle where – at least outwardly – social manners and graces were extremely conservative.

Nina meanwhile couldn't keep from smiling or staring at the expensive bauble on her hand.

'I'm really pleased for you. It's all a bit sudden, though, isn't it?' Phoebe said lamely.

Nina nodded. 'You could call it love at first sight,' she said in an undertone. 'We met at this club in town—' She stopped and blushed furiously. Phoebe wondered if Nina had any idea that she had seen their 'meeting' first hand.

'He's so lovely. Gottlieb introduced us, he said we were made for each other.'

'What about your degree?'

Nina pulled a face. 'Degree? What degree? You don't really see me ending up in some office somewhere, do you? Gareth says he wants me to stay at home and look *beautiful*.' She emphasised the word beautiful and sat back in the armchair, curling a stray lock of bleached blonde hair into a springy tendril.

Phoebe stared at her. 'Beautiful,' she repeated.

Nina nodded enthusiastically. 'We have a lot in common. You'd like him.' Nina glanced round the flat. 'Where's Shaun? I thought maybe you'd have moved him in by now.'

Phoebe winced as if Nina had struck her. She collected a pile of books off the coffee table, forcing a smile. 'He's not here at the moment. Look, I'm really pleased for you, but I've got to be going soon. Maybe we could get together some time next week?'

Nina got to her feet. 'You've got another lecture today?' she said with surprise. 'I thought everyone had given up for the weekend.'

Phoebe nodded, avoiding Nina's eyes. 'I've arranged to meet some of the others for a revision session in the resource block.'

Nina pulled a face. 'Rather you than me, I'll be glad to put all that stuff behind me.' She grinned. 'Not that I ever did that much. I'll walk over with you if you like.'

Phoebe's heart sank. Lying didn't come naturally to her. 'No, that's fine, thank you,' she began. 'I don't want to put you to any trouble.'

But Nina was already by the door. 'No trouble at all.'

Phoebe pulled on her coat and glanced at the clock; a couple more hours and she would be picked up by her nameless host. She shivered. Nina, left to her own devices was staring absent-mindedly at the diamond on her finger.

'Come on then,' said Phoebe, 'there's no need to walk all the way, just to the corner would be great. Were you on your way home?'

Nina nodded. 'That's right, Gareth is picking me up after he finishes work. I suppose I just wanted to kill a bit of time.' She paused, simpering. 'I hate having to be away from him.'

The walk through the grounds towards Phoebe's fictitious meeting was almost more than she could bear. Nina, having hit her stride, talked on and on about Gareth – his wealth, his wonderful personality, the house he'd bought, how much he loved her ... The only thing she didn't mention was his sexual prowess, which was unusual for

Nina, though Phoebe understood why. Not content with walking along the block to the corner where their routes should have parted Nina insisted on coming the whole way, saying it would take up another half-an-hour before she met her beloved Gareth.

Phoebe sighed in resignation and fell into step, it was pointless to fight. The only thing she was relieved about was that if Nina was safely engaged to Gareth, presumably she would be beyond the clutches of Joe Blenheim or Gerrard Gottlieb.

When, finally, she extricated herself from Nina and hurried back across the campus her mind began to toy with the possibilities for the evening. Her mind wandering, she barely noticed the girls hanging around the phone in the entrance hall.

'Phoebe?'

She looked up in surprise. One of the girls grinned at her. 'I took a message for you about ten minutes ago. I told him you'd just gone out. Shaun Rees?'

Phoebe felt her colour rising. 'Thanks, what did he say?'

'He said he needed to talk to you.'

Phoebe stiffened; another couple of hours and she would be out on her last date. She forced a smile. 'Did he say when?'

The girl shook her head. 'No. I asked him if he was going to ring back and he said no.'

Phoebe had to ring him. There was a queue outside the phone booth, two or three girls waiting who she couldn't expect to push ahead of. Phoebe cursed Nina and then rebuttoned her coat. The nearest phone boxes were either four streets away or back across the campus. Outside it was dark and uninviting. In the few seconds she had been inside the rain had turned from miserable drizzle into a continuous downpour. She sighed and headed back outside.

She ran along the pavement wondering what Shaun wanted. Maybe it wasn't too late after all. The phone box in Calden Street was empty. Shivering, Phoebe dialled Shaun's number from memory, pressed in a few coins and waited, listening to the distant lonely ring. Just as she was about to hang up someone answered the phone.

'Hello?'

Phoebe groaned inwardly; it was Tony Goodman, she would have recognised his oily little voice anywhere. She took a deep breath. 'Hello, is Shaun there, please?'

It was obvious from the soft laugh at the other end of the phone that Tony recognised her voice too. 'No, I'm afraid he isn't in at the moment.'

Phoebe could almost hear him grinning, though at least Tony did sound sober for once. 'How's it going? I've been thinking about you,' he said in an undertone.

'I'm fine, can you tell Shaun I rang?' she said briskly.

Tony laughed again. 'Maybe, maybe not. What are you going to do to make it worth my while?'

Phoebe stared at the receiver in disbelief and then slammed it back into the cradle.

Tears of pure frustration trickled down her face. 'You miserable little rat,' she whispered.

Outside under the street light an elderly man tapped on the glass, making Phoebe jump.

'Sorry, love, didn't mean to frighten you,' he said with

279

an apologetic grin. 'I just wondered if you were going to be very long?'

Phoebe shook her head. 'No, no, I'm all finished,' she said and picked up her bag.

Chapter Fifteen

Gottlieb poured Shaun another glass of wine. The young man was hunched miserably in front of the fire in Gottlieb's sitting room, his face ashen. It was a shame Phoebe hadn't been in to receive Shaun's phone call. He would have liked to have been privy to the young lovers making up their misunderstanding.

'Drink this,' he said quietly.

Shaun took the glass instinctively and swallowed back the contents in a single gulp. 'Thanks for letting me use your phone, Professor. Do you think I ought to go round there now?' he said unevenly.

Gottlieb glanced at the clock. 'No, leave it until tomorrow. It will give you more opportunity to consider what you're going to say.'

Shaun shook his head. 'I feel so bad about this, I can't believe I let it happen.'

Gottlieb made sympathetic noises. 'Sometimes events get away from us. You should be kinder to yourself.'

He paused and studied Shaun's face. He could see what attracted Phoebe. The boy's face had a kind of sculptural beauty, his dark soulful eyes enhancing an erotic mix of strength and vulnerability. A stray curl of dark hair hung into the curve of his muscular neck. Gottlieb was not attracted to male flesh but he could see the boy was desirable. Shaun had broad shoulders and a well-muscled athletic build. Despite his adult exterior, Shaun retained a certain boyishness; a perfect match for Phoebe Williams' slight lithe frame.

He couldn't resist the temptation to imagine them together; the boy's handsome face contorted in pleasure as he impaled the delightful Phoebe again and again. Gottlieb could almost see the fine beading of sweat lifting between Phoebe's breasts as she ground her hips against her lover, moaning softly, her mouth open, begging him to take her higher and higher. Her eyes, glittering unfocused, all her consciousness centred on their wild ride towards oblivion.

Gottlieb shivered at the erotic fantasy. Across the room, Shaun stood the wine glass down in the hearth.

'I think I've taken up enough of your evening, Professor,' he said with forced joviality. 'I really ought to be going home.'

Gottlieb nodded. 'Take my advice,' he said, 'go round and talk to Phoebe tomorrow. Don't leave it too long or it might be too late.'

Shaun nodded, and extended his hand. 'Thank you for your time,' he said with genuine gratitude. 'And your advice.'

Gottlieb shook his hand firmly and then waved him away. 'Don't mention it. My pleasure.' And indeed it had been. He had come across Shaun alone in the refectory and invited him home to talk about Phoebe. To his surprise, when he had spoken Shaun's eyes had betrayed such pain and discomfort that it had been simple to persuade the young man to accompany him home. He could hardly believe it.

All week, since meeting Joe Blenheim, Gottlieb had been toying with a variety of plausible but ultimately spurious reasons to corner Shaun Rees. What he hadn't expected was a confession – or an outpouring of guilt.

After showing Shaun to the door he allowed himself a smile; perhaps restoring the status quo wasn't going to be as difficult as he had first feared.

Shaun headed across the campus barely noticing the cold – all that he could think about was how awful he felt, in spite of Gottlieb's encouraging words. Along with the pain were the vivid memories of the job he had done for Bad Company.

He'd picked up the client from a big house out on Burbeck Avenue. She was a tall woman in her forties. Walking towards the limousine everything about her whispered wealth. Dressed in a full-length evening coat, with a discreet gold necklace at the throat, she looked perfect, but there was something about her, a sexual awareness, a self-assuredness, that was impossible to ignore.

'Good evening ma'am,' he'd said, touching his cap as he opened the door for her.

'You're new, aren't you?' she said, in a low musical voice.

Shaun nodded.

They had driven in silence but all the time Shaun had been aware of her watching him in the rear-view mirror.

He tried to concentrate on driving, ignoring the smell of her perfume and the enticing rustle of silk as she moved.

When the car pulled up in front of the theatre she leant forward and tapped on the glass that divided them.

'Don't stop here,' she purred, as he slid the panel aside. 'Take the next right into Chase Street. Do you like Italian food? I hate eating alone.' Before Shaun could reply she continued, 'We can park at the Metropole Hotel. The restaurant is only a few minutes walk from there.'

At the restaurant, when the waiter offered to take the woman's coat, she declined with a wave of her hand.

'I'm cold,' she murmured as the *maître d'* guided them to a secluded corner of the restaurant. Even then Shaun hadn't guessed that the table must have been booked in advance. The food was delicious. The woman laughed at his jokes, talked about his hopes and dreams, making him feel more and more relaxed. Refilling his wine glass, her dark eyes had flashed with a subtle mixture of amusement and an erotic charge that drew him further into the trap.

When they left the restaurant she slipped her arm through his.

'Such a beautiful night,' she said staring up at the stars.

She was stunning, and so close to him that Shaun could see the tiny beat of the pulse in the pit of her throat. When she leant against him, he felt a great surge of desire. As if reading his mind she turned and kissed him. Without thinking he pulled her closer.

Smiling wolfishly, her body moved against his, hips pressed close to his belly, so the ridge of her pubis brushed his cock. He felt it hardening and stepped away, apologising, trying desperately to regain his composure.

'Still hungry?' she whispered, the smile playing on her lips.

It seemed to be only seconds later that they were in her hotel room. Every time he moved towards her she shimmied away until he was desperate to touch her.

'No,' she said firmly. 'I'll tell you when, just relax and let me take the lead. I'm good at this.' Her eyes twinkled mischievously. 'This is what I'm paying you for after all.'

The woman unwrapped him like a birthday present, exploring every inch of his muscular frame. She undid his belt, unzipped his trousers and, freeing his aching cock, ran one long pink painted nail along its length. It was almost more than he could bear.

'My God,' she whispered appreciatively, stroking his shaft. 'You really *are* exquisite.'

She sat him down on the edge of the bed and unbuttoned her coat. It fell open with a sensual sigh, framing her voluptuous body. Underneath, she was naked except for a black suspender belt, sheer black stockings and a pair of high-heeled sandals.

She smiled lazily, cradling her heavy breasts, caressing her nipples until the peaks were as hard as cherry stones. She stroked the lips of her sex, easing a single finger inside, then slid it out and smeared the shimmering juices over her nipples.

Shaun couldn't take his eyes off her. Slowly she walked towards him.

'There,' she said, guiding a ripe nipple into his waiting mouth. 'Isn't this what you wanted?'

His reply was a hungry moan. The taste of her sex mingled with the scent of her body was electrifying. He pulled her down onto him. The caress of her skin against his felt magical. As he lapped at her breasts she straddled his hips, guiding the head of his cock deep inside her pulsating quim. Moving in time with his eager thrusts, she threw back her head and laughed.

'Storm promised me you would be good,' she whispered. For an instant Shaun froze, but it was too late to stop, too late to draw back from the mounting spiral of lust.

Alone, in the darkness of the university grounds, Shaun could still feel the tightness of the woman's sex sucking him dry. In the distance he could pick out the lights of Phoebe's flat. He shivered and hoped Gottlieb was right.

When Shaun had gone Maya came in to clear away their glasses. For once she was dressed, wearing a soft wool dress that accentuated her curves. Her long hair was caught up in a sleek chignon, her full mouth emphasised by the lightest touch of lipstick.

He smiled. 'You look very beautiful tonight.'

Maya's eyes sparkled. 'Thank you. How did it go?'

'Very well, better than I had expected.'

Maya glanced up at the clock on the mantelpiece. 'What time is your appointment with Phoebe?' There was no hint of accusation, no resentment or anger in her voice.

'Eight.'

Maya nodded. 'You're taking her out to dinner then?' She paused. 'Are you going to bring her back here after you've eaten?'

Gottlieb hesitated. At first, when his plan had been just an unlikely possibility, it had been part of the fantasy but he was reluctant to risk upsetting Maya.

He shook his head. 'No,' he said slowly. 'Not this time.'

She smiled. 'I won't wait up then.' She paused. 'Enjoy her, won't you?'

Gottlieb stared at Maya; she really was an astonishing woman.

She smiled selfconsciously. 'If I hadn't have found out about Phoebe for myself, when were you planning to tell me?'

Gottlieb shrugged. In his mind they had been separate, it hadn't occurred to him to tell Maya about his fascination with Phoebe. The Eurasian girl stooped to pick up the glass from the hearth. From the way her body moved it was obvious she wasn't wearing anything under the wool dress. With some difficulty Gottlieb struggled to drag his mind away from the way her breasts moved and the soft inviting orbs of her rounded backside.

'How did you get on with your interview today?' he said.

'Oh, I got the job.' She looked at him thoughtfully. 'I told them I needed a place to live. They're going to see if I can share with one of the other girls for a while, until I can find a place of my own.'

'You can stay here for as long as you want, you know that. There's no hurry to leave—'

Maya nodded. 'I know,' her voice betrayed a hint of sadness, 'but I think it's better for both of us if I move out.'

'I'm going to miss you,' said Gottlieb slowly, voice thick with emotion.

Maya smiled. 'I know.'

There was a strange sense of resignation in the air between them. Knowing something was right still didn't mean it was easy to do.

Gottlieb swallowed hard. 'When are you leaving?'

Maya tidied the wine and glasses onto a tray. 'Tomorrow.' She turned so that her slim frame was caught in silhouette. 'So I'll still be here when you get back.'

Momentarily Gottlieb saw her as the teenage girl he had first discovered in Bangkok, innocent but with a delectable sexual awareness. She had looked up at him from under heavy black lashes, a stunning face amongst a hundred others in a busy Bangkok café. She had glowed with the enticing ripeness of youth. She had been wearing a thin cotton dress, bought before her body had begun to blossom. The faded fabric stretched across her little rounded belly, pulled tight across her newly swelling breasts.

Quickly, Gottlieb looked away, feeling a gut-wrenching sense of loss. He wished that there was some way to go back in time, to undo all the things he had done and recapture that sweet moment.

She smiled. 'Don't be so sad. We have a lot of good things to remember. I will always remember you.'

He shook his head, wondering what strange female alchemy she was using to read his mind.

'Would you like me to run you a bath?'

Gottlieb grinned, fighting to retain a sense of control. 'What on earth am I going to do without you, Maya?'

She smiled coquettishly over her shoulder. 'I'm certain you'll think of something, Gerrard.'

Phoebe wondered if Shaun would come round to the flat. She couldn't settle, eyes on the clock, watching the minutes tick by. He said he needed to talk to her. She closed her eyes – what was it he wanted to say? She was torn between getting ready for her date and hoping that he would appear. Finally she couldn't want any longer, she had to get ready and take the chance that Shaun would turn up.

She struggled not to think about what she would say if he discovered her dressed to go out on her dinner date. Perhaps she could convince him it was for his benefit. The thought chilled her – she loved him too much to lie but she doubted he could stomach the truth. Tony Goodman's unpleasant little face flickered through her mind. She'd forgotten – thanks to Tony, Shaun already knew the truth about her. She sighed and turned on the shower. Whatever happened it was time to get ready.

A little while later, wrapped in a bathrobe, Phoebe stared into the bedroom mirror, studying her reflection as if fixing the image in her mind. This was the last time this face, exquisitely painted, framed by soft tendrils of hair, would stare back at her with such assuredness. This was the last time she would sell her company or her body. Storm Brooks was right, she really could be anyone. After tonight the person she would be was herself.

She tugged the belt of the robe undone and turned to study her body in the lamp light. Storm had trimmed the V of dark hair between her legs into a short glittering pelt that accentuated the heavy outer lips of her quim. Her belly was flat, the muscles taut while, above, her breasts lifted, the nipples flushed and hardening rapidly as she admired her reflection.

Until she had met Gottlieb she had been almost unaware of the beauty and magic of her body. She turned so the light caught the creamy roundness of her hips and sleek buttocks. Whoever her companion was tonight he would not be disappointed. She felt a glittering sense of anticipation. Tonight would be one last grand finale, one momentous celebration of the things she had discovered about herself. No more Bad Company, no more Joe Blenheim or Storm Brooks.

She dressed slowly, as if enacting an ancient ritual, pausing as she added each piece of her outfit to admire the effect. As a final touch, Phoebe added a little perfume and glanced at the clock. Five minutes and the car would be arriving. Five minutes and the curtain would go up on the final act of her performance as an escort. She took one last look in the mirror, swallowing down the flutter in her stomach.

It was hard to reconcile the sophisticated woman she saw there with her own self-image. Perhaps Storm was right, maybe she was Cinderella after all. She smiled, Storm mightn't have been too happy to be cast in the role of fairy godmother. From outside she heard a car horn and picked up her coat and bag.

'Show time,' she whispered under her breath and hurried towards the door without a backward glance.

The sleek black car was driven by a uniformed chauffeur. He opened the door as Phoebe made her way across the pavement. On his lapel she noticed a discreetly embroidered logo: the letters BC entwined. He was one of Bad Company's drivers – like Shaun. She took a deep steadying breath, struggling not to think about Shaun's soft caring touch or what it was he might want to say to her.

Tomorrow she would see him and sort everything out once and for all.

'Good evening,' she said pleasantly, feeling the driver's eyes assessing her.

'Good evening,' the man replied, touching his cap and grinning as she slipped into the back seat. His perusal of her was discreet but disturbing.

'Thank you,' she murmured, tidying her coat around her.

'Nice place, The Seaton,' the driver said, turning the ignition. In the car the sound of the engine was barely more than a low hum.

Phoebe nodded, presumably that was their destination – she had no way of knowing.

The man turned to glance back over his shoulder. 'Feel free to make yourself at home in there. There's a cocktail cabinet – help yourself. Tell me if you'd like it a bit warmer. A big car like this tends to be a bit draughty in the back.'

She wanted to ask him how long it would take to get to their destination. Was it a house? A hotel? A restaurant? For the first time since she had began working for Storm she felt truly vulnerable. She seemed a million miles away from the companionship of Storm or the other girls. Phoebe sat back, trying hard to control the growing panic in her stomach. She would be all right, she reassured herself.

The driver seemed to sense her unease.

'It won't be too long before we get there – about another fifteen minutes. Would you like some music?'

Phoebe made an effort to control her voice. 'That would be great,' she said lightly.

The man nodded and switched on the tape deck. An instrumental version of an easy listening tune filtered through the speakers.

She couldn't imagine Shaun doing this job but then again hadn't his been straight clients, not escorts on their way to a paid date? She felt her colour deepening and tried hard to concentrate on the view from the windows.

Finally the driver pointed ahead into the darkness. 'There's The Seaton, up ahead. Been here before have you?'

'No, I haven't.' In the distance she could just make out a cluster of lights on a hillside. 'What's it like?'

'Bloody expensive,' said the man with a dry laugh.

'Is it a hotel?'

'Yeah, but a lot of people go there just for the food.'

Phoebe realised with a start that she had no idea whether her client intended her to stay overnight.

'What time are you booked to take me home?'

The driver snorted. 'Don't worry about that. I'm on standby. Whenever you're ready to leave, just go to the front desk and get them to buzz me. When you want me, I'll be there.'

'Right,' she said. 'Thank you.'

The car began the climb up a steep hillside road that ribboned back and forth along a forest road. After a few minutes Phoebe could see the hotel more clearly. It was set amongst a dark canopy of trees. The main building looked like an old country house, subtle lighting throwing the frontage into dramatic relief. By the main doors, under an ornate portico, two uniformed doormen, complete with top hats and white gloves, stood waiting to greet the guests.

As the car purred to a halt the doormen stepped up to open the door for her. Phoebe let them guide her out into the night. Standing between them on the gravel she hesitated for a few seconds to watch the tail lights of the car vanish around the corner of the impressive house. She suddenly felt desperately alone but did not resist as the two uniformed men shepherded her into the warmth of the hotel foyer.

The Seaton was impressive; decked out like a Victorian country house at the height of England's glory. Everywhere was richly finished in mahogany or draped with heavy fringed fabrics. A wealth of brass glowed in the soft lighting. The main hall was lit with gas lights, while behind the main desk a man with an imperious expression watched Phoebe's arrival with interest. Dressed in a frock coat, his eyes never left her as she crossed the plush maroon carpet.

Phoebe stared around her in amazement, wishing she had known her destination – the temptation would have been to dress for the occasion.

The man smiled coolly. 'Good evening, madam. How may I help you?' Even his voice seemed to come from a different era with its rich rounded vowels and deferential tone.

Phoebe glanced around the large room hoping to spot a familiar face. The only people beside herself and the man were two young page boys, similarly dressed in period costume, who were standing by the main staircase. From somewhere close by she could hear the restrained tones of a waltz and the low murmur of voices.

She coughed to clear her throat. 'I am expected,' she said. 'My name is Phoebe Williams.'

The man glanced down at the book on his desk and then nodded. 'Ah yes.' He waved towards one of the young boys. 'Perhaps you would be good enough to show Miss Williams to the Chinese Room.' He stopped and studied her for a few seconds. 'Your gentleman friend is waiting for you in the dining room but he thought perhaps you might like to change first. Your maid is waiting.'

Phoebe found herself blushing. 'My maid?' she repeated.

The man nodded and handed the page a key. 'The Chinese Room.'

Phoebe thanked him and followed the boy. On the first floor he led her to a set of double doors, which he unlocked with a flourish. She stared at him, unsure whether she was supposed to tip him or not and then fumbled in her bag for a handful of change.

He grinned. 'I'll wait for you out here,' he said pleasantly and then stepped aside so that Phoebe could go in. Inside the Chinese Room was a revelation. The room was stunning, with a huge ornate canopied bed, rich oriental designs on the walls, a log fire burning low in the grate. It was quite overwhelming. She gasped and then turned around in surprise as a young woman, dressed in a severe but beautifully cut black dress, came in through a side door.

'Good evening, miss,' the girl said with a polite smile. 'I'm Carter. I'm here to help you dress.'

Phoebe nodded dumbly. The girl turned up the gaslight by the dressing-table. She beckoned to Phoebe, who was still completely bemused. She gently directed Phoebe in front of the mirror and unzipped her dress.

'First time at The Seaton?' she said conversationally as she slid Phoebe's dress down over her shoulders. Her manner was so matter of fact that Phoebe didn't consider protesting.

'Yes. I'd never heard of it—'

The girl smiled again. 'It's a really lovely place, very exclusive. It was one of those houses that remained untouched, you know, shut up and forgotten about except for a family retainer keeping the place aired and tidy. Mr Seaton thought it would make a wonderful hotel.' She opened the top drawer of the dressing-table. To Phoebe's surprise it was laid out with a collection of underwear. 'We get all sorts here, honeymooners, film stars, the lot,' she continued conversationally.

Phoebe was barely listening.

The girl selected a laced, boned corset and a pair of white cotton drawers, richly trimmed with broderie anglaise and then looked at Phoebe's silk teddy. 'That'll all have to come off too, I'm afraid.'

The girl made no attempt to leave so Phoebe slipped off the teddy, blushing slightly. Naked except for her stockings and shoes, she was glad of the heat from the log fire. Finally she relinquished even her shoes and stockings under the unflustered eyes of her maid.

The girl helped her into the drawers first, tightening the draw string around her narrow waist and then into the corset. The top was soft cotton with a low neckline, held in place by another draw string. The lower edge of the corset finished just below the swell of her hips. Phoebe wriggled into it, letting the girl adjust it so that it covered her breasts.

The maid smiled. 'You look quite the part already.

We'll just get you laced into this and then I'll get you some silk stockings and button boots.' She gave Phoebe an appraising glance. 'Then when I've dressed your hair I'll get your gown.'

Phoebe stared at her. 'Gown?'

The girl nodded. 'We've got some beautiful ones. You'll look a real picture in it once I've got this tightened up. Now, can you stand still? This takes some doing.'

Phoebe gasped as the girl started to fasten the corset, pulling with steady pressure at the laces and hooks until Phoebe could hardly breath. No wonder Victorian women used to have such perfect posture. Phoebe felt as if she was in a straitjacket but when she turned to look into the mirror the effect was truly stunning. Her waist was cinched in to barely more than a hand span. Above the boning, her breasts swelled provocatively like ripe fruit. Below, her hips seemed to have taken on an eroticism all of their own. She stared at her reflection, while the maid slipped on a pair of finely knitted silk stockings held in place by garters. Next she opened a cupboard and scanned a rack of button boots until she found a pair that would fit.

A few minutes later, curling tongs in hand, the maid transformed Phoebe's hair into an elegant concoction of bun and delicate tendrils.

The girl smiled at her. 'What do you think?'

Phoebe couldn't resist the temptation to laugh, though she could hardly breath. 'I'm amazed, what next?'

'Your gentleman ordered jewellery for you.' The maid opened another drawer in the dressing-table and pulled out a flat leather box, the shape indicating it held a suite of ladies' jewellery.

'They're only costume, of course, but they're exquisite. Here, let me help you put them on.'

Phoebe stared into the open box. Inside was a stranded choker of *faux* emeralds and diamonds, with matching earrings and bracelet. The lamplight reflected in the facets. Paste or not, they looked incredible. The maid helped Phoebe into them and then disappeared to get her dress.

Phoebe stared at her unlikely reflection. The outfit was a confection of erotic images. She turned, looking at the way the corset pressed her already slim frame into a wild fantasy. She touched the gems around her throat, wondering who would go to so much trouble to garnish his companion for the evening. One name sprang to mind: Gerrard Gottlieb.

When the maid returned with the dress, Phoebe suddenly felt surprisingly light-hearted and at ease. The gown was a picture though Phoebe wasn't certain it was genuine. It smelt of rosewater and lavender; the exquisite green shot-silk and mass of stiffened petticoats rustling as she stepped into it. Without the corset Phoebe couldn't have worn it, in the corset it turned her into a tempting erotic morsel. She could barely take her eyes off the mirror as the maid buttoned the long narrow cuffs.

'I'll put your things in this,' said the girl, slipping Phoebe's handbag inside another that was made from the same fabric as her gown. She smiled. 'And all your clothes will be in the wardrobe. The page will take you downstairs now to meet your gentleman friend.' She paused. 'You know, you look lovely in that dress, it really suits you,' she said, watching Phoebe's face.

Phoebe smiled, turning round very, very slowly. 'I feel lovely, like a princess.'

As she spoke, the service door to the suite opened and Gerrard Gottlieb strode into the room, dressed in period costume, his mane of hair swept back, his broad chest resplendent in a brocade waistcoat, and dark frock coat. Phoebe smiled nervously at him and turned again for his inspection.

'Perfection,' he whispered in an undertone, his eyes lingering on the narrowness of her waist before moving up to the curves of her breasts, nestling behind their discreet flurry of lace.

'I had intended to wait for you downstairs but the temptation was just too great,' he said. Behind him, the maid discreetly slipped away.

'How long have you been watching me?' Phoebe said quietly.

'Long enough.' His eyes were dark with barely veiled desire. His expression sent a ripple of excitement through Phoebe, so strong and so unexpected that she shivered.

He smiled disarmingly and extended his arm. 'Shall we dine, my dear?'

Phoebe nodded. When her fingers touched his she felt a tiny electric pulse; a low earthy hum that set every nerve-ending in her body alight.

'You're trembling,' he said softly.

There were no words she wanted to say. Instead she turned to look up into his eyes, astonished by the waves of anticipation that flooded through her. She saw her own passion reflected there, her own eyes as bright and dark as his. His lifted her fingers to his lips. The gentle pressure of his kiss was like white lightning. She swallowed hard, trying desperately to drive away the heady feelings that filled her mind.

'Tonight,' he said in an undertone, 'you will give me the power. Tonight I am your master.'

She shivered. It was not just her sex that responded to his low voice, it was her whole body.

'Yes,' she murmured. Her voice sounded as if it came from a thousand miles away, distant, unnecessary. He stroked her neck, a single finger tracing the curve of her throat. She closed her eyes, letting the sensation engulf her.

He made a soft noise of approval as she leant into his touch, savouring his caress. She stepped into the circle of his arms, surrendering herself entirely. He tipped back her chin and brushed her lips with his, a chaste, dry kiss that made her feel faint with need.

'Let's go downstairs and eat now,' he said. 'We have all the time we need.'

Slowly she stepped away, the gesture had been made. He linked his arm through hers and guided her out into the hallway. She felt as if she were floating, her entire consciousness centred on the electric desire that burnt inside her. Every step, every pressure of his body against hers sent a starburst through her mind. She had no idea that desire could be so all-consuming.

They ate in the magnificent dining room; the food was sublime but she was hardly aware of eating, hardly noticed the opulent surrounding or the other diners. Every thought was centred on Gerrard Gottlieb and the anticipation of the things he would show her. After dinner they danced to the strains of a string quartet. Even then, all she was aware of was the heat of his palm resting in the small of her back, the touch of his fingertips on hers.

As the medley of tunes finished Gottlieb turned to her. He said nothing, there was no need for words. Phoebe shivered and fell into step beside him, relishing the lightest touch of his hand on her waist.

While they had been dancing and dining the staff had lowered the flame in the gas lamps. Away from the dining room the rest of the hotel was cloaked in rich velvety shadows. With every step Phoebe felt her anticipation growing.

Chapter Sixteen

At the door to the Chinese Room Gottlieb hesitated and turned to Phoebe. 'Are you sure?' he murmured. 'I want you to be sure about this.'

Phoebe nodded, following the gesture with the words. 'Yes,' she said softly. 'Yes. I'm sure.'

He smiled, undoing the lock and stepping to one side to let her pass. 'Then why don't we go inside.'

The fire had been stoked, a single lamp lit on a side table. The flames from the grate cast shadows on the high ceilings. Phoebe stood nervously by the hearth wondering what would follow. Gottlieb tugged the bell pull.

'What are you doing?' she said anxiously.

Gottlieb grinned. 'Trust me,' he said and from a box on the side table removed a cigar. He made himself comfortable in one of the armchairs by the fire and let his eyes rest expectantly on Phoebe. She blushed under his unhurried examination, unsure what he expected her to do. Her expression must have reflected her uncertainty.

Gottlieb lifted his hand. 'Just wait,' he said gently.

A few seconds later the maid arrived. She bobbed a discreet curtsey. 'Yes, sir? You rang?'

Gottlieb nodded. 'Could you arrange for the night

porter to bring up some brandy.' The girl nodded and was about to leave when Gottlieb added. 'And then could you come back to help Miss Williams undress?'

The maid hesitated and then her face betrayed a flicker of comprehension. Gottlieb took a note from his wallet and handed it to her. The girl smiled. 'Won't be half a tick, sir.'

Gottlieb drank his brandy while the girl disrobed Phoebe. Although nothing was said the maid seemed to have sensed the scenario being played out between them. The fingers that had been nimble and quick when she had been dressing Phoebe now lingered provocatively over every fastening. She helped Phoebe out of her jewels, before beginning to slowly unbutton the gown. When it finally slithered in a rustle of petticoats to the floor, Phoebe heard Gottlieb's breath quicken.

The maid indicated Phoebe should sit in front of the mirror and, with languid strokes, brushed Phoebe's hair until it shone, finally twisting it up into a simple knot.

Phoebe could see Gottlieb's reflection. He was sitting by the fire, twirling the brandy balloon between his fingers. She sensed his relaxed attitude was a pretence; she could see the colour rising in his face and the pulse throbbing above his winged collar.

When Phoebe's toilette was complete the maid turned to Gottlieb, brush in hand.

'Would you like me to help the lady off with the rest of her clothes?' she said in an artful voice.

Gottlieb shook his head. 'No, thank you, that will be all.'

The girl smiled, replacing the brush on the dressing-table. 'Right you are, sir. Anything else you want, don't hesitate to ring.'

He nodded.

As the door closed silently Phoebe turned to face Gottlieb, well aware of the picture she presented to him. Her shoulders were bare, hair arranged in a soft knot, her breasts barely covered by the thin cotton top of the corset, her nipples jutting dark and hard through the fabric.

Below her impossibly tiny waist her hips rounded out into a sumptuous arc. Every fraction of her body felt alive under Gottlieb's rapt attention. Between her legs she could feel the moist kisses of her sex, pressing against the cotton drawers.

'Come to me,' he said in a voice barely above a whisper.

She moved slowly, aware of every breath, every tiny movement of her body as his eyes drank her in.

It seemed to take an age before she stood in front of him on the hearth rug, unable to control the slight tremble in her body. His fingers lifted to stroke the moist junction of her sex, lingering, exploring the places where the delicate fabric clung to her, betraying her arousal.

'Take them off,' he said in a guttural voice.

She pulled the drawers down over her hips in a single uncomplicated gesture, letting them fall, stepping out of them, revelling in her exposure.

Gottlieb groaned and sank to his knees, pressing his lips to her mount of Venus, breathing in her scent. His first impassioned touch was electrifying. Phoebe threw back her head, giving herself to him totally, whimpering as his tongue parted her lips, seeking out the tiny throbbing pleasure-bud.

She began to writhe against him, the anticipation she had felt all evening amplifying every sensation. One of his hands lifted to join his tongue, holding her open, exposing every secret fold, every sensitive crease. The other hand snaked round her buttocks, pulling her closer and closer. His fingers slipped inside her, easing her open, diving again and again into the throbbing depths.

'My God,' he whispered, his tone almost reverent. His tongue began to circle her clitoris, lips nibbling at its tiny crown with the practised skill of a master.

Phoebe thought she would die. Tangling her fingers in his hair she rode out on a spiralling, spinning voyage of pure sensation – it seemed as if an inescapable orgasm began the instant his lips touched her, going on and on in an endless intricate pattern, threatening to drown her sanity and every shred of reason and reserve.

Just as she thought she could take no more Gottlieb pulled her onto her knees. His lips searched for hers. His kisses were no longer chaste or cool, they tasted of her excitement and the rapturous aroma of her pleasure. Her senses reeled as his tongue explored her mouth, renewing her desire in a way that she had thought impossible.

He pulled away, eyes dilated, his expression almost unnerving. 'You know what I want from you?'

She nodded. She could still see the glitter of her juices around his full sensual mouth. He got to his feet, stiffly, holding his excitement in check, though she sensed retaining control was a struggle. He opened the wardrobe and then turned back to face her. In his hands were a pair of manacles.

Phoebe felt a thrilling shiver of apprehension. This was

what he really wanted; she had always known that. Nervously she picked up the discarded lacy drawers, holding them against her belly like a shield. He smiled and held out a hand. She knew she wouldn't resist him and stepped closer, wincing as he slipped the bracelets around her wrists, the little clasps snapping shut with an unnerving finality.

He pulled back the drapes on the bed. Set into the posts at just above shoulder height were two small rings. Phoebe stared in astonishment.

'You knew they were here?' she said in disbelief.

Gottlieb grinned. 'Of course.'

She dropped the drawers onto the floor, a final gesture of abandonment; what was there left to hide?

Gently he took her hands and snapped the first length of fine chain into place. Phoebe shivered uncontrollably. Beside her, Gottlieb's eyes were ablaze. She knew he could sense her fear and – more than that – that her fear excited him. The second chain snapped into place. She heard him sigh as he stepped back to admire his handiwork and closed her eyes. She knew what would follow and while part of her was desperately afraid, another instinctive part of her nature relished the possibility of total surrender. Tonight she was Gottlieb's alone – he could do with her exactly as he wanted.

Gottlieb refilled his brandy glass and turned to drink in the scenario he had so carefully engineered. It was so like the print in his treasured album: a pale, dark-haired girl manacled between ornately carved bed posts. Facing away from him, her body was caught in silhouette, revealing the sumptuous curves of her hips, the slimness of her waist, the dimples on her alabaster shoulders – an erotic hour glass that gave him a little shiver of pleasure.

Phoebe turned, peeping back over her shoulder, glittering eyes revealing a heady mixture of fear and expectation. He had studied the print so often he knew every detail: the discarded tumble of clothes at her feet, the small tasselled lamp throwing a delicate glow onto her rounded buttocks, the dark inviting places betwen her milk-white thighs, almost, but not completely, obscured by shadow.

He had always been reluctant to recreate the senario in the print in case, in the flesh, he was disappointed. There had been ample opportunity over the years. He had wanted to wait for the perfect woman – and now, finally, he had found her.

Tiny crystals of sweat had risen between Phoebe's shoulder-blades. They glittered, revealing the slightest tremor in her body. Gottlieb opened the wardrobe and brought out an old-fashioned carpet-beater made of twisted wicker with a clover-leaf head. In the sepia print it stood by an elegant *chiffonier*, waiting unused, but Gottlieb had always sensed that it had been this the young woman was meant for. Her eyes held an understanding of the unspoken promise. Casually he tested its weight, letting the head swing back. It made a satisfying hiss as it cut through the air. Across the room he saw Phoebe Williams stiffen, her whole body tense and expectant.

For an instant he sensed her panic, she tugged helplessly against the manacles and then she was still, her eyes shining.

Gottlieb swallowed hard and let the head of the carpet-beater swing back again, this time in earnest. It flashed past him, its face cracking against the soft rounded cheeks of Phoebe's backside. She shrieked wildly, lunging forward. Before she could recover he swung the beater again, relishing the way she strained and turned to avoid him and yet at the some time he knew she was longing to feel its kiss. He felt a rush of excitement and affection that took his breath away. He stared at the girl tied for his pleasure and realised with an unnerving certainty that he had fallen in love with her.

Red hot pulses of pain coursed through Phoebe's body, the sting and the sound of the beater were almost overwhelming. Her struggle against the restraints was instinctive. She bucked and twisted, letting out a thick sob as the beater found its mark again. The second stroke intensified the glow from the first, re-doubling the sensations. She moaned, stunned by the addictive paradox of pain mingled with a sense of pleasure.

Between her legs she knew her sex was brimming, creamy juices trickling down onto her thighs. She knew, in an abstracted part of her mind, that it was the act of total surrender that excited her far more than the pain. She had given herself to Gottlieb totally, without protest. The realisation excited her beyond anything else she had ever experienced.

The third stroke shook the thoughts from her head, replacing reason with a compelling image of being pure sensation. Every fibre of her body concentrated on the soft hiss of the beater, followed a split second later by the explosive heat as it made contact with her skin.

She shrieked again, imagining the picture she presented to Gottlieb; her legs open, buttocks crimson, the glittering droplets of excitement clinging to the intimate curves of her sex. She felt as if she was observing the scene: the man and his maid, compliant and eager to serve her master, writhing and gasping under his cruel attentions. She could almost see the straining arc of Gottlieb's cock, confined in his breeches, and sense its hunger. She longed to touch him, feel him press deep into her, making her cry out for more.

She whimpered, praying he would set her free so that she could take him – take them both into the realms of pure pleasure. The head of the beater exploded against her again, but now it was merely an echo as she imagined Gottlieb impaling her again and again.

She sensed him moving closer. Afraid to turn around she held herself taut, knowing that he would see the excitement in her eyes. Gently he parted her legs, fingers seeking out the hot wet places, hands snaking round to tease her flushed tingling breasts. He traced her nipples with his fingertips, rolling them delicately between thumb and forefinger until she sobbed with delight. Against the raw heat of her backside she could feel the terrifying engorged press of his cock, begging for entry, angry at being denied.

She held her breath as he fumbled with the fly buttons on his trousers and then gasped as she felt the scintillating brush of his cock against her inner thigh. He was wet. His cock felt like a dark oily force, slowly easing into her, opening her in its path. He was as big as in any of her wildest fantasies, filling her to the brim as he pressed home.

Her body closed around him, drawing him deeper and deeper. He moaned as she ground her hips against him, willing her body to accept everything he had to offer. When she began to move she felt her whole body respond, matching him stroke for stroke. It seemed as if every thought was centred on the junction of their bodies. His hands slid over her, cupping her breasts, teasing her nipples, his lips on her neck in her hair. She fought to retain some degree of control and then realised it was pointless – better to give herself entirely to the moment, let the feelings and the pleasure consume her.

Gottlieb's breath roared in her ears, a roaring storm wind that drove her wild, while his fingers pulled her back onto him. It seemed to go on and on for ever until suddenly she felt her sex convulse, sucking at Gottlieb like a mouth, sucking in pure pleasure. A split second later a sheet of blinding light filled her mind, eradicating her sense of self. For an instant they were one pure white hot flame of sex.

Coming back to reality was like waking from a deep sleep. Phoebe began to shiver while with gentle hands Gottlieb unchained her and guided her onto the soft feather mattress. She lay back while he undid the laces of her corset, not resisting as his fingers and lips pressed kisses and caresses to her exhausted trembling flesh. Slipping into the bed beside her he pulled the crisp linen sheets and the eiderdown up around them. She fell asleep in his arms, while he stroked her hair.

Deep in thought, Gerrard Gottlieb watched the dawn break. He had found it difficult to sleep. He ran his fingers through his hair. Being selfless was not something that came naturally to him, he thought with a wry smile; by burning Joe Blenheim's tape he had set Phoebe free. By talking to Shaun Rees he had smoothed their path back to reconciliation. He shivered, he'd already set Maya free – so where did that leave him?

He glanced back towards the bed. Phoebe Williams was lying amongst a snow storm of crisp white sheets, her dark hair spread like spun silk over the linen pillows. Her breast rose and fell with the soft easy breath of sleep. Her skin was slightly flushed, soft, warm and inviting. She looked almost edible. His heart contracted sharply. It would be so easy to ensnare her – and the possibility was tempting: take her away from Shaun. With the right words and his skilled touch, he knew he was more than halfway there already.

He stared out into the newborn morning. When Phoebe Williams had first walked into his office he had been playing with an abstract fantasy of seduction not love. He wondered how it had happened. He'd meant to teach her, manipulate her, even use her – and now, just when he had her, he knew he had to set her free. In doing so, he had to surrender himself. He smiled grimly. It was ironic really; the victor turned victim – and all of his own doing. He glanced at the bell pull and wondered if the staff were up yet, he could really do with a coffee.

When Phoebe woke it was light. She was instantly aware that the bed was empty and turned anxiously to find Gottlieb. He was standing by the window, dressed in a long nightshirt, looking out into the morning.

'Good morning, my dear,' he said softly. 'Did you sleep well?'

Phoebe nodded.

He ran his fingers back through his mane of hair. 'I think it may snow later.'

Phoebe slipped out of bed and, pulling the counterpane around her like a cloak, joined him by the window. Outside the sky was tinged with a strange grey light that augured the approach of winter.

He turned and kissed her gently on the forehead. 'Soon everything will be as it was,' he said in a low voice. 'And what isn't quite the same the snow will disguise.'

She looked up at him. 'What do you mean?'

Gottlieb smiled, though she thought she detected a flicker of regret and sadness in his eyes.

'We'll leave after breakfast. Shaun told me he would come round to see you some time today.'

Phoebe stared at him in surprise. 'Shaun?'

Gottlieb nodded. 'Yes, I spoke to him last night. Your unpleasant friend Tony has said nothing to him about you. The reason he has been avoiding you is because he slept with his last fare for Miss Brooks.' Gottlieb snorted. 'I think it would be reasonable to assume that she seduced him and he didn't know how to face you. He felt he had betrayed everything you'd built together.'

Phoebe shivered. 'You knew this before you brought me here.' She stared at the carpet-beater where he had discarded it on the floor, even now her buttocks still stung from its kiss.

Gottlieb nodded. 'Of course.'

Phoebe looked up at him. 'But Tony could still say something.'

Gottlieb shrugged. 'I don't think so. According to Shaun, Tony and his wife are now reconciled. I'm sure he wouldn't want her to know that he had been picking up whores at the Starcor convention. Anyway, you both have as much to lose if he is foolish enough to say anything. No, I'm sure your secret is safe. In fact everything will soon be as it was.'

'Why do you keep saying that?'

'Well, Dr Manley will be returning next week. Shaun Rees will be reunited with the woman he loves and I will be back—' he stopped and then continued more briskly, '— back at Morrahills with my research. After Christmas I may reconsider taking up the invitation I've had to return to America.' His eyes were distant. She stared up at him. 'I think it would be better for all concerned, Phoebe, if this is our first and last encounter, don't you?'

Phoebe nodded, though inside she felt a sense of loss.

He smiled. 'I would also suggest that you resign from Bad Company and avoid Mr Blenheim.'

Phoebe nodded. 'I'd already decided that before I came here last night.' She struggled to sound normal.

Gottlieb nodded. 'Good.'

'What about my final paper?'

Gottlieb snorted and slowly turned back towards her. He slipped the blanket off her shoulders, revealing her breasts. In the cold morning air her nipples hardened dramatically.

'I have already recorded my approval of your rather worthy thesis on the social effects of nursery provision on the economic structure of post-war industrial Britain.'

Phoebe gasped. 'But what about Bad Company? My research—'

Gottlieb traced the pattern of her areola with a long finger. 'I think it would be better for all of us if we closed the door on that. Your original idea will no doubt produce an excellent and very relevant paper, Miss Williams. Something I'm sure Dr Manley will be very proud of.' He paused, sliding the blanket lower. 'But perhaps we can forget the halls of academe for a little while longer. Why don't we go back to bed?'

Wordlessly Phoebe followed him across the room.

Gottlieb drove Phoebe back to university. It was mid-morning when his car pulled to a halt at the end of the road. Phoebe spotted an ageing VW parked against the kerb outside the flats. Her heart leapt when she spotted Shaun Rees sitting on the doorstep. She turned to Gerrard Gottlieb who lifted a hand to silence her.

'Forgive him, Phoebe, and yourself—' he said softly.

Phoebe stared at him. There were so many things she wanted to say but he waved her away. As she bent to say a final word of farewell he grinned wolfishly.

'I'll send you a postcard from San Francisco.'

She swallowed back a wave of tears. 'That's where you're going?'

Gottlieb slipped the car into gear. 'Maybe. Now, for God's sake, go and talk to your Mr Rees before he decides to run away again.'

Shaun looked up at the sound of her footsteps and scrambled to his feet. If he noticed the elegant clothes and high heels under her coat he said nothing, instead his eyes filled with tears.

'Oh Phoebe,' he said in a thick voice. 'I'm so sorry, have you spoken to Gottlieb?'

Phoebe nodded. She felt a great wave of tenderness and stepping closer pressed her fingers to his lips. 'It's all right,' she said softly. 'Don't say anything. Why don't we start again?'

Shaun pulled her into his arms and kissed her hard. She shivered with desire as she felt his body against hers. This was real, this was the kind of love she truly wanted. He held her tight against him, almost as if he were afraid to let her go.

'I love you,' he murmured, his voice thick with emotion. 'I love you more than anything.'

Phoebe didn't see Gottlieb driving slowly along the street behind them, or the sadness in his eyes as he accelerated away.